THE HAMMER AND THE ANVIL

David Trower & Jeremy Hubbard

Published 2007 by arima publishing

www.arimapublishing.com

ISBN 978 1 84549 237 3

© David Trower & Jeremy Hubbard 2007

Cover designed by WriteDesign (UK) Ltd

All rights reserved

This book is copyright. Subject to statutory exception and to provisions of relevant collective licensing agreements, no part of this publication may be reproduced, stored in a retrieval system, or transmitted in any form or by any means, without the prior written permission of the authors.

Printed and bound in the United Kingdom

Typeset in Garamond 11/16

This book is sold subject to the conditions that it shall not, by way of trade or otherwise, be lent, re-sold, hired out, or otherwise circulated without the publisher's prior consent in any form of binding or cover other than that which it is published and without a similar condition including this condition being imposed on the subsequent purchaser.

This book is a work of fiction. Names, characters, businesses, organizations, places and events are either the product of the authors' imaginations, or they are used fictitiously. Any resemblance to actual persons, living or dead, or to events or locales, past or present, is entirely coincidental.

Swirl is an imprint of arima publishing.

arima publishing
ASK House, Northgate Avenue
Bury St Edmunds, Suffolk IP32 6BB
t: (+44) 01284 700321
www.arimapublishing.com

The Authors are indebted to their friend Benedict Butler for his unfailing enthusiasm, encouragement and hard work, without which it is doubtful that this book would ever have been published. David would also like to thank his wife, Frances for her suggestions, and Jeremy would also like to thank his partner Diane Pattison and his daughter Anya for their helpful comments, encouragement and support.

I

Blythburgh, Suffolk.
16th. October, 1962

The ragged line of rooks tightened formation as the gulls, screaming and wheeling, attacked. High up in the crisp, cold air of a cloudless Suffolk sky, the gulls mobbed and scattered the intruders before swooping to settle back down behind the red tractor that was ploughing the large field below.

Wally, engrossed in his folded newspaper, ignored their squalling return. Steering his tractor along with one hand, he left a trail of slightly erratic furrows stretching out behind – of which both his father and his grandfather would have been ashamed. In their day, the shire team would have forged the plough's coulters unswervingly through the soil.

Attending to the news instead of the horizon, Wally did not hear the church bell in nearby Blythburgh toll eleven. His empty belly would tell him well enough when it was noon – and time to uncork the bottle of cold tea to wash down his lunch of bread and cheese.

Glancing away from his paper briefly, he twisted around in the metal seat to look behind, steadying himself against the curved, high mudguard to check the progress of the plough. The gleaming shares, set at the depth of sixteen inches because of the early October frosts, churned the chocolate earth open to the greedy gulls.

Turning back, he eased himself up a fraction from the folded sacking cushion. Blood flowed back into his numbed buttocks. Taking a bearing on the huge horse-chestnut tree rising up out of the hedgerow at the edge of New Delight Wood, he nudged the tractor into true then settled back down to scanning the paper. The bold headlines proclaimed 'Cuban Missile Crisis. Castro: Thorn In Kennedy's Side?' Wally followed the complexity of the growing international situation that, the paper promised, threatened to engulf even Blythburgh and its surrounding arable fields in the unfolding global drama. Wally, struggling with the unfamiliar Russian names, wondered if his wife had remembered to pack fruitcake in with his bread and cheese.

Eighty yards from the towering horse-chestnut tree, the tractor lurched. As the front wheels slewed, the engine's shrill protest scattered the feeding gulls. Shutting off, Wally clambered down. The plough had snagged – he had heard the sharp metallic scrape – and it would mean a sweating struggle with the obstruction. Another large flint, probably. The third that week. Treading the turned earth carefully, Wally cursed his bad luck. He hated ploughing deep. The muttered oath froze on his lips as he stooped to inspect the tip of the leading ploughshare. It was not the gleam of flint but the glint of metal that winked in the bright, cold sunlight. Wally staggered backwards, stumbling, against the tractor wheel. Terror rose up and choked him. He had unearthed an unexploded bomb. He was sure of it. The land hereabouts still held them – everyone in the pub who worked the land knew that, or knew someone who had turned one up beneath the plough.

Blowing hard to steady his thumping heart, Wally cupped his hands to his mouth, calling out across the wide field to where Mick was tightening the discs of the harrow.

Mick stood up, stretched and shielded his eyes against the glare of the low, October sun.

'What you want?' he bellowed.

'Come you here, bor,' boomed the reply.

'What's up? What is it?' Mick countered, reluctant to wade across the ploughed earth. 'Tractor broke, is she?'

Wally waved frantically. 'Come you here, bor. I've maybe brought up a bomb.'

'I'm now coming,' Mick yelled excitedly, dropping his spanner. Loping awkwardly from furrow to shining furrow, his heavy boots toppled their smooth, ploughed crowns.

'Hurry,' Wally roared.

'Hold you hard,' Mick panted, approaching. 'What you got, then?' he demanded urgently, steadying himself against the silenced tractor.

Wally pointed down towards the edge of the leading ploughshare. His finger trembled slightly. Mick snatched off his cap, pocketed it and rubbed his hands together briskly in eager anticipation. The small shed behind his cottage already housed some World War II wreckage – a tail wheel, live and spent ammo, shards of fuselage from a B-17 and an altimeter from a Mustang.

Wally stepped back, skidding on the soft earth in nervous haste as Mick crouched down to examine the find.

' 'At a bomb?' Wally whispered hoarsely.

Mick rose up. Rooting into the exposed soil with the toe of his boot, he shook his head.

' 'At be no bomb, bor.'

'Sure?' Wally insisted, unconvinced.

'Sure I'm sure. Look. Bit of an engine block, see? And this here is what they call cowling.'

Kneeling back down to his task, his large hands entered the earth to further uncover the metal. With a delicacy of touch, Mick's thick fingertips gently brushed away the crumble of friable soil.

'Not shift her without tackle,' he pronounced, his face reddening with effort inches away from the engine block. 'She'll weigh some and more when she's up and out. We'd better be getting back for the lads and a winch. American by the looks of her, see?'

An enthusiastic collector of wreckage since his boyhood, Mick was quick to spot and decipher the production line plate. His fingertips, still quivering with excitement, traced the series of letters and numbers dye-stamped into the metal.

'Pratt and Whitney', he said, adding hesitantly, 'R – 1830 – is that a seven, no it's a nine – 90. Pratt and Whitney,' he repeated, 'R – 1830 – 90.'

'Might be that bombs came down with it,' Wally warned.

'Ten, maybe twelve feet under, if they did,' Mick shrugged unconcernedly. 'This won't harm us,' he murmured, scrutinizing the find. 'American. Liberator, most like. Seen something the same a while back. Yes,' he nodded. 'Liberator.'

'Liberator? Weren't them bombers?' Wally countered anxiously.

Mick nodded slowly. He remained silent. Looking up, as he knelt beside the plough, he saw the horse-chestnut tree rise up from the hedgerow. The hedgerow he had explored and enjoyed so often as a boy… seeking cobnuts, 'nesting' in April, blackberrying in late-September. His eyes narrowed with concentration and the sudden flood of memories. In his mind, the horse-chestnut tree loomed up in full summer leafage.

'What's up with you, bor?' Wally rasped, still rattled, his fear sharpening his voice. 'You sure and certain we be safe?'

Mick did not hear the question. Eyes closed, he was far away, some eighteen summers back in his wartime boyhood. A boyhood spent along the hedgerows, beneath horse-chestnut trees.

Liberator. The heat of his exertion and excitement became the warmth of a hot summer day. It would have been July. Or August. Yes, that would be right. Back end of summer, 1945. No. 1944. Mick and the lads from Blythburgh village, sockless in their Utility boots, tramping along the edge of New Delight Wood, a mongrel dog scampering at their heels. He remembered it all. This field, with that hedgerow, and that horse-chestnut tree – huge to a small boy – towering up into the blaze of the summer sun.

Mick started to breathe faster as he remembered the blue sky filling with the noise of approaching planes. He remembered squinting up into the sun, all the boys shielding their eyes with protective hands. The sudden showing of three Liberators, the heavy throb of their engines making speech impossible. Excited squeals and pointing fingers. Then, to their delight, a Mosquito. The fighter-bomber now gracefully high above the USAAF Liberators. Whoops of joy from the boys – now charging around in dizzying circles, arms outstretched as they mimicked the formation above. More joy – unbelievable! Mustangs, fighter cover, sweeping down, their high pitched whine clear above the bombers' thunderous roar. Tipsy with delight, the boys below had screamed their cheers. At their dancing feet, the excited dog had snapped and barked.

For a moment, Mick blinked then closed his eyes tightly as his recollections of the sudden, huge explosion roared in his mind.

'You all right there, bor?' Wally demanded, puzzled by the kneeling man's shiver. Mick was remembering the ear-splitting crack high up above that had caused the ground beneath their feet to tremble. The sudden rush of hot air blasting down. The boys and their dog had been punched flat into the turf as the Liberator in the centre of the formation had exploded and disintegrated. Spread-eagled and winded, deafened and terrified, they had remained sprawled face down as tiny shreds of scorched debris drizzled all around them.

Mick opened his eyes, drawing a deep breath. Rising up onto one knee, he patted the chunk of exposed engine block.

'Liberator,' he whispered, recalling how he and his frightened pals had remained flattened on the ground until the last of the horse-chestnut leaves blasted from their branches by the fireball above had fallen to earth.

'Pass us that,' Mick muttered, pointing into the tractor cabin.

Wally handed his newspaper over. Mick scrunched it up into a ball, wiping his soiled palms clean on the crushed map of Cuba.

WASHINGTON D.C.
Dateline: 16 October 1962
08.23 am Eastern Standard Time

In the White House, the US President ignored his breakfast. His waffles and coffee were cold. He only had appetite for the up-to-the-minute briefing sheets from the teleprinter. Outwardly calm, he read and re-read the latest intelligence update. In his right hand, a heavy rolled-gold pen turned over and over. He used it briskly to initial a paragraph or to delete a single line. He paused for a sip of cold coffee. The teleprinter ceased its chattering. Only the delicate chink of the china coffee cup returning to its saucer broke the silence of the room.

The high-ceilinged office had an air of austere grandeur. Dark, heavy drapes remained drawn. From antique crystal chandeliers, dozens of electric light bulbs blazed. Large paintings – sombre portraits in sober oils – adorned three walls. The eyes of presidents past looked on as the present incumbent pondered the future. The Stars and Stripes filled most of the fourth wall. White clocks studded the rich wallpaper above the mahogany bookcase, one for each time zone.

The president drained the last of his strong coffee and gazed up at the clocks. Time was passing. All too quickly. He knew that he had everything he needed. An arsenal to command and deploy. The resolve to do so if necessary. But had he got enough time? The president grunted, concentrating hard. He had grown accustomed to balancing both reflective and problem-solving skills, allowing him to remain calm yet alert. He eased back slightly in his chair.

The president had arranged to have his desk moved on his first day so that he could be aware of anyone entering his office – as they dealt with the double doors – before full eye contact was established. The split second advantage was always with him. He shifted his gaze from the three telephones on the right of his desk to take in the name plaque which, facing the double doors, came to the aid of sometimes over-awed and tongue-tied visitors. Such visitors were always greeted with his charming smile and found it easy to speak with him, frequently relaxing enough to use his first name within minutes of their meeting.

To the president's immediate left, almost at his elbow, was a model of a World War II Liberator bomber. He noted with rueful pride the Ace of Spades insignia. He turned to the photograph next to it. The silver-framed picture was of a conventionally pretty blonde. Not a Hollywood belle, the Ivy

Leaguer was in her late-thirties. There was more than a hint of matronly maturity about her sensible smile. From behind the glass, her shrewd eyes gazed back into his. The clothes were good. Quality. Expensive and chic. Refined and reserved, they indicated taste but more importantly, sound judgement. The clothes were typical of the attire worn by American women of standing and social eminence – society hostesses, senators' wives who craved the Paris look but who had no appetite for traveling to France. A grim smile played briefly across the president's pursed lips. No, he reflected. American women of distinction seemed perfectly content to remain uninterested in what lay abroad, 'across the pond.' Set in the regular features of his square-jawed, handsome face, the eyes of the president gazed down dispassionately into the face of his wife fixed behind the glass.

Tentatively – then with a sudden snatch of impulsive resolve – his fingers gripped the handle of a desk drawer then drew it open. It slid out silently. Looking down, his eyes darkened and softened. After removing the eagle-embossed State Department file carefully concealing the photographs from accidental discovery, his nostrils flared slightly at the sight of the two smaller pictures. Black and white and now yellowing with age, the snapshots were framed in plain wood. Slightly askew, one showed a grinning face. The fleshy jowls were a shade too heavy for the youth of the man, broadening the unmistakable Slavic features. Beneath the jaunty cap of a Soviet junior military officer, the pale eyes sparkled intelligently. Two short lines were scribbled across the photograph. Above, the calligraphic Russian script held its secret. Below, the meaning was revealed in a few simple words. The president grinned as he savoured the 'Good Luck' penned with a flourish.

A small flame flickered into life with his grin, a flame of contempt for overbearing authority from his younger days. He suddenly relished the thought of the panic and alarm knowledge of the existence of the snapshot would bring to Capitol Hill.

Nodding gently, the president dipped his straightened forefinger down into the drawer to tease out the second picture and lightly stroke the face behind the glass. It was a face and figure – of striking beauty. A dark-haired young woman whose graceful curves were somehow more revealed than concealed by the narrow-strapped, floral-print summer dress of 1940s English style. The dress seemed to echo the personality of its wearer. Demure yet alluring. Shyly provocative. Mutedly seductive.

A spasm tensed the president's firm jaw-line as he felt the present colliding with his past. A short tap-tap at the double doors announced the arrival of an aide. Instantly conscious of the burden of duty, he slid the drawer shut before giving permission to enter. The doors opened to admit the perfectly groomed aide, who was closely followed by the robust form of General Maxwell Taylor. They approached the presidential desk.

The aide hovered at a respectful distance. General Taylor, stepping closer, scanned the remains of the breakfast tray. Scorn twitched to curl his lower lip but tact kept it straight. The General detested untidiness. Damn all Democrats, he thought.

'Sorry to disturb you, Mr President,' the General began in a voice devoid of contrition, 'but I guess you need to look at these.' He broke off abruptly, pressing the sheaf of papers to his impressive row of medals while jerking his closely cropped head sideways.

'You still here?' he barked at the hovering aide.

The aide, avoiding the irate General's glare, looked directly across the desk. The president nodded. The aide departed in silence.

'Too many goddam eyes and ears about,' General Taylor remarked pointedly, slamming down the sheaf of large, square aerial surveillance photographs. His splayed fingers fanned them out.

'I pick my team very carefully,' came the gentle rebuke.

General Taylor reddened slightly and swallowed hard.

'Look,' he countered urgently, attempting but failing to make the imperative an invitation rather than an instruction.

A decade or so senior to the president, the General struggled to hide his contempt for the younger man's self-assurance. What others saw as graceful charm, Taylor felt to be arrogance. As he spread the aerial photographs out across the desk-top's polished surface, his heavily gold-braided cuff accidentally swept away the presidential name-plaque. Bending to retrieve it, his red face grew crimson more in anger than exertion. Reading the gold lettering resentfully, his mouth twisted slightly as he replaced the plaque on the desk. President Joseph P Kennedy. The words always provoked him.

'Seen enough?' General Taylor snapped, prodding his finger awkwardly at the fuzzy images. 'Commie bastards.'

Still smarting over the stalemate in Korea, the grizzled old warhorse blamed the politicians for the dishonourable impasse. Politicians. They had screwed up in Korea. Badly. Were they about to screw up again in Cuba?

President Kennedy refrained from answering his general directly. He resented the overbearing presence of the older man. He found the implicit impatience and patent lack of trust irksome. Other older men had showed the same mixture of impatience and mild contempt towards him. Among them, his father.

'Whatdya think, eh?' the general challenged.

President Kennedy remained silent. To answer directly would acknowledge – or at least concede to – the military man's expertise. Ask the questions, don't answer them, he thought to himself. The general was bullish. Bullish and bullshit.

'Well?' General Taylor demanded, hating the silence across the desk that somehow diminished him.

'U-2s?' the President asked, tapping the aerial shots.

Slightly mollified by the ground skillfully restored to him, the general replied promptly. 'Can't hide so much as a coyote from those babies, no sir,' his voice throbbing with pride. 'Had them rushed over. They're as fresh as eggs and sunny-side up. Take a look, Mr President. There. And look at those, there.' Again, the stabbing finger came down.

President Kennedy nodded his agreement. For a brief interlude, the military man before the desk and the politician seated behind it struck a truce – united by the sheer gravity of the situation. Overflying Cuba, the U-2 spy plane had captured in graphic detail clear evidence of Soviet military installations.

'New York know we've got these?'

The General knew that by New York his President meant the United Nations.

'They know, Sir.' He refrained from adding that those peaceniks would be still searching for a warm place to shit when the ICBMs* started to rain down.

'Launch sites. Any doubt about it? Silos?'

'No doubt about it whatsoever, Mr President. Nuclear capability confirmed. We've got,' he lowered his voice respectfully, 'CIA guys on the ground down there.'

Shaking his head, Joseph Kennedy Jnr. gazed down at the missile pods. Long, cigar-shaped images showing white against the grainy grey background. Cigars. His mind flashed automatically to his father, Joe Senior, puffing greedily on a Romeo y Julieta.

'Those bastards have a known range that could wipe everything from Dallas to Denver off the map, Sir. What you see there could make Pearl Harbour look like trick or treat.'

'This should never have happened,' Kennedy said, almost to himself. What the hell had the CIA been doing? Sleeping in the sun down there?

General Taylor stepped back from the perilous brink of a clash. Swallowing down his many views on politicians in general to democrats in particular, he forced his mind to stick to military matters.

'Just give the word, Mr President.'

Kennedy looked up.

'For an air-strike. B-52s in at 40000 feet. Carpet-bombing. Take every damn thing out, Sir.'

'Carpet-bombing?' Kennedy echoed, checking on the jargon.

---
* *Inter-continental ballistic missiles*

'Wall-to-wall destruction, Mr President. Don't leave a blade of grass standing. Like the Allied raids over the Ruhr. And Berlin.'

Dresden. Cologne. President Kennedy pursed his lower lip doubtfully.

'Follow up with an amphibious landing, Sir. Send in the Marines.'

And Bob Hope will be there to sing for Thanksgiving, Kennedy thought to himself. He shook his head slightly.

Pressed into the desk top, the general's hand clenched into an angry fist. 'Only thing for a nest of wasps is gasoline, Sir. Gasoline.'

President Joseph P Kennedy remained silent. The silence of a man not yet convinced.

'You only have to give the word, Sir,' the general urged, struggling to bury his rising impatience under a deferential tone.

Kennedy nodded, accepting the fragile olive branch. But he remained silent. Skillfully, he handed the olive branch back after a lengthy pause.

'If it comes to it, General, I know that you and your boys will not disappoint us.'

The general flushed pink with pride. Kennedy bit his lip to conceal his smile. Jesus, he reflected, if only his troublesome senators were so easily placated.

'The sooner we go in…' General Taylor urged, emboldened.

The president remained silent. He would not be brow-beaten into igniting a regional powder-keg. Gasoline for wasps. That is how his general liked to describe it. But it was larger than that. It was a global kerosene can. Closing his eyes, he blotted out the glimpse of Cuban coastline on the desk before him and thought of a larger map. A map which included Europe. The Middle East. China. And the vast Soviet Empire. The USSR. The biggest land mass on the globe. All held in a delicate cat's cradle of equilibrium. A balance all too easily blasted away by a few B-52s.

'Sir?' the general challenged, mistaking the president's silence for indecision. 'Do we go in?'

Kennedy reached across the desk and picked up one of the three telephones. The green one. 'Get back in here.' He spoke softly into the mouthpiece, avoiding the general's angry glare.

Before he had replaced the phone the double doors had opened and closed to admit the aide. Still considering the evidence supplied by the U-2 spy plane, the president beckoned his aide over to the desk. General Taylor gave no ground, forcing the aide to hover uncertainly.

Kennedy glanced up. Stretching out his arms, he made an encompassing, inclusive gesture, drawing the two men together before his desk.

'I need you two guys in harness on this,' he murmured.

It did the trick. Years on the fund-raising 'rubber chicken' dinner circuits had taught Kennedy how to yoke different beasts into a single team. He had perfected the political knack of gladhanding poets and pig-breeders and leaving them life long friends.

'Put together a team for me. Advisors. Top security clearance. I want the best. USAF. CIA. Be sure to bring in the Pentagon.'

'Nothing to the press boys?' ventured the aide.

The president nodded emphatically. 'Nothing. Bob McNamara will brief the press corps before noon. Give them a UN tie-in. But I want this team in play as soon as possible. Understand?'

'Yes, Sir, Mr President,' the aide and the general chimed together, the general glancing skywards, momentarily exasperated with himself.

'Keep me updated. That's all.'

Dismissed, the two men left the presidential office, their departure leaving the president feeling isolated.

Joseph Kennedy Junior reached out across the desk to straighten his name plaque. Taking a deep breath, he shuffled the splayed surveillance plates into a red folder which he placed in a wire tray marked: IMMEDIATE ACTION.

He bent forward, joining his hands together as if in preparation for prayer. A brief smile, then a wry grimace, twitched his full lips. His thoughts returned to the snapshot buried in the drawer below. Across it, scribbled in both Russian and English, the words 'Good luck, Joe. Anatoly.'

Good luck... something he knew he was going to need. His gaze rested on the model of the Liberator bomber.

Fersfield US 8th Air Force base, Norfolk, England.
9th July 1944

'Good luck, Joe,' the USAAF chaplain murmured, almost shyly. 'I've been posted.'

Lieutenant Joseph P Kennedy, serving officer in the US Navy Special Air Unit No. 1, responded coldly but politely. Both men avoided direct eye contact. Both were secretly relieved to be parting company.

Joe Junior knew perfectly well that the base chaplain fed back a full report of all Joe's missions and off-base escapades to his father in the States. Although Joe Kennedy Senior had served as US Ambassador in London, the wily father by-passed diplomatic channels. The Catholic Church had a more reliable communications network. Joe Junior knew what the chaplain had been doing in the guise of pastoral care. And the chaplain suspected that Joe Junior knew. They shook hands with brief formality.

Joe wheeled away, heading for the briefing scheduled for 1400 hours. It was a gloriously hot English summer day. Beneath the Liberators parked on the concrete hard-standing, the shadows were dense and dark. Up above, a golden sun blazed in the broad, blue Norfolk sky. The heat haze shimmered in the distance at the end of the vast runway. As he strode across the concrete apron, Joe sniffed the air, catching the mix of dust, fresh paint and aviation fuel. The heat drew a prickle of sweat from his neck. As he raised his arm to use a handkerchief, a dark patch showed at his armpit.

Inside the briefing hut it was stifling. Stepping into the dark interior after the blazing sunshine, his eyes took a few seconds to adjust. Blackouts were in place at every window, despite the daylight outside. Black cloth had been firmly pinned over the charts and maps at the far end of the low, curved-ceilinged Nissen hut. Above, the iron-sheeted roof clicked as it expanded under the sun. Joe Junior, late as usual for briefings, tried to ease down silently into a canvas-backed chair. It creaked in the gloom. Without turning from the blackboard onto which he was busily chalking figures, Colonel Forrest growled, 'Glad you could make it, Lieutenant Kennedy. Now you're here, perhaps I can get on.'

Joe Junior, alert to the echo of his father's sarcasm in the CO's jibe, glanced up angrily. A spasm of annoyance plucked along his tense jaw-line, registering the resentment he bore towards such overbearing authority.

Colonel Forrest returned to his briefing. Joe, itching for action, closed his eyes and tried to concentrate. The CO's voice drawled on, peppered with terse, sardonic asides. These drew polite, sycophantic laughs from the air crews – and made Joe wince. Guys from the press and little nobodies from City Hall used to reward his father just like that when Joe Kennedy Senior held court.

'Like I say,' Colonel Forrest concluded, 'just an observation patrol. Not a medal-mission, fellahs. No silverware…'

No medals. The words seemed to burn in Joe's ears, transporting his thoughts back to Hyannisport, the family estate in Massachusetts. The blaze of lustrous chandeliers. The huddle of excited household staff at the front double-doors – opened wide in welcome. And there, astride the threshold, Joseph Kennedy Senior, smugly satisfied behind his dress shirt and cigar, rubbing his hands expectantly as the US Navy staff car scrunched to a halt on the gravel drive. Then, the entrance of Jack, the younger son, self-conscious and grinning. The medal winner. The second son bringing home the first of the silverware of the war.

The citations recorded Jack's heroics in rescuing the crew of the Motor Torpedo Boat PT 109, lost in the waters of the

Ferguson and Blackett Straits on the night of August 1st 1943, along with the injuries he sustained. The Navy and Marine Corps and Purple Heart medals glinted and danced on the young hero's chest, jolted and rattled by the flurry of back-slapping and hand-pumping on the entrance steps. Jack, stranded shyly in the throng of his father's dark-suited friends and political connections – with Joe Junior standing ignored beyond the noisy reception.

And then later. Later, at the family dining table, when coffee had been served and Joe Senior had sat at the head of the table musing over the fortunes of war – and a fine old brandy. The father had well-mapped political plans for his first-born son's future in public office. High expectations that led directly to the steps of the White House and the Oval office within. A Kennedy as king at the court of Washington D.C.

But against his father's hopes and expectations, his second-born had won the medals. Potentially upsetting the smooth progression of Joe Junior's path to the presidency.

From where he was seated at the table, Joe had seen the frustration in his father's eyes. He had read and understood Joe Senior's unspoken disappointment in his first-born son.

The excitement still ran high around the dining table, with Jack – shrugging off his success modestly – unpinning and passing around his medals into eagerly outstretched palms. Joe Junior, gazing up along the white clothed table, glimpsed the look in his father's eyes through the pale blue wreath of cigar smoke. Joe felt the flame of resentment rise up in his face as he sensed his father's acceptance of Jack's success as Joe Junior's failure.

Then: the sudden squall of a family storm. The father, masking his feelings towards his namesake's failing, relishing his second-born's success. Rising from his chair, flushed with brandy-fuelled pride, he raised his crystal balloon glass up in tribute to Jack.

Joe Junior had remained seated, frozen in sullen resentment. Hating both his younger brother's fortune and his father's disappointment.

Joe Senior had glanced angrily down the table. 'Up, son. Up on your feet.'

Reddening, Joe had obeyed.

'Raise your glass, Joe, and congratulate your brother.'

Joe, reaching clumsily for his brandy, had accidentally spilled it. A furious tirade of abuse broke out from the head of the table as the angry patriarch gave vent to his pent-up emotions.

Joe Junior strode out of the dining room, ignoring his bellowing father's commands to remain. Snatching at the dining room door handle, Joe turned and saw the looks of confusion and concern around the family table. He left the room abruptly, slamming the door behind him. It did not shut properly, allowing his father's abuse to follow him as he hurried upstairs to his room. There, in the darkness, sprawled on his bed, his hot face pressed into the cool pillow, he punched his fury into the fat, silk counterpane. Moments later, the bedroom door opening abruptly, the reek of cigar smoke filling the room together with his father's stern voice. Joe Senior's ranting switched from mocking his son's tears to berating his lack of achievement. Joe Junior remained face down in the pillow, helpless before the scalding tide of his father's contempt.

'You'd better get back downstairs, son, and I want to see you shake your brother's hand. Understand?'

Joe remained face down in the pillow, glad the room was in darkness. He would have hated to have had to turn a tear-stained face to his father. But then the light was switched on. Sniffling, Joe hurriedly wiped his eyes.

'And when you've done that, you and I are going to have a little chat. Man to boy. Yeh?'

The growl of a nearby Liberator's engines broke into Lieutenant Joseph Kennedy's painful memories. He opened his eyes, blinking away the scene of Jack's triumphal return.

Colonel Forrest had finished. The briefing was over. Joe found the atmosphere in the briefing room oppressive. He needed fresh air. His CO lit up the customary post-briefing cigar. The aroma stabbed at Joe's nostrils, stirring up more disturbing feelings of resentment and shame. He needed to get away...

Out in the heat, the engines coughed and spluttered to rest. Under the huge, cloudless sky, Joe stretched and breathed in deeply. He relaxed, letting the surge of anger seep out of his tense body. The sounds of shouts and laughter drew his gaze to a group of men over by the far perimeter fence. Even the spasm in his tightened jaw-line ceased as his handsome face cracked open with a wide grin. Shirtless in the heat, they were enjoying a boisterous game of softball. The last of the tension drained from his hunched shoulders.

'Hey! You guys!' he yelled out, breaking into a trot towards them. 'Cut me in.'

The sudden roar of a Mustang fighter-plane banking round above made Liz start.

'It's only the Americans, darling,' her companion laughed, drawing back her friend's arm to link it within her own. 'London has made you jumpy.'

Liz nodded. Down from Cambridge for the summer, she had spent two weeks near London with relatives before joining her fellow undergraduate and close friend at the Rectory in Fersfield. 'You didn't say you had an air base on your doorstep.'

After their salad lunch, the two young women had left the austere Rector to his ecclesiastical crossword in The Church Times. He had struggled with the Hildegard von Bingen clue (Sibyl of the Rhine kindled this musical flame; 1, 5, 8) pulling a face as sour as the pudding prunes during lunch. Liz had surprised and pleased him with her suggested: O ignis spiritus.

'So very glad Jane has such a... suitable young companion for the holidays,' he had beamed. It was the ultimate approval from a protective father for his daughter's friend. 'You must stay,' he added indulgently, 'as long as you wish.'

'I'd better take your ration book, my dear,' Jane's mother remarked, echoing her husband's approbation. Retiring to her sweet peas, she had suggested the afternoon walk for the two friends, 'On such a splendid day.'

A narrow lane divided the rectory from the church and its unusual but beautiful tower. The lane led the girls towards the USAAF air base. They took a turning to their left, avoiding the heat in the shade offered by a coppice.

Liz produced a small packet of Senior Service cigarettes and deftly lit one. Snapping shut the green jade lighter, she exhaled luxuriously.

Jane sighed.

'I know you disapprove,' Liz murmured, 'but I promise I won't smoke in the rectory. Or put on lipstick for evensong.'

Jane giggled – Liz seemed to be able to read her mind. She blushed, feeling gauche and inexperienced beside the pretty, frizzy-haired redhead who was so much more worldly and yet almost exactly the same age. It had been like this from their very first encounter up at university. Liz throwing Jane occasional glances which left Jane feeling on the very edge of something possibly quite naughty but not knowing exactly what or why.

'Don't worry, darling,' Liz soothed. 'I won't kick off my shoes in gay abandon and shock your father with my views on The Modern Girl or shame you by asking your mother for a sherry at tea-time. Like we have at college…

'Shush, Liz, please,' Jane wailed.

'Relax, only teasing.'

'Oh do promise me please that you'll be… be…'

'No politics, no mention of modern art, French existentialism, foreign policy in India or Ireland, trade unionism, contraception for the working classes…'

'Oh, please, Liz.'

The redhead attempted to blow a smoke ring as she relished her companion's anxiety.

'No Marxism, no Socialism – nothing, in fact,' she paused, considering, 'that keeps us all up talking until past midnight in college halls,' she teased.

Jane bit her lip.

'Jam,' pronounced judiciously, 'for your dear mother. The making and the labeling and the storing of it... and Jerusalem,' she broke down, giggling, 'for your stern but sweet papa.'

'Beast,' Jane retorted, hugging Liz warmly. 'I knew you'd understand. I do love them,' she added quickly, 'and they do love me, it's just...'

'It's just amazing that you ever managed to persuade them to allow you to go up to Cambridge.'

Jane nodded ruefully. It had been a struggle. There had been difficulties, but her calm resolve and sweet reasoning had gradually worn down her parents' objections and misgivings. An only child, she had been favoured with her father's cool intellect and had inherited her mother's sound common sense. Both had been used skillfully to gain her a place at Cambridge.

'Which of them gave you the Beware Of Boys talk?' Liz murmured.

Jane blushed. She remembered the slight awkwardness between her mother and herself during the embarrassing exchanges over a kitchen table crowded with pickling jars.

Liz, sensitive to Jane's silence, rattled on lightly. 'My aunt says men are the problem. Boys,' Liz observed drily, 'scare too easily.'

'Elizabeth!' Jane laughed, scandalised.

'Ask any Light Blue to secure you a pair of nylons for the May Ball and he'll simply go to pieces despite having just gained a First in Mods and Greats. Start muttering about not wanting to brush with spivs and black marketeering. All very silly and quite useless,' Liz purred reminiscently. 'Men are much more practical. One actually offered to paint my legs for me. Seams and all.'

'Liz,' Jane squealed, shocked yet secretly thrilled. 'You... you didn't...'

'Neither did he. But he offered,' Liz laughed happily.

'Who? When?' Jane demanded.

'Rupert.'

'Rupert? But he's... he's...'

'A forty-six year old classics Don with lovely eyes and a tin leg from the last war who lives alone in his ivory tower – well, cottage, actually, close by the quad – and who is nevertheless a man. Exactly like the men your good mama warned you about, no doubt.'

'Sally Cato had supper with him,' Jane announced.

Liz frowned. 'The Cat. So Rupert suppered The Cat, did he?' she mused. 'How do you know?' she demanded.

'She nearly got gated coming back in so late. I heard all the whispering and giggling as her pal let her in through a jake's window. It was the evening of the Herrick lecture. We all stayed behind for tea and buns...'

'And The Cat sneaked off?'

'I heard her being beastly about him afterwards. Mimicking his stammer. Very cruel.'

'Cruel?' Liz queried, suddenly alert. 'Jealous, were we?' she teased.

Jane blushed. 'No, of course not. It's just...Well, he is rather sweet.'

'Just don't ask him to procure a pair of nylons, my girl, or he'll be in your rooms paint brush in hand.'

'Liz!' Jane protested.

The redhead finished her cigarette and trod it out carefully. She eyed her companion shrewdly.

'Come along, innocence.'

Arm in arm they strolled contentedly, emerging from the coppice and side-stepping the occasional brambles that threatened their thin summer frocks. Jane promised that they would soon reach a favourite path which would take them around the edge of the airfield and offer them a panoramic view of the open, Norfolk summer landscape. At their feet, daisies, corncockles and purple knapweed provided a colourful carpet. Up above, larks were trilling sweetly. The girls shaded their eyes as they peered up to spot them. Wood pigeons murmured softly in a nearby clump of elms.

'This is so beautiful after London,' Liz confided in a soft, almost sad voice.

Jane squeezed her friend's hand understandingly.

Ahead and to their right lay a different horizon. Beyond a wire fence, the vast, leveled expanse of the airbase, with its closely cropped green grass, gave way to the seemingly endless stretches of pale grey concrete runways baking in the sun.

A sudden thunderous roar above them left both girls squealing and cowering. A Mustang fighter plane, the sound of its piston engine changing from a thumping growl to a rising snarl as it climbed away, reclaiming the sky for another circuit before attempting to land.

Liz, laughing, brushed her knees clear of the dry, prickling earth she had knelt in as the fighter plane had zoomed over them.

'Nice neighbours!'

Jane smoothed her shoulder-length, dark brown hair back into place. 'You'll get accustomed to it. Even the hens have started laying again. Daddy, of course, was worried about the church tower. Such delicate tracery. But the Base Commander came to tea and explained about the runways. The bombers – they are called Liberators – would not be flying directly over the church. He was very well mannered but a Mormon so Daddy didn't show him his butterfly collection, but Mummy did present him with a pot of greengage jam and he said "Thank you kindly, Ma'am," just like they do in the cinema. But he has left and now there's a new chap in charge there, a Colonel Forrest I believe and – Oh!'

The two girls were forced to stop abruptly by a stretch of the wire mesh fencing that cut across the grassy pathway, blocking further progress.

'Oh!' murmured Jane doubtfully. 'Gosh. This wasn't here when I was home for Easter.'

'What now? Hadn't we better go back?'

Jane shook her head then tossed it back decisively. 'Of course not... there, look! The path picks up again over by those gorse bushes, see?'

'Well, we could go that way,' Liz agreed. 'It will take us towards the airfield.'

They explored the enforced diversion, threading single-file through the dense bushes while following the line of tall, forbidding fence. In the distance, the Mustang had taxied to a halt after landing. It seemed no bigger – or more threatening – than a tiny painted toy. The pigeons had returned to their soft murmuring and high up above the larks resumed their song.

Despite the strong sunshine, Liz shivered when she glanced up at the gleaming coils of barbed wire riding the top of the high barrier. The harsh intrusion of the war into their peaceful summer afternoon reminded her of her recent visit to London; of bomb craters, air raid sirens and hideous shelters.

The bushes thinned and the ground became open grass again. They saw a group of tanned, athletic young American airmen enjoying a game of bat and ball. Jane glanced away shyly from the wire mesh but Liz gazed appreciatively – giggling when their presence at the fence was celebrated with the happy shout of "Dames!" A piercing wolf-whistle followed. Jane turned to go but Liz stood her ground.

Their softball game abandoned, the airmen dashed across the grass up to the fence. They yelled their appreciation out loud, filling the air with "Hi! Honey!" "Hubba Hubba" and – for Liz – "Get a load of that redhead". Jane blushed while Liz laughed.

'Come along,' Jane whispered primly.

'I'm staying, darling. Just a bit of fun. No harm in it.'

Jane, still blushing and with her head bowed, veered away as a full and frank compliment acknowledging her charms flew through the wire. Liz skipped up and grabbed her companion's arm gently but firmly to steer her back to face the fence. The buzz of excitement increased. Above the din, a young officer saluted them smartly, introducing himself as Lieutenant William Ford. He apologized for the rowdy airmen with a shrug.

'Hi, honey,' he said, speaking easily through the wire mesh to Liz.

Liz nodded. Jane averted her shy gaze.

'No need to be shy, honey,' Will continued. 'Where you folks going on such a fine day, hmm?'

Suddenly, bursting through the airmen pressing up against the fence, a short, thick-set young man launched himself up the wire mesh, clinging to it a few feet up. Tossing his head back, he uttered a coyote howl.

Flinching, Jane shrank back.

'Now don't you mind him, honey. That's just Lou.'

Lou slithered down the fence to the cheers of those surrounding him. A scrummage followed with Lou in the thick of things as the others wrestled, then pinned him to the grass.

'We need a nurse here,' a voice shouted, laughing. 'This guy needs the kiss of life.'

Liz grinned then turned to catch up with Jane who had walked away along the barrier. On the other side, breaking away from the horseplay, William Ford caught up.

'Sorry, honey. You OK?' he asked Jane, his tone soft and respectful.

Jane paused, then turned decidedly to face Will directly through the wire mesh. They were almost nose to nose.

'We're fine, thanks. But,' she added waspishly, 'don't call me "honey." OK?'

'OK' murmured Will, momentarily taken aback. 'I sure didn't mean no offence.'

The girls walked on, Jane drifting slightly ahead. Will tracked Liz pace for pace.

'So what may I call you?' Will ventured, bouncing back.

Two paces later – before Liz had framed her reply – the wire mesh fence ran out abruptly. Over Will's shoulder Liz noticed another tall, good-looking officer approaching across the grass.

'I'm Liz. Liz McCoy. How do you do?' She offered Will a tentative hand.

Will took it and kept hold of it. 'The real McCoy,' he murmured, smiling.

Jane returned to join Liz. 'I think your friend wants you,' she said to Will, watching the approach of the lithe young man.

Will looked around. Liz sensed Jane's awareness of the handsome officer striding towards them.

'That's not my friend,' Will grinned engagingly. 'I'm joking. Guess he is. He sure as hell ain't my boss.'

'You'll never have a boss riding you, William Ford, not in this life. Now will you be good enough to introduce me to these charming friends of yours?'

Liz noticed that Jane had patted her hair as the young officer approached to join them.

'Sure thing. Girls, this is Lieutenant Joe Kennedy. US Navy pilot. And this is Liz. Liz McCoy,' Will nodded, adding as he turned to Jane, 'And… I didn't quite catch…'

'I'm Jane,' she said, her voice cool and distinct.

But Liz caught the almost imperceptible quiver in her friend's tone.

Lieutenant Kennedy took her hand and pressed it firmly.

'Jane,' he echoed.

II

29th July 1944
Fersfield US Air Force Base

Joe and Will approached the colonel's office with mounting interest. The July sun was pleasantly warm in the cloudless, blue sky.

Seeing the staff cars drawn up alongside the flat-roofed, low, brick building, Will nudged his friend.

Joe nodded, his eyes narrowing as they took in the four armed guards at fixed posts.

'Gee, something big,' Will whispered excitedly.

Again, Joe merely nodded.

'Come in, gentlemen,' Colonel Forrest barked.

Joe, to his amusement, sensed that his CO was ill-at-ease in the presence of the visiting officers from central HQ.

Joe and Will gave their names and ranks, saluting smartly – much to their colonel's evident relief – before sitting down in the chairs prepared for them some feet away from a large desk. Joe's gaze swept briefly over the classified documents arranged neatly on the desk-top before settling to appraise the senior ranking officers seated behind it.

'Lieutenant Colonel Lieb,' Colonel Forrest began the introductions. 'Major Randel.'

Nods were curtly exchanged. 'Kennedy, eh? Know your father, son. And your kid brother did well out there in the Pacific.'

Will sensed Joe's stiffening at the mention of Jack's medals. They never spoke of it but Will guessed the truth.

'As you gentlemen, strictly speaking, should not be, but probably are, aware,' Lieb began dryly, his slow but precise voice taking command, 'the USAAF began flying Project Aphrodite missions some weeks back –'

'As from June twenty third.' his colleague supplied.

Lieb nodded, a slight frown signalling his annoyance at the interruption. 'The purpose has been to go after the Nazi V-weapon sites.'

Will stirred slightly in his seat.

'That's right. Hitler's desperate gamble. The so-called terror weapons. Almost impossible to stop them in the air. London is wide open and civilian casualties are mounting.'

Joe and Will leaned forward expectantly as the major unsheathed a bundle of black and white photographs from a sealed envelope. 'Sir?'

Lieutenant Colonel Lieb nodded.

'Our informants tell us the V-1 was developed by two clever Krauts called Lusser and Gosslau and that a new weapon, the V-2, is being developed by a team led by a guy called Wernher von Braun,' he continued as Randel presented the photographs across the desk – holding them up in turn for Joe and Will to see but not touch. 'Hitler is believed to have commissioned them personally. The whole terror-weapon circus is run by a Lieutenant-General Schneider, but there are even bigger onions in this stew. Major General Dornberger keeps a watching brief and our intelligence boys suspect he has the ear of Heinrich Himmler.'

'The British call the V-1 the 'doodlebug', don't they, sir?' Will ventured, nodding to a black and white grainy snapshot of a cigar-shaped missile, winged, rear-finned and with a tail-mounted rocket engine.

'They sure do,' Lieb countered. 'Peenemunde was knocked out last year but they were soon back in production.'

'And they have improved the range and accuracy,' the major broke in. 'The V-1 is getting cheaper to make by the week. We estimate that production costs have come down from ten thousand to fifteen hundred Marks a shot. And the assembly line is slick. Only 270 man-hours to get each baby out onto the launch site.'

'And the V-2?' Joe murmured.

'13000 man-hours at a cost of seventy five thousand Marks each is our current estimate,' Randel replied, relishing his moment to divulge the details.

'They'll run out of time, if not money,' Joe said.

The major shook his head vigorously. 'Slave labour, underground production sites in the Harz mountain-range and with Hitler bankrolling the…'

'No need for all that,' Lieb broke in sharply, keen to progress the briefing. 'These are weapons of terror and, once launched, are unstoppable.'

'But can't we jam the bastards?' Will demanded.

Colonel Forrest reddened slightly but Lieb grinned indulgently.

'Over to you, Major.'

Major Randel spread his hands out. 'No can do. The V-1 is not radio-guided so we can't deflect its trajectory by jamming. It's pretty basic. No electronic guidance system on board. They just point them and fire them. They come down when they run out of fuel. The range is set by calculating the amount of fuel they'll need. Very hit-and-miss. Now and then some brave RAF guy will manage to fly alongside and flip it off course with a wing roll but that's too dicey and unreliable.'

Will, chin in hand, nodded appreciatively.

'And the V-2 will come in at something like over 4000 feet per second…'

Joe and Will whistled in unison. Forrest stiffened, anticipating a stronger, earthier response.

'Faster than a tracer bullet,' Major Randel affirmed.

'Only a slight increase in payload over the V-1 but the high pressure shock wave when it slams down could more than double the kill factor.'

Joe and Will sat in respectful silence, each nursing his own thoughts on the further horror soon to be raining down daily on the people of London.

'Impossible to effect interception,' Lieutenant-Colonel Lieb said softly, breaking the silence. 'So we're fighting fire with fire.

Project Aphrodite means to wipe out these babies once and for all.'

Leaning forward urgently across the desk, emphasising each point with a stubby forefinger – its nail whitening each time he jabbed it down – the Lieutenant-Colonel gave Joe and Will a terse summary of the missions so far. Subdued by the enormity of what they heard, the two young airmen sat in attentive silence despite their eagerness to get busy and strike a blow back at the Nazis.

'Project Aphrodite's aim is to fly unpiloted planes – our own kinda flying bombs – by remote control and crash them down onto the launch sites and the production centres.'

Lieb explained that war-weary planes, close to being decommissioned, were deployed after being stripped of all armour, turrets and other weighty features. The auto-pilot was wired up to a radio-receiver.

Will was about to ask a technical question. Lieb anticipated him.

'It works. The radio control unit we're using has been adapted from the recent bomb experiments at Horsham St. Faith, but Major Randel will fill you two in later on the specifications.'

'Payload?' Joe inquired.

'Ten tons. Torpex.'

Joe pursed his lips. He had heard of the British high-explosive. It sure as hell packed a powerful punch.

'We need it,' Lieb explained, 'to go after them deep underground.'

Joe nodded. A pilot, he wondered aloud about the dispersal of such a huge payload.

'Tough to fly by remote,' he reflected. 'Does the payload shift?'

Lieb nodded approvingly. 'Good point, son. Aphrodite first used B-17s, but stripped right down to the bone. Gave us a 5000 lb weight reduction.'

Joe calculated rapidly. 'Unloaded weight of 32,000 lbs.'

'Exactly. Then it's loaded up with the Torpex. Very securely.'

Joe grinned.

Lieb briefly explained how the Torpex was dispersed. The bomb bays had been strengthened by reinforcing cross-beams to support the ten-ton payload.

'A B-17 will take 335 63-pound boxes. That's 21,105 pounds tops. 25 boxes on the flight deck. 210 boxes in the bomb bay and…'

'100 in the radio room,' Joe concluded.

Lieb was impressed. 'You guys catch on quick.' He turned to Colonel Forrest.

'Seems like you've found me a couple of real peaches.'

The Colonel accepted the compliment, but grudged Joe the tribute. 'Still a bit raw but I'll lick them into shape.'

Joe's scowl of resentment disappeared as Lieb continued. 'Standard take-off, of course. Once airborne, the Torpex must be armed.'

Will looked up quickly. 'Primacord?'

Lieb assented. 'With a double check on the connections. The electrical circuit must be completely intact.'

'And then?' Will almost whispered.

'And then,' Lieb spoke emphatically, 'the crew bales out.'

For the first time since they had entered the briefing room, Joe and Will smiled at each other.

'Glad to see you gentlemen approve,' Lieb commented dryly. 'Now, to business. Trials to date have all been A-OK. Adjustments have been calibrated to ensure optimum flight characteristics and everything is apple pie, just like momma makes them.' Lieb paused. He stared intently across the desk.

'Look here, you guys. These goddam terror weapons have got us worried. Sure, the Soviets are doing their bit and now we've opened up a second front in Normandy and Italy is collapsing it is just about end-game for the Nazis. But there's more.'

Joe and Will looked up expectantly. Major Randel nodded gravely.

Lieb drew in his breath and exhaled slowly. He spoke deliberately, as if reluctantly.

'Does the name Mimoyecques mean anything to either of you?'

Will shrugged. Joe shook his head. Lieb had turned to Randel as if to seek approval of his pronunciation. The major merely nodded.

'Mimoyecques,' he repeated, more confidently. 'Word has gotten to us from the French Resistance of a different type of terror weapon being built there.'

'Another rocket?' Will hazarded.

Lieb shook his head. 'No. Not another rocket. A supergun which will soon be able to pound London with…' he broke off and nodded to Randel. 'Give them the facts.'

The Major tore open an envelope marked "Top Secret" and took out folded sheets of paper, handing one each to Will and Joe. They read the closely typed script quickly, conscious of the eyes across the desk on them.

'Got the picture?' Lieutenant-Colonel Lieb drawled softly as Randel reclaimed the briefing sheets.

'When our Intelligence first got wind of the "London Gun" they couldn't believe the specifications. Just couldn't be, our back-room boys said. This baby, let's call it the V-3, has a barrel length of 150 yards…in fact, it is a composite battery of 25 individual barrels…'

Will whistled softly.

'And it's only 90 miles from the heart of London. When fully operational – and our sources say that will be soon – it will be capable of firing 150 mm rocket-assisted projectiles, one every 12 seconds…'

This time, Colonel Forrest did not mind the whispered 'Jesus' from his two young airmen.

'You said it, guys,' Lieb countered grimly. 'We've just got to take this goddam V-3 supergun out of action. Pronto.'

'But what's the Navy's stake in this?' Joe wondered aloud.

'Leave the politics to your father, Kennedy,' Colonel Forrest rasped.

Joe flushed and scowled. Lieb chuckled.

'We're here, and you're here, because the US Navy means to deploy radio-controlled drones out in the Pacific theatre. We want to launch planes from carriers on one-way missions against the Japs. So here we are at Fersfield for Project Anvil.'

'Anvil?' echoed Joe and Will in unison.

'Glad to see you can keep the lid on some things, Colonel,' Lieb remarked dryly. 'Yes. Anvil. We're going after that V-3 at Mimoyecques from Fersfield under the code name Anvil and,' he paused, 'you'll be flying PB4Ys not B-17s. It's a dry-run for the Pacific operation. And some. Any questions?'

Joe grinned. PB4Ys. The US Navy's version of the Liberator bomber. Joe had flown these out over the Bay of Biscay in hundreds of hours of anti-submarine patrols.

'Why Fersfield, sir?' Joe's tone was respectful. He liked Lieb. Liked his frank, forthright approach.

'Our best option. Project Aphrodite ran out of the Woodbridge base under Colonel James Turner. Woodbridge has long runways. Gave the pilots a little extra length to get those B-17s up in the air. But we hit a snag...'

'Woodbridge is the crash-strip, isn't it?' Will queried.

Lieb nodded. 'Exactly. Bombers that had taken flak or fighter damage over the Continent were being directed to Woodbridge to give them more runway for their emergency landings. If one of them had slewed into a B-17 loaded up with Torpex...'

Lieb left his audience to imagine the results of such an occurrence.

'That's why we're all here at Fersfield,' Colonel Forrest remarked.

'Yes,' Lieb agreed. 'US Navy Special Air Unit No. 1 with our PB4Ys all primed for August twelve.'

Major Randel twisted around in his chair, as if the date was news to him.

'August twelve. Confirmed. Came down the wire yesterday.'

Colonel Forrest spread his arms out wide. 'But they'll need time to...'

'There's an Aphrodite mission going out on August four, Colonel. These two guys will be up there with the observers.'

'In the mother-ship,' Randel explained, answering Will's frown. 'No need to bale out just yet. We aim to bring you two back to Fersfield.'

'That's right. Anything else, boys?' Lieb asked.

'The guidance system, sir,' Will began. Joe, alongside, nodded quickly.

'Now strictly speaking that's all still classified information. Codename Block. But,' he considered, 'I guess you need to know the basics. Major?'

Major Randel cleared his throat before choosing his words carefully. 'OK. It's this way. The mother-ship, a PV-1 Ventura, is fitted with a nose-mounted television screen.

The controller, squeezed right up-front in the Ventura, works from that screen. Signals will be sent from the mother-ship to your plane, the PB4Y, through a BC 756 Control Box using a whip-aerial fixed to the fuselage. With me so far?'

Will nodded.

'At a predetermined point, your task will be to arm the Torpex payload and then bale out. The controller in the mother-ship guides your pilotless Liberator out over the coast and across the Channel to the V-3 site at Mimoyecques.'

The briefing drew to a close after Will had sought and received further clarification on a few more technical points, and Joe had been assured that their aircraft would have its exit hatches enlarged to accommodate both the back and chest parachutes each airman would need in order to abandon their plane safely.

Chuckling, Lieutenant-Colonel Lieb bent down and eased the left-hand drawer of the desk open gently. Both Joe and Will heard the bottle of rye roll sluggishly, but the promise of a post-briefing drink was quickly broken by Colonel Forrest's 'That will be all. Dismissed.'

Joe could have sworn he heard a muted 'Aw, shucks,' from Lieb as the drawer was closed. After saluting their superior officers, Joe and Will withdrew.

'Forget it,' Joe laughed, releasing the tension in a brief but furious bout of play-boxing with Will. 'Let's get us a couple of coffees in the PX.'

That evening, bathed and closely shaved, Joe gazed steadily into the small mirror. Smart as new paint, he thought. The youthful face reflected in it, though broad, handsome and lightly tanned, already showed signs of both character and maturity. Tiny lines, etched by hundreds of flying hours, crinkled the skin at his eyes. His full, almost petulant mouth, had been tightened by the responsibilities of his rank.

Tonight would be his fourth date with Jane. Joe and Jane, Will and Liz had become regular items every chance they had got since that brief encounter at the perimeter wire almost a month ago. Joe closed his eyes, remembering how the base security, headed up by the blustering Sergeant Braddock, had roared up in a Jeep to break up their unauthorised encounter. Braddock, as tough as a teamster, had bullied the two girls but had met with the cool logic of Jane, who had gently pointed out to the red-faced Sergeant that not only had there been no notices forbidding public access – but half the fence was missing. Remembering, Joe grinned.

Then, an unaccustomed stab of keen apprehension – unusual for Joe Kennedy, who had always been pencilled in on the Prom cards by hopeful mothers and their daughters.

Jane, he thought. He smoothed his hair down nervously for the third time. Despite the pressure and excitement of Project Anvil, Joe felt her presence in his mind nearly all the time. Her gentleness. Her loveliness. Her grace. Composed and a little serious, Jane was cool but not cold. Yes, damn it, he suddenly admitted to himself. She excited him. Her innocence intrigued him. Will and Liz had clicked – remaining together alone long after Joe had escorted Jane back from a drink or a dance to the gate of the Rectory opposite the church. Will and Liz had become very close – as Will's grin clearly betrayed when referring to his nocturnal activities over his first cup of coffee the following morning.

Jane was not that sort of girl, Joe sensed. What was that old saying? I want a good girl – and I want her bad. Joe grinned sheepishly into the mirror at the double meaning. For the first time he had actually found himself almost tongue-tied with a girl – or at least reluctant to incur her crisp response should he indicate that they might take their deepening friendship a little further along the path of pleasure.

Her innocence. A perfect English rose. Unblemished. Joe had grown to enjoy teasing Jane. Liz always cottoned on, flashing knowing looks but Jane seemed to remain completely unaware of any innuendo. Once, when Liz had giggled and whispered the explanation to one of Will's more dubious jokes, Jane had merely given both Will and Joe a 'don't be childish' look – and it had been Joe who had reddened.

Jane. That fragrance of hers. It stirred him. Maddened him. Rose water – so light, so fresh. Joe allowed his mind to wander, wondering if she dabbed it not just at her wrists but at her throat…

'Now darling I'm sure I don't have to remind you to be… well… careful…' her mother had said to her earlier as they had been washing the dishes after tea.

'Yes, Mummy.'

'Men, you must realize, can be so difficult to…well…to manage. Especially,' her mother had added significantly, 'when they grow fond.'

'Yes, Mummy.'

Then there had been a change of tack.

'All this dashing into Diss or, for heaven's sake, up to Norwich, at the drop of a hat.'

'There is a war on, Mummy.'

'And you haven't actually introduced him to us.'

'Everything is changing, Mummy... becoming more informal, more relaxed...'

'Exactly my point, darling. And after all, he is an American.'

'Yes, Mummy.'

'One has viewed such peculiar things in picture shows.'

'Joe calls them movies and anyway he prefers a decent book. He can quote from both Ovid and Petrarch.'

'In translation, no doubt.'

Yet another change of tack.

'Kennedy. Now surely,' her mother had continued, after returning from emptying the tea leaves on the compost heap, 'that denotes Irish ancestry. Would he be Catholic by any chance?'

'Mmm. He calls the chaplain 'Father' but for some reason doesn't seem to like him very much and he has the sweetest little silver rosary his mother gave to him before he left for England.'

'Now your father...'

'Oh Mummy, please – Joe's Catholicism or being of Irish descent or being an American pilot means nothing...'

'Jane, darling, there are certain pitfalls in life it is wiser to sidestep, perhaps avoid altogether.'

'He... we... he isn't in love with me or anything like that,' Jane blurted out. 'We... we just sort of jog along together as good pals and he is so polite, Mummy, so wonderfully well-mannered...'

'So you are becoming fond of him.'

Silence from Jane who had merely blushed, resenting her mother's shrewd insight into her secret.

There followed a slight softening in her mother's voice.

'Oh dear, it's worse than I thought. My darling, do please be careful. If there were to be any... scandal...'

'Mummy,' Jane squeaked indignantly.

'Now I'm sure you know perfectly well what I mean, Jane. It simply wouldn't do. It would of course quite ruin your poor father. Ruin him. And there are whispers in the Cathedral Close that our rural Dean may be taking up a placement in Salisbury, leaving a vacancy...You do understand?'

'Yes, Mummy. I understand,' Jane retorted coldly.

Nothing more had been said.

She thought of Joe. And Will. And that madcap Lou with the peculiar, possibly Italian name, Pontillo, and the others in Joe's circle of friends. Jane gazed into her looking glass as she brushed her hair, blushing slightly. In a moment of abandonment, after bathing and towelling herself dry, she had sprinkled herself with copious amounts of expensive rose water. Joe had once, in a moment of tenderness, kissed her and called her his English rose. Jane closed her eyes, blushing a little more deeply as she remembered the kiss.

Naked after her bath, in the evening sunshine behind the chaste white chintz at her bedroom window, Jane steadily brushed her hair as she recalled the exchange after teatime between her mother and herself. Her body shone with the rose water which had slightly stung her, leaving her tingling.

Polite. Jane bit her lower lip. Joe was certainly polite. Infuriatingly so. She shuddered as she thought of his restraint. All that power under control. He hardly touched her, avoiding direct physical contact except for helping her somewhat diffidently out of that funny little Jeep he drove. Will, she reflected ruefully, took blatant advantage of such opportunities to let his eager hands enjoy Liz.

Courteous. Joe, without being affected, was as old fashioned as any Junior Don she had encountered at Cambridge. Good breeding, there, surely, undeniably – as Jane's mother would have said.

Jane pressed her naked thighs together and shivered deliciously. Joe. For all his courteous restraint there was a boldness, an assuredness, in him. Jane had sensed his eyes fully appraising her on more than one occasion. She dropped the brush. It came to rest in her lap, the bristles prickling her skin. She parted her lips in surprise at the sweet discomfort.

'Jane?' her mother's summons rose from the foot of the stairs. 'Aren't you ready yet? What on earth are you doing?'

'Nearly ready, Mummy.'

They were in Norwich. Will had taken Liz off to some dubious nightspot for some hot jazz and dancing, leaving Joe to escort Jane gently up along the star-lit cobblestones of Elm Hill, away from Tombland, towards the heart of the blacked-out town.

After the warm summer day, the cloudless night brought with it an unaccustomed chill. Jane pressed unselfconsciously against Joe as she told him of her childhood. A childhood of simple – although it seemed to Joe somewhat lonely – pleasures. Walks along the river bank and, later, summer sailing on the Deben at Woodbridge when her father had been the vicar of St. John's there. Joe learned of her favourite spot at Kyson Point, where she had filled her hours contentedly collecting wild flowers and reading poetry.

Suddenly anxious that Joe might become bored, Jane regaled him with stories of her friend, Liz. The red-headed Ulster girl, who was reading Classics at Cambridge, had inherited her wealthy father's robust approach to life. Jane shyly alluded to Liz's cavalier attitude to relationships and her very hectic social life.

'And what about you?' Joe broke in, turning the tables on her.

'Me?'

'Yes, you.'

She glanced away shyly.

'Do your studies leave any time for other activities… clubs, drama or the debating society,' he asked in mock solemnity.

'Oh, I see… yes… clubs and societies…'

Sensing her awkwardness, Joe gave Jane a gentle squeeze, reassuring her that he had been teasing her – not imagining her to be like Liz.

Talk of her studies moved into politics and took them, arm in arm, to the foot of the Norman castle that rose up proudly from its grassy mound. Skirting the ticklish Irish Question, they fell into a heated discussion of the Empire. Joe's democratic instincts rushed hot-headedly to the fore.

'Capitalist expansionism,' he concluded, with a vigour Harvard would have approved of whole-heartedly.

'Really?' murmured Jane. 'I think you'll find it is the textile Trade Unions here keeping India on a short rein.'

Joe contested the point with fervour – until Jane impishly predicted that the Stars and Stripes would no doubt be replacing the Union Jack as Britain slowly retreated from her colonies after the war. The acuity of her perception rankled, but Joe relished the cut and thrust, admiring her candour. True, her digressions into Walpole and the Whigs and the bicameral system seemed another world away from the politics of his father – wheeling and dealing and 'fixing' in cigar-smoke filled backrooms. Her sudden return to the immediate future – the defeat of Hitler and possible Soviet expansion into Europe startled and intrigued him. He held her tightly, relishing her irony.

'We had centuries of communism, and it didn't do us any harm,' she observed laconically. 'Only it was called the feudal system and our commissars were kings.'

'Aren't we a little too close to the castle,' Joe murmured, after silencing her suddenly with a kiss.

Jane thrilled to the protective squeeze of his encircling arm. She answered him with a questioning, open-eyed look.

Joe wondered aloud if Norwich Castle presented any Dornier bomber with too easy a target.

'We are quite safe here,' she whispered, returning his kiss, lightly, on the tip of his nose. 'I promise.'

'Sure?' he drawled, unconvinced. He kissed her firmly.

'Mmm,' she managed.

'Guess you've got that in writing. From the Luftwaffe.'

'As good as.'

He pulled back, looking at her quizzically.

Jane relented. 'It's supposed to be a secret but I can tell you,' she whispered in a sudden bout of confidentiality.

'Spill the beans.'

'Spill the... Oh, I see what you mean. You say the funniest things, sometimes, Joe.'

'The castle?' he prompted.

'Our Home Guard,' Jane announced proudly, 'detained the crew from a Heinkel that was brought down just near Diss in 1940. The head of the patrol was one of Daddy's vergers...'

'Verger?'

Jane explained. Continuing, she told Joe that papers on the pilot indicated that Hitler himself had forbidden the bombing of Norwich castle. When questioned, the Luftwaffe pilot had told his captors that all bomber pilots had been instructed to avoid the Norman castle as Hitler had plans to use it as something of a weekend retreat.

The authorities were doubtful at first but after several pilots had been captured and interrogated it seemed that it was true.

'So we are safe here, don't you see?'

'I should have thought that, by now, Hitler would have given up on that idea... and anyhow, doodlebugs don't have brainwashed pilots flying them,' Joe countered grimly. 'Hitler has an arsenal of terror weapons and there's no Geneva Convention about targets.'

Dismayed by Jane's seeming complacency, Joe startled her with his vehemence. Seeing the alarm in her eyes, he softened his tone.

'But we're going to knock out the launch sites. Soon. Eliminate them once and for all...'

'You make it sound like taking petrol to a wasps' nest.'

'Something like that,' he grunted, suddenly aware that he was on the brink of saying too much. Projects Aphrodite and Anvil were still 'top secret'. He returned to the future of the Norman castle.

'Maybe Hitler will occupy it after all.'

'Joe?'

'Get a room all to himself,' Joe continued, his tone hardening. 'Down in the dungeons. Before he's put on trial.'

His mind brooded in the ensuing silence on the Blitz over London's East End, on doodlebugs and on the V-3 lurking in the hill-side across the Channel at Mimoyecques.

Sensing his melancholy, Jane snuggled closer into his tunic.

'They'll put him in the Tower of London if they ever capture him alive.'

'I guess so,' he smiled, his mood lightening. He kissed her. His lips left hers and visited her cheeks and eyebrows before settling on her nose. He inhaled slowly, drawing in her sweet, soft perfume.

Jane spoke solemnly. 'There's something I must share with you. Give you.'

Joe swallowed noisily in the darkness.

'Come with me,' she said abruptly. 'Come on.'

She grabbed his hand impulsively. They raced back down along the streets, skittling down the cobblestones of Elm Hill. Joe's mind was in a whirl. Was this it? Was this to be their night? Did she know of some quiet, secluded spot beneath the stars?

Hand-in-hand, they cannoned into Tombland, slowed down to a walking pace and – led by Jane – joined a queue lined up beneath the starlight before what seemed to Joe to be a single-decker bus. A bus with no seating but with a stove-pipe chimney sprouting from the roof. Joe stared, frankly puzzled.

'Special treat,' Jane whispered, squeezing his hand.

The queue shuffled patiently up to the side of the bus. A hot, sizzling sound filled the night air. Joe caught the pungent aroma of frying. Reaching her place at the narrow counter, Jane murmured the order for their suppers. Joe joined her and peered in. He caught a glimpse of a pale faced young man busy at the fryers. In the eerie light, his oiled hair glistened. Teeth set into his lower lip, the young man whistled a Glenn Miller swing tune. Joe's fist tightened. That's one of our tunes... and why the hell wasn't this guy in uniform... the angry thoughts flashed across his mind.

'Say, fellah, is this your night work? Do your fighting in the daylight only, eh?'

'Joe, no…' Jane turned, pressing a finger to her lips anxiously.

The young man turned towards them. Joe saw the missing left arm. From the shoulder, the empty sleeve was pinned back.

'Dunkirk,' he said evenly. 'Could have used some help from you Yanks then. Wrapped, Miss?'

'No, thanks. Salt and vinegar, please.'

'Help yourself, Miss.'

Joe attempted an apology but, gathering up their suppers, Jane bundled him away.

'Gee, I'm sorry…'

'Hot head. Always go at things like a bull at a gate, Joe Kennedy.' Her tone was reproachful.

Joe sulked, hating his mistake and wincing under her sarcasm.

'Didn't mean to shoot my mouth off like that…'

'Oh, come on. Instead of "shooting your mouth off" as you so quaintly put it, fill your mouth with these.'

Joe glanced down dubiously at the fried fish and chips.

'Try. Go on,' Jane giggled. The dark moment had lifted, they were close again.

Joe hesitated. He bent his head down and sniffed.

'Coward,' Jane teased. 'I suppose you are more used to finer fare. Sole and lobster?'

Joe squinted down suspiciously at his battered fish.

'Go on, try some. After all, you say you live near Cape Cod.'

'This is cod?' Joe exclaimed, his voice a mixture of surprise and relief.

Jane nodded. She giggled again as Joe swore – sucking on his fingertips after burning them. Grinning, he managed a mouthful.

'Say, that's good,' he pronounced approvingly.

Under the arched stone entrance to the cathedral they munched contentedly. Joe finished first.

'Say, what do I do about these?' he shrugged, offering up his greasy fingertips.

'Baby,' Jane teased, dabbing first at his shining chin and then at his fingertips with her handkerchief. 'I thought all you brave pilots were taught survival skills.'

Their hands remained touching. Soon, their fingers were entwined. They both spoke at once.

'No, you go on,' Jane encouraged.

Pulling her gently towards him, Joe spoke softly. Almost hesitantly. He spoke of his growing love for Jane. Of his need to see her. Be with her. Of his hopes, perhaps, of a future together.

Jane quelled his impetuous words with another kiss. He responded, his hands capturing and squeezing her slender waist.

Her hands gently prised his away. 'Not now, my darling. And not here.'

Joe looked puzzled.

'Holy ground.'

They had wandered into the Cathedral Close.

Joe grinned sheepishly. Jane reminded him that she would not be returning to Cambridge until October.

'We still have over two months of summer.'

'I'll have a bit of flying to do,' Joe argued.

'But they won't move you to another base. Or make you go over to bomb the Japanese, will they?' Jane asked suddenly.

'Nothing doing. I've got a mission to fly.'

'Will said something to Liz about that…'

'Will talks too much.'

'A secret mission. That means it's dangerous, doesn't it?'

Joe's voice softened as he caught her anxious tone. 'No, not really,' he shrugged.

Jane persisted. 'But what about their fighters? They're surely faster than your bomber. And,' a catch in her voice made him wince, 'there's that terrible ack-ack.' She clutched his hands, squeezing hard. 'You will fly high, very high, and keep safe, won't you?'

There was a new urgency in her voice. Their usual teasing and playful banter had evaporated. He struggled to reassure her, bound as he was to secrecy.

'Can't say much but don't worry about ack-ack. Wil and I will be baling out long before we reach the French coast and their anti-aircraft defences. It has all been carefully planned. I'll be back. Safe and in one piece.'

'Bale out? Oh, you mean a parachute. But... but who will fly the plane?'

Joe bent his face down to meet hers, silencing her questioning with a long, firm kiss.

The mood lightened. Happily, they squabbled about where they would live after the war.

'You'll love the States,' he pronounced.

'You seem very sure, Joe Kennedy.'

'Sure I'm sure.'

'That I'll marry you,' she reasoned teasingly. 'I'd have to marry you before I could go and live with you in America.'

4th August 1944
Fersfield USAAF Base

'Yessir.' Joe and Will saluted snappily and turned away from the Jeep to walk across the hot concrete towards the B-24. In preparation for their imminent Anvil mission, they had been scheduled to ride as observers on one of the Aphrodite mother-planes.

Colonel Forrest brought his gloved hand down smartly against the side of the Jeep. 'Move it,' he barked, slapping twice.

Avoiding the odd drop of oil dripping from the converted bomber's inner port engine, Joe and Will sought the sheltering shade beneath the huge wing as they waited to mount the ladder and clamber aboard the B-24. Stepping out of the bright August sunshine into the deep shadows beneath the wing caused them to blink. The smell of high-octane aviation fuel hung heavily in the air.

His eyes accustomed to the shade, Joe gazed down into his open palm.

'What's that you keep looking at, Joe?' Will asked.

Joe Kennedy closed his fist protectively, but then opened it again to show Will the pressed flower Jane had given him.

'Gee, that's real cute. Gotta name for it?'

'Oxlip. *Primula elatior*.'

'Helluva long name for such an itsy-bitsy bud,' Will mused.

'Her favourite. Ever since she was a girl,' Joe remarked.

Will scratched his head. 'Nothin's simple over here, eh? All the names and the words kinda confuse me. Take that crazy game they have. Cricket. You're out when you're in and you're in when you're out. Crazy game.'

'Liz took you to watch cricket?' Joe laughed.

'Like watching paint dry. We kinda strayed over the boundary into the long grass...'

Joe shook his head, still laughing.

'Afterwards,' Will protested, 'we trailed back to some flaky hut called a pavilion for bread and jam which back home Mom calls jelly...'

Primula elatior. Joe carefully pocketed the oxlip Jane had kissed before giving him. I want to share my garden with you, she had said, offering him the flower and telling him its name. I want to introduce you to all the flowers in my garden and teach you all their names.

'... and this thing they've got over here with tea. Tea, for Christ's sake. It looks and tastes like old maid's...'

'That's us,' Joe broke in. 'Let's move it.'

Minutes later, Joe and Will were strapped into their crew seats. The four piston engines coughed and spluttered into life one by one and soon the entire airframe of the mother-plane, a B24 for this mission, was shuddering as the pilot eased the throttle open.

On the control panel, the needle on the rev counter flickered and climbed. The propellers became a blur – glinting silver discs slicing the air. Joe nodded his satisfaction, recognising the quivering of the bomber straining against its brakes. It was a grudging satisfaction only. Joe Kennedy hated being a passenger.

THE HAMMER AND THE ANVIL

Final clearance came just as full throttle was achieved. The B-24 rolled out, gathering speed. Seconds later, the mother-plane was lumbering along the runway, its heavy wheels buzzing on the concrete. Joe glimpsed the tree-line almost a mile-and-a-half away. Deceptive, he thought. Distances at this speed. They would be there in about twenty-five seconds. Joe's thoughts turned to the moment when, in a week's time, both he and Will would be rumbling down along the same runway heavily laden with Torpex.

With plenty of concrete to spare, the B-24 clambered up into the air, banked to the left and started an ever widening, climbing spiral that would take it up to its operational altitude.

Designed to be flown with a payload, the empty mother-plane proved a little skittish in the air. Joe sensed that the slightest touch of the pilot's gloved hand at the controls caused the bomber to respond alarmingly, despite the perfect flying conditions and negligible headwind.

Impatient, Joe grew restless. He knew it would be another 43 minutes before the formation would be complete and the mission fully underway. He knew it for a fact – pre-mission briefings had been exact in every detail – but his imagination and thirst for action had already flown him across the Channel to their targets.

The pilot, adjusting to flying an empty bomber, flew the B-24 in a configuration that framed Fersfield below, holding his plane at a level height. Twice Joe strained to see the church tower and rectory, knowing that down there in their garden both Jane and Liz would be shading their eyes and gazing up into the blue.

Below, parked on their hard standings within the protective shelter of raised earthworks, two war-weary B-17s were being given last minute inspections. Particular attention would be given by the armourers to the intricate pattern of fuses linking the Torpex payloads distributed throughout the fuselage. Loaded up to their maximum capacity and finally given the all clear, the bombers were being boarded by their Aphrodite crews.

The B-17F, nicknamed 'T'aint A Bird', pensioned off by the 95th Bomb group, had First Lieutenant Pool at the controls with Staff Sergeant Enterline alongside as his engineer.

All four engines would now be roaring lustily, and then the heavily laden bomber would trundle out and nose its way onto the runway. Joe knew that Pool would already be feeling the sluggish response as the bomber took the strain – with vibrations from the engines rattling the entire airframe.

The vibrations increased as, at full throttle, 'T'aint A Bird' unwillingly accelerated down the concrete runway. Pool's gloved hands tightened their grip on the joystick. He thought to himself, as the RAF boys would say – this was not going to be a 'piece of cake'. Alongside, Enterline wriggled within the irksome parachutes strapped to his body. He crossed himself, praying under his breath. The end of the runway was just visible beneath the shimmering heat haze. Pool swore softly. 'T'aint A Bird' thundered onwards, its heavy payload pressing it to the concrete. Enterline's mouth opened – then closed with a deep sigh as, just when it seemed that catastrophe was unavoidable, the nose glinted as it rose in reluctant obedience to Pool's bullying. The B-17F, with all the inelegance of a fat swan struggling to get clear from the surface of a lake, groaned as it rose sluggishly and climbed. It was a shallow climb, and, for those watching its progress, the bomber seemed to hang in the air too close over the Norfolk fields and treetops.

Almost immediately, Fersfield began to echo with the reverberating roar of four more engines reaching full throttle as B-17G, nicknamed 'Wantta Spar', followed in the lumbering wake of the B-17F. Piloted by First Lieutenant John Fisher, with Technical Sergeant Ed Most alongside as radio control engineer, 'Wantta Spar' struggled off the concrete runway and laboured noisily in its climb to join the formation of planes above.

The B-24 in which Joe and Will were riding as observers was the mother-ship to 'Wantta Spar', with another airborne B-24 detailed to perform the support role to 'T'aint A Bird'. These four bombers, two bristling with radio guidance systems, two laden with deadly Torpex, achieved their rendezvous position, converging at the altitude set by the carefully calculated flight plan. A Mosquito, chosen for its range, speed and agility, was already airborne and well ahead of the mission, observing and relaying back wind speeds, cloud levels and weather conditions. As an additional measure, two more B-24s, both equipped with full radio control guidance systems, took off and joined the Aphrodite formation. Their role was to supply immediate back-up to each mother-plane should either experience technical malfunction.

Joe and Will, passive but pensive observers to the unfolding drama, craned their necks to scan the blue sky above and around them through their Perspex bubble to spot the arrival of the shepherding squadron of Mustangs deployed to provide protective fighter cover. They did not see the fighters arrive but understood from the tightening formation of 'mothers' and 'babies' taking up their east-south-east flight path that the Mustangs were in position and the mission had 'green for go.'

Joe felt the adrenalin flow. He was in an unarmed bomber carrying no payload. He was not even at the controls of the B-24. He was merely an observer – but in a ringside seat. He was taking part in a mission that was about to deliver a fatal blow to Hitler's terror weapons across the Channel in Northern France.

The 'babies' of the Aphrodite mission had been painted white on their upper surfaces to enhance visibility. From their B-24 mother-plane, Joe and Will could easily spot and follow the progress of the two highly visible cruciform shapes against the greens, browns and golds of pasture and arable land below. But Joe was not entirely convinced, and had angered Colonel Forrest at a recent briefing. Had the decision to paint the 'babies' white on their upper surfaces been fully thought through? Had there been a full assessment from the mother-plane's pilot's point of view? How would the white paint stand out against a sheath of ghostly nimbus cloud? What would happen when the planes passed over the silver dazzle of the Channel?

First Lieutenant Pool, flying 'T'aint A Bird', had been assigned the V-weapon site at Watten in the Pas de Calais. 'Wantta Spar' was heading for its deliberate crash-landing on the terror weapons located at Siracourt. Valuable targets – if the guiding mother-planes successfully nursed their soon to be pilotless 'babies' safely and accurately through the skies across the Channel to Northern France.

Suddenly, the tense monotony was shattered by a squall of activity. The distance between 'Taint A Bird' and her escorting mother-plane shrank rapidly before their eyes. Joe saw the pilot of their own B-24 tense at the shoulders as he peered down at 'T'aint A Bird'. Joe followed his gaze and watched as two tiny specks – the heads of the two crew – emerged from the enlarged escape hatch. The specks grew into recognisable human forms. Joe tensed as he followed the full emergence and immediate cartwheeling and plummeting of the crew. His throat felt tight and painfully restricted. His mouth dried, rendering his tongue thick and useless. Christ. They had both survived the slipstream. Just. He knew that there had been no puffs of smoke around the bomber from deadly flak. No scream of predatory Messerschmitts. But his mind dictated that crew baling out of a plane signalled imminent danger. Those watching could not but flinch. Flinch, grit their teeth and pray. Hard.

The chutes opened, allowing Pool and Enterline to descend gently as planned midway between Woodbridge and Orfordness. Joe dragged his eyes away reluctantly from the two parachutes and trained them unswervingly on the pilotless 'T'aint A Bird'. Joe stared down upon the deliberately abandoned bomber speculatively. It was all uncanny, slightly unreal. The Torpex-laden bomber, being shepherded by remote control, by its B-24 'mother'.

Will's hand tapped Joe's shoulder gently. Joe turned away from 'T'aint A Bird' to join Will's concentration on their own 'baby' below. 'Wantta Spar' was responding to her mother-plane's guidance system but it was becoming clear – Joe and Will were privy to the radio traffic between both planes – that First

Lieutenant John Fisher was experiencing unexpected difficulties. As soon as he relinquished control of his plane to the B-24 above, 'Wantta Spar' started a perverse shallow climb.

Joe listened in eagerly as Fisher acknowledged that he was resuming control, shivering slightly as he heard Fisher's curt command to Ed Most to bale out.

Joe and Will exchanged glances. Something was wrong. Fisher's voice held a sharp note of anxiety in it. Things were not going to plan. Joe felt the knot in his belly tighten as Fisher's voice suddenly shouted that 'Wantta Spar' was pushing her nose up the instant the mother-ship took control. The voices of both Fisher and the radio controller in Joe and Will's B-24 rose in mounting anger and alarm.

'More power. Gonna give it more power,' the radio guidance controller shouted. 'Switching in and taking control for the third time. Repeat. Taking control. Do you read me? Over.'

'I read you. Boost the juice. Over.'

Joe thought that Fisher still sounded enthusiastic – but again heard the sharp tone as Ed Most was ordered to jump. Pronto.

In the confined space of the mother-ship, Joe watched as the radio guidance controller depressed a switch and adjusted two dials.

'You have control... oh, shit...' they heard Fisher cry out in anguish. Down below, the white upper surface of Fisher's bomber became a blur of pale grey as belly and under-wings revealed themselves: the bomber had yawed, turned into a tight spin and was now out of control.

They heard Fisher scream 'Jesus'. The bomber was now in a spinning dive. Joe's heart felt as if it had frozen between beats. His mind remained alert. 'Wantta Spar' had been flying beyond its heavily laden capability. Even devoid of such a payload, it would be very hard to pull its nose up now.

Joe watched as a parachute opened above – now high above – the falling, stricken bomber. Ed Most had got clear of the doomed plane.

'Bale out, John. Bale out,' Joe yelled impotently.

'Jump. For Christ's sake jump,' Will echoed frantically.

'Abandon. I say again. Abandon. Over,' intoned the dull, scared voice of the radio guidance controller.

Joe snatched a glance at him. His face was grey. The headphones seemed to be squeezing the sweat from his forehead.

'Abandon. Over.' A mechanical chant.

Joe's instinct was to close his eyes. Tightly. He did not want to see John Fisher die. But he kept them open, out of respect. He did not want to but he knew he had to – observe and record the final moments before the death of their 'baby.'

Three seconds later, the dark and brooding wood smothering the undulating ground below swallowed up the vertical descent of the bomber. Joe could not hear the explosion that coughed up flames, debris and a shockingly thick plume of smoke.

Numbed, Joe gradually became aware of an irritation. An irritating noise. It was the dazed, useless voice of the radio guidance controller tonelessly repeating the vanished bomber's call sign.

Next to him, Will was jerking slightly as he retched. Joe averted his gaze, reluctant to see Will having to swallow down the vomit surging up inside his throat.

Then their hollow eyes met. No words were spoken, no gestures made. The silence between them said it all. What had just happened to John Fisher could be their fate in a few days' time.

III

White House. WASHINGTON D.C.
DATELINE: Wednesday 17th October 1962

Down in the kitchen the duty staff stretched and yawned. Black coffee and orders phoned down from upstairs had kept them going since midnight. It was now just past seven thirty and an unusually large order for breakfasts was expected imminently. Sleek limousines had been creeping up the gravel drive all night, disgorging the various members of the hurriedly convened meeting of EX-COMM* scheduled for eight that morning.

Upstairs, his footsteps muffled by the thick carpet, a presidential aide strode down along the long corridor leading to the president's private quarters. The armed brace of marines on guard duty, now grown accustomed to his frequent coming and going, scarcely gave him a second glance and nodded him through.

Pausing at the panelled door marked 'Strictly Private', the aide adjusted his perfectly knotted tie before raising his hand and slowly turning it into a fist. The knuckles hovered for a moment before knocking with an urgency that atoned for the brief delay.

No response came from beyond the panelled door. The aide frowned as if presented with a problem to which he had no solution. He was about to knock again when the door opened a fraction.

'Yeah? Oh…'

The door opened wide. President Joe Kennedy stepped out.

'It's you, Richardson. Well?'

'The EX-COMM meeting, Mr President. They are all assembled and waiting, sir.'

'Give them breakfast…'

---

* EX-COMM: Executive Committee of the National Security Council

'All arranged, sir.'

'I'll be along,' the president grunted, buttoning up a crisply laundered white shirt.

Richardson, whose role and function never gave him access to the inner sanctum of the presidential private quarters, surreptitiously strained to peer beyond the president and snatch a glimpse of the room within. The fleeting view he caught of full ashtrays, empty glasses and a litter of maps and briefing documents was instantly blocked by the president who had stepped out into the corridor, closing the door deftly behind him.

'So what have you got for me, eh? I don't want any damn surprises sprung on me by intelligence up there in front of EX-COMM.'

'No, sir, Mr President,' Richardson nodded vigorously.

'OK. Shoot.'

'There have been some... serious developments, sir. SS-5 missiles...'

'How many? Do we know?'

'Two SS-5 sites at San Cristobal and Sagua la Grande. Two SS-4 sites at Juanajay. The SS-5s have double the range of the SS-4 missiles, sir. Eleven hundred miles. That puts Houston, Dallas, Washington and even New York within range.'

'Jesus!'

'And we've got evidence that two airstrips are being built. They'll be for bombers. Ilyushin 28s.'

'Nuclear capability?'

'Affirmative, Mr President.'

'Our U-2s get all this?'

'U-2 high level surveillance, sir, plus F84s and PF101s on low-level, high speed runs, sir.'

'Location?'

'Sir?'

'Airstrips. For the Ilyushins.'

'North shore, sir.'

'Bastards.'

Turning, President Kennedy entered his room, closing the panelled door behind him firmly. Three minutes later he re-emerged, fully dressed and alert – but Richardson noticed the strain, the tiredness, showing in the slightly crinkled skin at the corners of his eyes. There was the ghost of a spasm in the jaw-line.

'Have they put up a worst-case scenario?'

Richardson responded immediately. 'Three million, tops.' His voice was devoid of emotion. 'It depends, Chiefs of Staff say, on which cities get hit in the first-wave strike, sir.'

'It depends,' President Kennedy murmured. Three million, he thought. Three million civilian casualties if we screw up on this. Christ!'

'Three million, tops, sir,' Richardson repeated.

Joe Kennedy reined in his sudden surge of impatient anger. The aide sounded like a corporate tax accountant discounting a pre-tax dollar loss.

'OK. Let's get this show on the road.'

The aide led the president down the thickly carpeted corridor. As they passed through the door, the armed marines saluted smartly.

A country lane near Fersfield, Norfolk.
Late evening, 31st July 1944

'Jeez, what was that?' Will exclaimed.

Liz giggled and patted Will's tousled hair. 'Did it scare you? It was only an owl. Tawny, I think. Too early for barn owls. Surely you have owls in America?'

'Knew a guy from Pittsburgh,' Will muttered, recovering from the recent shock of being startled by the swooping bird, 'who took the pants off me at poker. They called him 'The Owl' as I recall.'

'Do you know many gentlemen from Pittsburgh who are successful in removing your trousers, hmm? Is there something you should tell me, William Ford?'

'Remove my trousers? Gee, honey, I meant took me to the cleaners…'

'I know, I know. Only teasing. So they called this card sharp an owl. Why? Did he have big eyes behind huge spectacles?'

'Nope.'

'Well?'

'Well what?'

'Why did they call him The Owl?'

'The guy had asthma but chain smoked throughout the game. Only stopped when he picked up his winnings. Then he'd cough, only sort of owl-like. Wheezing. Kinda whoo-whoo, you know.'

They laughed and continued strolling down the lane in honeysuckle scented darkness. The night sky was cloudless, allowing the crescent moon and a scattering of stars to shine brightly against the deep indigo. On the horizon, Venus hung like a wet pearl. Under the inky branches of an ancient oak tree, they paused to embrace and kiss.

'Mustn't be back too late,' Liz murmured reluctantly.

Will ignored her, his caressing hands drawing her soft body against his. The sharp bark of a fox broke the intense silence. He rested his chin gently on her bowed head.

'You ever been caught sneakin' back in late?'

Liz shook her head. 'Jane's a sport. She pretends to lock up but leaves the scullery door on the latch. I slip my shoes off as soon as I get to the Rectory gate and tiptoe in.'

'She sure is a pal,' Will whispered into Liz's perfumed hair.

'Mmm. And she's getting terribly fond of Joe.'

'You think so?'

'I know so. Is Joe fond of her, do you think?'

'I guess he sure is,' Will replied. Oxlip. He suddenly remembered Joe with the little flower. What was it? Primula. Sort of suited Jane. Prim and proper. *Primula elatior.* 'Yep,' he spoke decisively. 'I guess he is.'

'Do you think… I mean… have they…'

'Well Liz McCoy. Shame on you.'

'No, really,' Liz protested, giggling. 'When one is so very happy…' she kissed Will impulsively, '… one wants to share it with one's dearest friends.'

'So 'one' is very happy, is 'one'?' he teased.

'Very,' Liz whispered.

'I guess one and one make—'

'Love,' she said simply.

He kissed her.

'So how many girlfriends does Joe have back home?'

'You ask a lot of questions, little lady. Working for his father, are you?'

'Will,' she cried. 'What a peculiar thing to say!'

She pushed him playfully. He caught her wrists. They swayed in a happy struggle before tumbling down onto the soft sedge.

'Oh, Will… I must get back…'

He peeled her dress off, placing it down as a pillow under her head. Three fields away, a vixen yapped in response to the bark of the nearby fox.

Afterwards, they shared a single cigarette. The night was warm. Liz remained undressed. Now their only touch was when the cigarette was passed between them.

The red glow gleamed as Liz placed it between her lips. She exhaled slowly.

She suddenly curled her knees up and snuggled into him. 'What did you mean? Was I working for Joe's father.'

Will laughed. 'Joe Kennedy Senior keeps his son on a short rein.'

'No! Really?'

'You bet! They're a big family back home…'

'Joe's got lots of brothers and sisters?'

'Sure thing, honey, but I meant politically big. And Joe's father has high hopes for Joe Junior.'

'High hopes? How high?'

'The highest.' He sat up. 'You know that Joe's father was the U.S. Ambassador in London a while back.'

'Gosh.'

'Didn't Jane tell you?'

'I'm sure she doesn't know.'

'Well I'll be…'

'And so I had no idea, Will. You mean Joe…?'

'The Kennedys are big news. Joe Senior is rich and ambitious. When all this is over, the plan is to put Joe into the White House.'

The next morning, Jane's mother took Liz out into the garden.

'The flowers in the drawing room are looking tired. I need to change them. Sweet peas, I think,' she had said, picking up her shallow wicker basket and firmly steering Liz out into the sunshine.

Somewhat bemused, Liz found herself assisting among the flower beds. She sensed that this early morning raid on the sweet peas was nothing more than a pretext. There had been a slight awkwardness late last night. Liz had stolen in through the pantry door just before one, clutching her shoes in her hands, only to stumble into Jane's mother descending the stairs en-route for warm milk. Liz had managed a convincing yawn, murmuring something less convincing about taking a turn on the lawn before bed.

'You know, my dear,' Jane's mother began, 'we are a very small community here in Fersfield.'

'Mmm, I expect so,' Liz replied guardedly.

'And in a small community such as ours… gossip, indeed scandal, spreads so quickly.'

Holding the shallow basket, Liz merely nodded.

'And it would be perfectly dreadful if scandal were to touch the rectory.'

Here it comes, Liz thought. She knows I was out late last night. She decided to go on the offensive.

'Jane is so lucky,'

'Lucky?' The echo contained a note of bewilderment.

'Being quite the Caesar's wife, beyond the reach of scandal,' Liz said sweetly.

'I did not mean Jane and besides I simply fail to understand…'

'Joe. Lieutenant Kennedy. Such a perfect gentleman and, he is, as you know, one of *the* Kennedys.'

Torn between her curiosity and her wish to conceal her ignorance, Jane's mother wavered.

'I mean, they are almost like our aristocracy. Joe's father is akin to an earl. Over there, of course.'

'Yes… of course.'

'Very wealthy, very influential.'

'The Kennedys are influential?' she prompted, intrigued. 'In which sphere?'

Liz concealed her triumphant grin. She said, almost casually, 'Imagine Joe's father being appointed to the Court of St. James.'

'Do you mean to say that Joe… Lieutenant Kennedy's father recently served as the American Ambassador to London?'

'Absolutely! And Joe… Lieutenant Kennedy is being groomed for future high office. The Presidency, no less.'

Liz relaxed, certain that her moment of danger had passed. Jane's mother tossed some sweet peas into the basket.

'Pick some more and bring them in, would you, my dear? I must go in and see to breakfast.'

Leaving Liz in the bed of sweet peas, she returned to the kitchen. Jane was at the kitchen table, slicing bread and buttering it.

'Please be careful with the butter, Jane, the ration goes simply nowhere.'

'Yes, Mummy.'

'My dear, I've been thinking.'

'Mmm?'

'Why don't we invite some of your friends around for supper.'

Jane, buttering the bread sparingly, looked up in surprise. 'But they are scattered all over the country, Mummy.'

Her mother swept such considerations aside. 'It must be dull, yes, rather dull for you here after university. I mean,' her mother's tone rose implacably in a manner Jane had come to know so well, 'it is almost August and as there has been no tennis to speak of …I thought perhaps a supper.'

'But who would I invite?'

'I was thinking,' her mother pressed on, carefully avoiding Jane's searching gaze, 'we should perhaps be more welcoming … yes, welcoming, to those brave young American flyers. Why not invite Lieutenant Kennedy?'

'Ask Joe to supper?' Jane gasped, surprised. 'And Will to partner Liz?'

This was answered with a frown.

'Settle it soon, darling. And for supper, which we'll have next week. We'd better make it the ninth, hmm? I think something not too ambitious. Something intimate, perhaps. Just the family and Liz and your young Lieutenant Kennedy.'

Jane, caught off-guard by the 'your' in her mother's surprising suggestion, gripped the butter knife tightly to quell the flickering pleasure rising up inside her.

Joe forked down his scrambled eggs with gusto. Will, fastening his cuff button deftly, strode towards the table. He sat down, helping himself to coffee.

Joe looked up from his breakfast. 'Good time last night?'

Will grinned and gulped his coffee.

'How's Liz?'

'She's swell.' Will eyed the table for toast and jam.

'And Jane? See her?'

'Nope,' Will replied, his mouth full.

'Liz mention her?'

'We didn't get round to much talking,' Will shrugged happily.

'Seems you two are gettin' kinda close.'

'Guess we are.'

'And girls like to talk when they get close.'

Will did not reply.

'Hope you haven't been shootin' your mouth off.'

'What about? Say, what are you…'

'About anything. I know you. Anything to impress the dames.'

Will took refuge behind his coffee cup. Shit, he thought. Joe did know him all too well. And Joe was suspicious.

'Never talk about work,' Will said.

That means he has been talking, Joe thought. Then a fleeting smile passed across his face. He himself had had to pacify Jane by telling her more than he should. A sudden fear sprang up.

'You haven't told Liz about my family. Sort of keep that stuff to yourself …'

'Hell, no,' Will lied easily. 'Anyway, Liz is smart.'

Joe fumed. Will had spilled the beans about the Kennedy dynasty. He knew it.

Will read Joe's thoughts. He decided to counter-attack.

'Say, what do you think your old man would make of you and Jane?

Joe flushed.

'Have you mentioned her to your folks?'

Joe shook his head.

'Her daddy being a minister … a vicar … and all. Not exactly kosher, if you know what I mean.'

'I know what you mean.' Joe smiled briefly at the idea of Catholicism being kosher. Then he frowned. What would his father say if he found out about Jane. If his father knew of Joe's deepening feelings for the relatively poor Protestant English girl. How would Jane figure in his father's plans for political power.

Will studied the frown on his friend's face.

'I guess if it came to it you could always hold Gloria over him. If it got rough.'

'What the hell do you mean by that?' Joe snapped.

'Hey, easy boy. Easy. Lookie here. If my pop didn't like my honey and I knew he had been cutting the rug with some dame I sure as hell would...'

'It would break my mother's heart,' Joe said flatly.

'Guess you know best but all I was saying was when you go to play poker you need all the chips you can get.'

'I don't play the game by my father's rules.' Joe's voice was grave. He hated the knowledge of his father's affair ten years back in Hollywood with the film star Gloria Swanson. He also sensed that despite Will's sound advice, he would never have the guts to confront his father about it.

'Guess what,' Will chipped in, eager to lighten the mood.

'What?' Joe grunted.

'Word is that a big... get this... a very big noise is now flying Mosquito planes out of a base not thirty miles from here.'

'Yeh? And just how loud a noise might that be?'

'How loud does Franklin Roosevelt Junior sound to you?' Will grinned.

'Bullshit,' Joe laughed. 'That'll just be the press boys cooking up a bit of hokum. Come on. Better get to the briefing.'

'Hey,' Will protested. 'I'm not done here. I'm starving.'

'Liz giving you an appetite? You'll just have to sing.'

'Sing?' Will echoed, baffled.

'If music be the food of love...'

'Asshole,' Will grumbled, snatching up an apple and hurrying to catch up with Joe.

Fersfield US Air Force base.
6th August 1944

'So, gentlemen, now we've all had plenty of time to evaluate Project Aphrodite,'

Colonel Forrest concluded, 'let's talk about Anvil.'

'They're flying the drones too high, sir,' Joe began. 'I think –'

'I know what you think, Kennedy. I've read all the observation reports. Good reports,' he conceded, tapping the folder on the desk top.

Joe nodded slightly, prepared to accept the tribute.

'But I'm not too sure about your ideas — especially flying the Anvil drone closer to France. You want to take the drone to mid-Channel, leaving only twenty-five miles or so to the target.'

'And at a lower altitude,' Joe broke in quickly. 'I'd like to go across at two thousand feet, sir.'

'Yes. I made a note of that. But I'm not convinced,' Colonel Forrest replied.

'Reduces the actual time the drone is under remote control, sir,' Will prompted, loyally defending Joe's proposal.

Colonel Forrest held his hand up for silence — a silence he broke after two minutes.

'Your idea has possibilities, Lieutenant, possibilities. But if we go ahead with this idea we'll have to reconfigure the pick-up operation. It'll mean bringing a Catalina within reach of Nazi fighter patrols. No. I'm not sure...'

'The flying boat could be sent up and held over the Kent coast, sir,' Will suggested.

'That's right,' Joe nodded. 'Then shadow Anvil and be in position to pick us up on the spot.'

'No.' The tone was emphatic. 'Can't change everything at this stage. Anvil goes out on the twelfth. We stick to the project routine as planned.'

'But we've got to get closer to the target,' Joe insisted, dropping the polite use of 'sir' in his urgency.

'Why? If the BC 756 Control Box system works, it works, OK? A few miles either way makes no difference,' Colonel Forrest snapped. 'Getting the drone to the target by remote control has been tried and tested and like I said a few miles here or there —'

'Makes all the difference. See here,' Joe argued hotly. 'I saw Pool's plane —'

'Yes, yes, it nose-dived just after passing Gravelines,' the commanding officer rasped testily. 'So?'

'The less flying time under remote control the greater the percentage for success. And I say we should –'

'This is a military operation not a political strategy, Kennedy. We don't deal in percentages, OK?'

Scowling, Joe flushed. The spasm in his jaw quickened.

Will took up the cause. 'Joe's right, sir. And another thing…'

'And? Another thing? You mean you've got another beef?' Forrest demanded.

'The white paint, sir. It's an asshole scheme.'

Forrest reddened.

'Painting the upper surfaces white, sir,' Joe spoke evenly, coming to Will's rescue. 'I don't like it. I don't think it –'

'I know you want a medal pretty damn quick. Or at least your father wants you to get one, Kennedy. But get this. You are paid to fly, not to think…'

'But Joe's right,' Will blurted out.

Forrest turned wearily to Will. 'Oh yeah?'

'Sure as eggs is eggs. We saw the Watten drone going into patchy low cloud. Just before the target. We were there, sir. We saw it all. Visual was lost and it missed completely. All a big waste.'

'OK. OK. You men may have something there but I'll have to convince our technical boys. I can't promise anything. Understand? If word comes back that Anvil goes ahead as planned, it goes ahead. As planned.'

'Yessir,' they replied, grimly.

Fersfield Rectory.
10th August, 1944

Liz, anticipating Will's call, snatched up the receiver.

'The rectory, Fersfield.'

Will chuckled. 'Gee, honey, you sound grand.'

'I am grand,' Liz giggled, 'or swell as you will keep telling me. Makes a girl think she's getting plump.'

'What's plump?'

'Fat.'

'I'd sure like to be the one to make you grow fat.'

'William Ford. You should be ashamed!'

'Hey, is it OK to talk?'

'Not like that, but, yes, if you behave yourself… it's OK… I'm alone. Jane's gone out with her mother and her father's –'

'Skip it, cutie pie. Just tell me, now that you are alone, that you miss me.'

Liz told him. Adding, 'Are you sure you can't wangle a pass?'

'No can do, honey. We fly soon.'

'I see,' she said.

'Now tell me that you want me.'

Liz obliged, remaining decorous.

'Now you wouldn't be holding out on me, would you?'

Liz teased him, wondering aloud what he could possibly mean.

'Tell me how much you want me. Come on, honey. Gimme details.'

'And tell the exchange as well? Just behave yourself, young Master Ford. There are laws, you know…'

'Say, honey, how did the supper go last night? Joe hasn't said much. Sure would've liked to have been a fly on that wall.'

'We had a bottle of pre-war sherry that fortunately wasn't corked, and we had trout off the best plates…'

'Jeez, sounds kinda grand. Say, did the old dame spill the beans?' Will asked anxiously.

'Don't be alarmed. Joe's family is still a closed book to Jane. The secret you shared with me is still safe. Jane doesn't know who Joe is and her mother was very careful not to let the cat out of the bag. Mothers with daughters to marry off are extremely clever, believe me. Although I must admit that she was extremely nice to Joe. Jane was completely baffled.'

'So Joe won't get mad with me?'

'Not a hope. And Joe's been invited to some pretty grand houses after the Glorious Twelfth…'

'Say, honey, get all that under wraps, pronto. The mission date's top secret and if…'

'The Glorious Twelfth, for your enlightenment, is the day when grouse shooting starts. When society flings open its country houses again – or at least those without billeted soldiers crawling all over them. So don't snap my head off like that.'

'Gee, sorry, cup-cake.'

'It was quite funny, really…'

'What was?'

'Listening to Joe being prepared for the ritual of after dinner port. In the time honoured tradition.'

'Say what?'

'Joe. Being coached. Jane's mother warned him that if the gentleman seated at his left inquired "Do you know the Bishop of Norwich?" it was polite request, in code, to pass the port decanter.'

'The hell it is.'

Liz giggled. 'Joe said it was all too complicated and that he would say "I've met the Dean of St. Paul's" and stick with the brandy.'

'The hell he did.'

'Jane's mother was a bit put out but Joe was only teasing. The rector, who underneath
the crust is really rather a sweetie, took to Joe very warmly. Showed him his butterfly collection after coffee.'

'And then the cops raided the joint,' Will laughed.

'I beg your pardon?'

'It's what we say back home when everyone's making whoopee. Oh, hell. What do I do now?'

'Put some pennies in. Four. The big, flat brown ones…and press button…'

The click and soft purring noise signalled the end of their conversation.

'Dear Will. You chump,' sighed Liz, replacing the receiver.

THE HAMMER AND THE ANVIL

Fersfield US Air Force base, Norfolk
The afternoon of the 12th Of August, 1944

The Jeep's tyres zipped across the concrete. The vehicle slowed before swerving onto a stretch of grass to pull up. Joe and Will hopped out. Beneath the port wing of their Liberator – bearing the 'Ace of Spades' insignia – Colonel Forrest waited for them, arms folded impatiently. Other airmen gathered around their commanding officer. Basking in the warm sunshine, a team of armourers watched the slow progress of a convoy of trucks approaching the Liberator. The GMC two-and-a-half ton, three-axle lorries each towed a three-ton bomb trailer laden with what from a diminishing distance appeared to be tea-chests. Crates of Torpex to be carefully loaded into 'Ace of Spades'.

The group beneath the port wing opened ranks to allow Will and Joe into the circle. Colonel Forrest began to berate Joe immediately. He accused Joe of arrogantly dismissing Will's concerns. Concerns shared by the technical boys.

'I understand that Lieutenant Ford feels the switch-over still isn't one hundred per cent reliable and that he wants…'

'I thought we didn't play a percentage game, sir,' Joe countered.

'Damn it, Kennedy, don't get smart with me, If Ford wants that mechanism fine-tuned in the workshop then…'

'But with Codename Block still top secret we can't even discuss the problems…' Joe countered. 'This is no time to be returning to the test-bench. That Nazi V-3 could be ready in days – hours – who knows? We can get this baby up and into France before dark, sir.'

'France can wait a day or two, Kennedy. This has got to be done right. On the button.'

'Hell, sir…'

'I know you want to get up this afternoon and I sure as hell know why, but I won't let your hunger for success spoil Project Anvil.'

'But…'

'When you go you've got permission to stay low,' Colonel Forrest rasped.

'2000 feet?' Joe queried.

'2000,' his commanding officer confirmed. 'And you've made your point, Kennedy. Word has come back giving the OK to your flying closer to the target. But not too close. We don't want you guys landing in France. Satisfied?'

The tone was nakedly sarcastic. Joe suspected that Forrest had stressed his reservations when making these requests to HQ and had bitten the bullet when over-ruled.

'Sure,' Joe shrugged, 'but I want...'

'Just be satisfied with what you've got – you and your damn powerful connections – and stop pushing me and your luck.'

The tension under the shadow of the Liberator's wing was tangible. The group of airmen shuffled uneasily.

Joe resented the 'powerful connections' jibe. His proposals to fly closer to the target and at a lower level were his mission-modifications. They were based on his appreciation of the situation as a pilot, not his father's political prowess. Six previous missions and their problematic outcomes had proved him right.

'You and Ford have both got your way, OK? But I say when...'

Colonel Forrest's words were drowned out by the squeal of the brakes of an approaching Jeep. It pulled up a few yards away. Lou Pontillo jumped out and trotted across to the group beneath the port wing.

'Signal just in for you, Colonel.' Saluting, he thrust a sheet of paper into Forrest's hand.

'Weather report radioed back from our scout Mosquito. Low, dense cloud...'

Joe swore. Will grunted.

'Thickening over the Channel. That's it, gentlemen. Mission postponed.'

Gesturing his impatience, Joe turned on his heel and strode away. Forrest watched his departure through narrowed eyes then turned back to Will.

'Lieutenant Ford,' Forrest barked.

'Sir?'

'Best put the rest of this goddam afternoon to some use. Get over to the test-bench and see if you can give those technicians a hand.'

'Yessir.'

'Lieutenant Kennedy,' Forrest yelled.

Out in the blaze of sunshine, Joe stopped then turned to face his commanding officer slowly. The buzz of conversation around 'Ace of Spades' died. All eyes turned towards where Joe stood, hands on his hips like a gun-slinger.

'Over here, Kennedy. I want a word with you.'

Will shot an anxious glance out into the sunshine.

It was Lou Pontillo who eased the tension. 'Gee, Will. Can you gimme a minute? I need some help.'

'Sure, Lou. I gotta minute.'

Lou's eyes darted swiftly from left to right. 'I've got me a problem and thought maybe you can help me.'

'Shoot,' Will encouraged.

'It's kinda a language thing, see? I mean, over here, they sure give their grammar star billing. Make a big deal outa little biddy words...'

Forrest turned, his interest engaged.

Lou scratched his head. 'Well, it's this way. Would you say "The yolks of eggs is white" or "The yolks of eggs are white" Uh?'

Will replied promptly. 'Are,' he pronounced decisively. 'The yolks of eggs are white.'

Forrest, following the exchange, nodded.

Lou shook his head, fingering his chin perplexedly.

'You got a problem with that, Pontillo?' Forrest demanded.

'Well, you see, Colonel, I always thought the yolks of eggs were yellow...'

Even Forrest had to laugh, joining in with the sudden evaporation of the anxiety that had built up in the shade of the

Liberator. The armourers, labouring in the heat to load up the 20,000 lbs of Torpex, were glad of the brief respite.

'Son of a bitch,' chuckled Forrest, wiping the sweat from his brow. 'OK Lieutenant,' he called across to Joe. 'We'll pull together to get this baby up in the air tomorrow.'

Will and Lou exchanged winks.

Fersfield US base.

Later, in his quarters, in the cool of the early evening, Joe was brushing his hair in readiness for supper with Jane when there was a polite double-tap at his door.

'Yeah?'

An airman entered. 'Phone call for you, Lieutenant. Stateside.'

'Thanks,' Joe said unenthusiastically. It would be his father.

At the phone, Joe remained defensive. His responses were terse and ungracious.

'Just caught me,' he replied, already searching for something to say. 'What? No. Just a drive out with Will. Will? William Ford – sure – I wrote you about him. Yeah. That's right.'

Then Joe's hand tightened around the receiver. His knuckles grew as white as his angry face. 'No. Yeah. Bad weather... sure, I was going to tell you. No. Low cloud.' A pause. 'Sure we are going ahead.' Joe's voice rose in anger. 'Tomorrow – but I guess you found that out already, huh?' At this safe distance, Joe was able to try out a little cautious sarcasm.

Another twenty five seconds passed. Joe's jaw spasmed with suppressed anger. He shook his head. 'Look, Pa, back off, will you? I'll bring you back some more silverware, OK?'

Joe slammed the phone down and punched the wall. It always seemed to Joe to go this way. Getting the needle when his father phoned – questioning, coaxing, domineering him. Reducing him to a sullen, angry adolescent. Goading him with paternal wisdom... and pressure.

THE HAMMER AND THE ANVIL

Joe slunk around the phone uncertainly for a few minutes. He hesitated, impotently. He was not going to phone his father back. He knew his father was not going to phone him again that night. No apologies from either father or son. No hope of patching things up. Even on the eve of Project Anvil.

In a fit of petulant fury Joe snatched up the receiver. 'And who gave you the green light to drag Gloria Swanson into the sack you old bastard?' he yelled down the dead line. He slammed down the receiver.

Two passing airmen avoided eye contact but Joe heard their suppressed laughter. He punched the wall again.

It was only a few minutes drive away and he wasn't late but Joe gunned the jeep along the narrow lane with unnecessary ferocity. Rabbits twitched in terror before scuttling into the hedgerow.

He still felt angry with his old man. Angry at Joe Senior's capacity to manipulate from afar. It was not just the physical distance, Joe realised. He felt that time itself seemed to collapse on every occasion when he tried to stand up to and confront his overbearing father. And every failure brought Joe vividly back to the struggles – and failures – of his childhood and early manhood. Times of frustration, tears and resentment.

The Jeep jinked. The offside tyre kissed the grass verge. Joe braked, changed gear and drove the Jeep in a more controlled manner. Suddenly, he realised and instantly accepted that the anger he felt was as much with himself as it was with his domineering father.

Was the father's bullying making a coward of the son? The idea seared his mind. Joe braked hard and stopped. Despite the evening's cool air, Joe flushed. Memories from his childhood flooded back. Can it have been like that, always? Being in his father's study, aged nine. Yes. He remembered. The first of so many of those suffocating man-to-boy chats. Joe winced as he heard his own thin, boy-voice piping up "To be Head Boy, Father" in answer to Joe Senior's stern question on ambition. Jesus. Had he really said that? Said that, to satisfy his father's demands. To meet his father's expectations. Joe suddenly hated himself – despised his willingness to appease and placate the bullying old man.

Eat with the domestics – if you fail. Yes. That had been the unwritten but understood forfeit holding sway over the Kennedy children. Public humiliation awaiting those who dared to disappoint. Joe had never actually been banished below stairs – but as he sat in the silent Jeep he remembered. He remembered the morning after Jack's triumphant return and his own tearful episode after the disastrous family dinner. The following morning, Joe had avoided the breakfast table. Stealing down the back stairs to the kitchens below, hoping for coffee and cinnamon toast, Joe had unwittingly fulfilled his father's forfeit for failure.

Joe punched the horn savagely. Slumbering rooks cawed their alarm, scattering from the branches high above. He closed his eyes as if trying to shut out the memory of his humiliation. Then he came to an abrupt decision. He could not see Jane in this state. He should not seek her company in this turmoil of angry resentment. He'd no right, as a coward and a failure, to pursue her for friendship, affection and – love.

Joe swallowed hard, as if bile had risen up inside his throat. Jane. Was the poison of his father to seep out and spoil even that secret friendship. And Jane was no coward – hadn't she successfully stood up to her possessive, protective parents? Hadn't she done the impossible, escaping the clutches of the rectory and getting into Cambridge? He felt diminished by her achievement. Jane had, against all odds, proved strong, while Joe still struggled to escape his father's controlling influence.

As he prepared to turn the Jeep, the soft lowing of cows began to fill the gathering darkness. The encouraging shouts of the boy driving the dairy herd to the milking sheds became distinct. Twisting in his seat, Joe saw the shadowy forms of the small herd approaching. It was not going to be easy, he realised, to head back. Conscious that he was technically AWOL on the eve of an important mission, Joe knew that his absence from the airbase would have already been reported up the line to Forrest and that he would be carpeted in due course. Surrendering to these final indignities, he started the engine and drove the Jeep through the deepening twilight, along the stretch of lane towards the rectory.

Jane greeted him delightedly at the gate.

'Oh my darling, you're back safe... and so soon!'

Joe did not correct her misunderstanding. He smiled and shrugged, noticing that the rectory was in darkness. She sensed the tension in him, thinking it was due to mission fatigue. Taking his hand, she led him around the side of the rectory. Together, in silence, they walked down along the cinder path towards the vegetable garden. There, in a darkening corner, herbs filled the night air with their pungency.

Bending, Jane nipped at the dark little leaves and squeezed them, oiling her fingertips with their juices.

'Mint,' she whispered, offering her fingertips to his nostrils. 'Sniff. It is believed to purge choler.'

'You don't say,' he said doubtfully. He sniffed obediently, then sighed.

They were standing apart. They drew a little closer.

'Borage,' she soothed, her fingers at his nostrils.

Sniffing, Joe lowered his face. Her fingers grazed his lips fleetingly.

Moments later, she tilted his chin up and held her fingertip just beneath his nose. 'Thyme. Inhale deeply.'

Joe closed his eyes. His heart raced as he sensed her shoulder pressing against his. He felt the slight, soft pressure of her breast. He swayed as the tension eased out of his taut frame. Jane steadied him, her hand, palm inwards, at his chest. Joe remained motionless and completely entranced. Jane's hand remained at his shirt, her splayed fingers weaving soothing, delicate arabesques through the cotton into his flesh.

'Once upon a time,' she murmured, 'all these herbs – then known as simples – had specific uses and applications. Marjoram, tarragon and basil. Basil,' she continued gently, 'must always be grown in a terracotta pot.'

The formality of her words – here in the darkness she spoke as she would politely to a stranger in daylight – beguiled Joe. He sighed as the slender hand at his chest pressed gently at his shirt.

'Camomile, of course, was administered in an infusion.'

She continued speaking in a somewhat detached manner, as if deliberately giving Joe the chance to recover himself from his brooding anger. Her clear voice lulled the rage he had brought to her. She stayed very close to him. Their bodies were now pressed tightly together. It was as if Jane awaited the communion of their minds.

'I had a bad day,' Joe started thickly. 'A very bad day…' Having understood and accepted her silent invitation to unburden himself, Joe found it strangely easy – wonderfully easy – to do so.

She stroked his face with a fresh twig of thyme. He caught it between his teeth.

'Jeez, Forrest was riding me hard…'

She listened to his account of the day, the aborted mission and fully appreciated his frustration at the delay to Project Anvil's execution. Joe was slightly guarded, more so when recounting the miserable phone call with his father.

'Harry Hotspur,' was all Jane replied.

'Huh?'

'Oh, just another hot-head beleaguered by difficult old men,' she soothed, bending down in the darkness to find with blind fingers a sprig of feverfew. 'Here,' she said, rising. 'Harry Hotspur. This will cool your heat.'

Joe inhaled. The feverfew bore a faint trace of aniseed in its medicinal aroma.

He did in fact feel calm. Calm and soothed. 'Hey, Harry Hotspur. I get it now. Wasn't he a warrior hero of yours that went across to France –'

Smiling in the darkness, she raised a finger up to his lips. Tossing the feverfew aside, she grasped his hands. 'Come. Come with me –'

She was leading him gently further into the shadows of the garden away from the rectory.

'But your folks?' he whispered.

'Don't worry,' she whispered back, conspiratorially. 'They're out. We've got enough time…'

He followed her trustingly as she led him gingerly around plant beds and between perfumed magnolias to the shallow wooden steps to the summer house. Inside, it was dark and cool. Scents from the sleeping flowers followed them inside and mingled with the sharper tang of dry rot and creosote. Cobwebs were brushed aside as leaves rustled underfoot. Joe worked a Zippo lighter out of his pocket, clicked it and held the small yellow flame aloft. Jane's slender shadow flickered against a dark wall behind her. Joe snapped the lighter shut. They knelt down, breathing rapidly, face to face. They could feel each other's warm breath. In the absolute darkness their fingers reached out and found a welcoming touch.

Joe spoke rapidly, his words tumbling out. Confused, he spoke of his need for Jane, his love for her – but how he mustn't… how he couldn't… she was a… it wouldn't be…'

She silenced him with a deep, warm kiss, taking his hands and placing them at her waist. He held her tightly, squeezing harder as his kisses grew hungrier, more demanding, more dominant.

They broke away, Jane trembling slightly in response to the pressure of his hand at her breast.

They knelt in the darkness, almost nose to nose, panting. Joe began to hurriedly unbutton his shirt.

'Let me.' Jane's hands reached out, her fingers replacing his as she slowly, hesitantly, undressed him.

'Come closer,' she murmured.

He inched towards her. Closer still. His nakedness bumped softly into her fully clothed body. In the darkness, she finger-tip traced the contours of his face. As each finger passed his mouth he kissed then caught them fleetingly, kissing harder now. Allowing her hands to follow the line of his shoulders down to his chest, she gripped and squeezed his firm flesh. Her right hand fell down past his belly. Joe grunted as her knuckles gently swept his arousal.

Jane gasped, withdrawing her hand instantly. Joe kissed her – catching up her hand gently and drawing it back to his manhood. He groaned sweetly as her flesh met his.

'I want to see you,' he whispered hoarsely.

Jane surrendered to his intimate touch as he carefully undressed her. The moon broke through the low cloud just as her breasts were bared. Joe held his breath in spellbound silence. He could not move. Jane whimpered gently, signalling her desire. Memories of the dark confessional every Saturday night rose up in Joe's mind. Pleasure, sin and guilt.

'Stand up,' he urged her, his voice thick with gruff tenderness. He remained on his knees.

Uncertainly, she obeyed.

Once more in darkness, he stripped her, casting her skirt and underwear into the corners of the summer house. He felt her smoothness.

Pleasure, sin and guilt. The unholy trinity branded into him since childhood.

Jane's soft feet trod the wooden floor impatiently, her fingers now buried in his hair.

She drew his upturned face into her – closing her eyes and tossing her head back as she felt the warmth of his breath invade her.

Kneel and worship. The sweet blasphemy exploded in Joe's mind. Fleeting memories of kneeling before cold, hard statues confounded his passion momentarily. Years of strictly supervised religiosity had brought him here, on this Norfolk night, in a darkened summer house, to kneel and worship.

Joe, eyes wide open, knelt and worshipped. At her warmth, he whispered profane prayers of adoration.

Moments later, using their clothing as bedding, they lay outstretched and entwined on the hard floor. Squeezing and caressing each other with fierce tenderness, they embraced urgently. Joe was drowning in his excitement, Jane almost suffocating in hers. Seconds later, she moaned softly as he blindly found her.

Suddenly, out in the darkness of the lane, a lorry thundered by. Lights dimmed – observing the blackout – it sounded its horn sharply, twice, as it approached a bend. Joe cursed in alarm.

Angrily ashamed, Joe attempted a muttered apology. Jane twisted onto her side and rummaged among their tangled clothing. To his surprise, she giggled gently.

'Got it,' he heard her sigh.

Retrieving the Zippo lighter, she held it aloft. She had to click it three times to get the flame.

She shook her head in mock severity. 'Harry Hotspur, my lovely hot-head. Always so impetuous…'

Joe grinned, relaxing instantly.

'Sorry… Jeez… I don't know what to say…'

'Not to worry, darling.'

He gathered her up in his arms and cradled her. They lay down once more, embracing closely. They talked, their frequent kisses silencing one another's words. Pledges to survive the war were followed by promises of a future lived together.

'God, I love you,' Jane sighed.

They fell silent, as if slightly overawed by Jane's solemn words.

Joe sensed – before he saw – the tears glistening on her cheeks. Breaking his vow, he reassured her that Project Anvil was a much safer mission than she feared. He confided in her more than he had ever meant to, explaining that the mission was not so much a dangerous adventure but a well rehearsed exercise. He repeated his promise of a safe return before kissing her tears away.

Then they made love.

Joe was patient and considerate at first. Planting the gentlest of kisses, he whispered his love into her ear. She hugged him to her – remaining silent even when Joe's naked body stiffened and tensed at his climax.

They lay together, then, enjoying their stillness and silence. Joe's fingers played through her hair while Jane sketched little circles on his chest with her fingernails.

They made love once more. This time Joe was more assured in the pleasure he both gave and took in their love-making.

IV

The White House, Washington D.C.
Thursday 18th. October 1962 08.55 am

The EX-COMM team was assembling round a large, oblong table in the centre of a pale-grey briefing room. Twelve of the chairs were occupied, eight remained to be filled. Despite the early hour, most of the men already looked strained and tired. Nine wore the uniforms of political or administrative office, their dark suits and bland ties almost identical. Three men had close-cropped grey hair confirming their military provenance; each wore the high ranking uniform and decorations of the armed force they represented. The US Army. The US Navy. The US Air Force.

'Which of these three guys represents the Marines?' a dry, legal voice asked laconically.

Faces reddened and throats were cleared. Like a joke at a funeral, the wisecrack had bombed.

Sitting directly opposite to General Maxwell Taylor (Chairman of the Joint Chiefs of Staff) – and impervious to the general's disdainful gaze – was the slight figure of George Ball, Under Secretary of State. Ball eased his tension by taking off his glasses and wiping each lens methodically with his handkerchief. It was a tactic that had got him through many a tough stretch on Senate Committee meetings. To those watching, the careful action suggested that Ball was turning important matters over in his mind, but the fingers fiddling with the handkerchief seemed to be upsetting General Maxwell Taylor. He frowned his frustration and was about to remonstrate when the double doors opened, allowing the presidential aide to enter.

Standing aside smartly to his left, he announced,
'Gentlemen, the President.'

They all rose from their seats as Joe strode into the briefing room.

The walk down the carpeted corridor behind Richardson had been a short but an anxious one. Joe needed to see a friendly face. His eyes swept around the oblong table.

'Where's Bobby?'

Richardson, always fully briefed, was about to reply when McGeorge Bundy (Special Assistant for National Security Affairs,) said that Robert Kennedy was on his way.

Joe nodded his thanks to Bundy before turning to his aide once more.

'I thought we'd agreed that this was a working breakfast. Some of these guys have been travelling all night.'

'Waiting for you, Sir,' Richardson replied adroitly. 'I'll inform the kitchens at once.'

'Fine. Make it snappy. See that we aren't interrupted once we get down to it.'

'As you wish, Mr President.' Richardson withdrew.

Joe surveyed the faces of those seated around the table. He felt a surge of relief. At least they had managed to take their places without any obvious wrangling. Joe knew exactly where each of the assembled men stood in the power hierarchy – but there was no protocol for EX-COMM. Perhaps the gravity of the situation had swept aside the need for such protocols.

Joe sat down.

'General?' he looked down the table at Maxwell Taylor, asking for an update.

The general cleared his throat importantly before informing the EX-COMM team of the deteriorating situation, telling those brought together to tackle and resolve the Cuban crisis nothing that Joe didn't already know. This gave Joe time to study the faces before him, allowing him to gauge their individual reactions and, more importantly, anticipate their responses.

Maxwell Taylor concluded by straying from fact to opinion.

'So the way I see it, we need to act. Pronto. Act fast and act first, gentlemen. The only way to keep ahead of the game with these commie bastards...'

The US Navy and the US Air Force representatives nodded their agreement enthusiastically.

Reinforced by their encouragement, the general pressed on.

'We've gotta bomb them. Today. Bomb them hard then spearhead an invasion task force with the Marines. Secure all objectives within forty-eight hours.'

Before Joe could reply – he had carefully avoided either nodding or shaking his head during the general's robust prescription – the President's Special Counsel broke in.

'We've gotta be very careful, Sir,' Theodore Sorensen said, pointedly ignoring the general and appealing directly to Joe. 'There's international law...world opinion...the United Nations. And unilateral action like that won't go down well with the Security Council and my view is, we're gonna need friends to help us pick up the pieces when this has all blown over...'

'Blown over?' the Navy supremo blustered, mouthing the words like expletives. 'Blow the bastards away, I say. Who needs goddam friends in the Security Council with the fire power we've got -?'

'Damn right...'

'But we've got the moral high ground...'

'Horse shit...'

'OK,' Joe barked. He nodded to Sorensen. 'You were saying?'

'I think we should set up a naval blockade.' He turned in appeal to the U.S. Navy's man. 'A tough call, sure, but your guys are the best.'

Admiral Staffort preened and nodded.

'Nothing in. Nothing out,' Sorensen continued. 'Keep them in like rats in a hole –'

'Then blast them out...' a bellicose voice interjected.

Sorensen shook his head, sighing wearily. 'No, no, no. A blockade will bring them on their knees to the negotiating table. And we get real tough at those talks. Real tough.'

Joe acknowledged his Special Counsel's contribution without, once more, revealing his thinking.

A sharp knock preceded the opening of the double doors.

Coffee, iced-water and fresh flowers quickly appeared on the table. As the two domestic staff swiftly withdrew, Richardson ushered in Robert Kennedy.

'Gentlemen, the Attorney General.'

'Another blasted lawyer,' muttered one of the uniformed men.

Bobby came in, slapping Joe briefly on the back before grabbing a chair and a coffee. He looked like a preppy freshman seated among the grizzled, tired men around him.

'Remind them of our position in international law, Robert,' Sorensen urged, anxious not to lose the momentum of his argument.

Joe held up his hand. The admiral was having a heated, ill-tempered exchange with the men seated beside him. Above his white collar, his red neck bulged. Someone had just thumped the table, rattling the coffee cups in their saucers.

'I'm with Taylor,' Air Force General Curtis LeMay snapped.

At the far end of the table, Bundy nodded his assent.

'So am I, I guess,' the National Security Advisor echoed.

His hand still raised for order, Joe shot a questioning glance down the table at his Secretary of Defence. Robert McNamara took it squarely and shrugged.

'I'm with Taylor and LeMay on this,' he said firmly.

'Secretary of State?' General Maxwell Taylor asked across the table, by-passing his president.

Joe, conscious that the EX-COMM team was in imminent danger of breaking up into entrenched factions, regained control.

'Now, gentlemen. Let's hear from the Secretary of State.', Joe said, and then, to his brother, 'You can sit down, Bobby, we'll hear from you in a minute.'

Dean Rusk sipped his coffee and, placing the cup down delicately, pressed his fingertips together and spoke with cautious deliberation. In principle, he favoured firm military intervention, but stipulated that such a course, if undertaken, should be done so with immediate effect. His preference was not for bombing, which could incur unacceptable civilian casualties, but for an invasion force. He spoke of US forces being seen on the world stage to police the situation. Just as the hawks in the briefing room chorused their agreement, Dean Rusk struck a more dove-like note.

'Unilateral action,' he concluded, 'may well, however, prove to be both incautious and injudicious on our part. Down the road, it could lead us into international condemnation and isolation.'

The hawks, feeling cheated out of his initial support, turned on him angrily.

Stung to defend himself, the Secretary of State dropped his legalistic tone and spoke bluntly.

'Can't you guys see it? We'd be the giant bullying the pygmy, huh?' he asked EX-COMM rhetorically.

A few heads nodded their appreciation of his point but many more shook their dissent.

Up to that moment, only two voices remained unheard: those of Bobby Kennedy and Adlai Stevenson, the unpopular US Ambassador to the UN. Joe invited the latter to speak.

Stevenson picked up on Rusk's closing remarks.

'The Secretary of State makes many points for us to consider and consider well, gentlemen. Britain and her neighbour France lost far more in the court of world opinion after their adventure into Suez…'

'True,' a solemn voice reflected.

'Cost Eden his job,' another added.

'Nasser sure gave that poor sap a pain in the guts…'

'Yup. But we got MacMillan in. Jeez, what a Christmas box, huh? Our man in Downing Street…'

Joe's mind flashed across the Atlantic. He liked Mac. Thought of him like an uncle. Mac being half-American probably helped. If only London would stop putting the squeeze on him for Skybolt.

'... and therefore, gentlemen, for the reasons I have outlined...' Adlai Stevenson's precise voice intoned, '... and with due regard to the international ramifications we have just discussed... we should, I think, strive to avoid military action and seek a resolution through diplomatic channels...ending this crisis through negotiation, compromise and inducement...'

'The hell we will,' roared Taylor belligerently.

'Pinko crap...'

'Inducement?' gasped Bundy, purpling.

Stevenson's temperate words ran into a storm of abuse and derision.

Joe groaned inwardly. Apart from Bobby's wry smile, he felt as anxious at the head of the table as he had when he had first walked into the briefing room.

Fersfield US 8th Air Force base, Norfolk.
13th August, 1944.

Earlier that morning, the mood in the CO's office had been purposeful as Joe, Will and Forrest had discussed the impending mission in a manner quite different to the heated exchanges of yesterday afternoon. Will's confidence in the reliability of the mechanism which would activate the switch-over to remote control was now strong enough to persuade Colonel Forrest to give Project Anvil the green light.

Now, a little after noon, Joe and Will were walking in the bright sunshine towards their Liberator bomber parked on the concrete hard-standing within the three-sided protective shelter of surrounding earth banks. Both had their eyes fixed upon the 'Ace of Spades' insignia painted on the side of the bomber's nose just below the cockpit.

They were getting uncomfortably hot in their flying kit, the sun drawing out the smell of leather from their jackets.

'The CO's confirmed that the MTB's* are on standby,' Joe said quietly. 'Word is there's a bit of a swell in the Channel, so they're ready to go ahead of schedule if necessary.'

'Head wind?' Will countered.

'Tail wind,' Joe replied easily.

Will nodded. The Motor Torpedo Boats would provide the essential support to the Catalina flying-boat during the pick-up off the French coast. With a swell, timing would be essential, and too great a swell could prevent the rescue plane from landing on the water.

'Forrest promised us a Catalina and he got us one,' Joe grinned.

Will shrugged. He did not voice his suspicion that the long arm of Joe Kennedy Senior might just have pulled a few influential strings in securing them the flying-boat.

Engineers were busy with their final preparations as Joe climbed aboard. A Jeep skidded to a halt and Colonel Forrest climbed out, striding up to Will. In silence, they briefly inspected the bomber's hold, surveying the tightly crammed fuse-linked crates full of Torpex. Moments later, with Forrest back in his Jeep, Will climbed into the cockpit and settled alongside Joe. They commenced the pre-flight checks, the routine suppressing their mounting excitement.

'Generator switches?' Joe asked.

'Off,' Will confirmed.

'Parking brake?'

'On,' Will nodded.

'Mixtures?' Joe continued, after Will had confirmed that the supercharger was disengaged.

'Idle cut off,' Will replied.

'Intercooler shutters?'

'Open.'

As Will and Joe donned their head-sets, the engineers withdrew. A sudden clatter of engines heralded a Lockheed Ventura's readiness for take-off. Joe and Will watched as their

---

* MTB: Motor Torpedo Boat

mother-ship tore down the runway, and climbing steeply, became airborne. They returned to their pre-flight checks.

'Wing flaps?'

'Down twenty degrees,' Will confirmed.

Seconds later, one by one, the engines coughed, spluttered and began to roar. The Liberator trembled as it strained at its brakes. Joe released them and the bomber began lumbering towards the runway. Joe turned towards Will. They exchanged nervous glances. Joe returned to the controls, setting the quarter-flaps for take off. They both saw the green Very light shoot up from the control tower and arc across the sky. Joe advanced the throttle right to the stops, knowing that with such a heavy payload, he'd need every drop of power he could squeeze out of his engines. The engines' deafening roar seemed to fill with a sharper, high-pitched note. The vibrations shivered the massive wings as the Torpex-laden bomber accelerated along the runway. At ninety five miles per hour, Joe felt for the lift from the wings. Nothing there. At a hundred and five, still nothing. At a hundred and ten, he tried again, but the bomber refused to leave the runway.

'Too fast to abort,' Will yelled.

The end of the runway was racing towards them. Suddenly, a slight lurch, accompanied by an empty sensation in the pit of his belly, told Joe that his ship was airborne.

'Wheels up,' Joe yelled, his gloved hands gripping the control column.

Will pulled the lever. A light on the panel flashed, signalling that the landing gear had retracted.

'Wheels up,' Will confirmed.

Joe snatched a quick glance at the ground racing past below. He saw that the closely cropped grass at the edge of the runway was sharply defined. Too sharply defined. Jesus, we're too low, he realized. Despite the speed, he could still see the daisies.

The retraction of the landing gear reduced their drag, allowing the bomber to stagger into the air as the end of the runway disappeared beneath them. But at thirty feet, the Liberator's

Number Three engine warning light flashed red and the bomber began to lose height. Twenty six... twenty three feet... they screamed over a thick hedge, scattering a herd of cows in the meadow twenty feet beneath them.

'Wheels down,' Joe yelled.

Will pushed the gear lever and the wheels were three parts down when the Liberator hit the grass hard and bounced back into the air.

'Come on, you bitch, come on.' Joe wrestled with the controls, draining every last drop of power from his engines as he battled to get the Liberator's nose up – and get the over-laden bomber higher into the air.

'Wheels up,' he commanded. They had climbed about thirty feet.

Will obeyed.

Slowly but surely the ship began to struggle drunkardly upwards... forty... fifty feet.

Will wiped the beads of sweat from his forehead.

'If we get outa this shit I swear I'm never, ever gonna fly again.'

Joe managed a weak grin. 'How much height we got?'

'One thirty... one fifty... we've done it,' Will shouted, slapping Joe's back in relief.

Joe nodded but did not respond. His thoughts were down below. With Forrest, Lou and the air crews who he knew would be watching tensely. And with Jane, and Liz, in the rectory garden, shielding their eyes against the sun as they gazed up at the Liberator.

The bomber streaked across a tree line, scattering rooks that wheeled away in a ragged formation below.

'Two hundred feet... two thirty...' Will called out, his voice now steadier.

Joe nodded but did not relax his grip. The Liberator still felt sluggish as he nursed it up, banking the bomber gently. To Joe's relief the oil pressure on the number three engine had stabilized and the warning light had gone out. When Will called out fifteen hundred feet, Joe leveled off.

They flew on, anxious eyes continually checking the instruments. Joe monitored the engines' temperature gauge knowing that the strain put on them by the difficult take-off had been immense. Will tuned into the correct radio frequency to make contact with the mother-ship flying above them.

'Test coming up in two minutes,' he informed Joe.

Joe replied with a 'thumbs up'. Will patted the newly installed dash-mounted black box. They both scanned the sky above through the Perspex cockpit canopy, eager to see the approaching flight-group converge in tighter formation.

'We got us some company,' Will yelled.

Joe saw the mini-armarda of aircraft circling high above. Two PV-1 Venturas, one of which was their mother-ship which would, after Will and Joe had set the controls and jumped ship, fly alongside the abandoned Liberator and by means of radio guidance, direct the Torpex-laden bomber right into their target at Mimoyeques. Joe saw the photo-reconnaissance Mosquito; two B-17s; two P-38 Lightnings and – in tight formation - their escort of sixteen P-51 Mustang fighters.

Joe's headphones crackled into life. 'Mother Hen calling T-11. Mother Hen calling T-11. Over.'

Joe exchanged tense grins with Will before acknowledging. The mother-ship relayed instructions.

'Mother Hen to T-11. When you've switched over to remote-control guidance, on your signal we'll feed in new co-ordinates. 150 degrees. Over.'

Joe repeated the information then turned to Will.

'OK, cowboy. Hit it!'

Will had been scanning the formation above them, and the vast blue horizon.

'No sign of that Catalina, Joe…'

'Mother Hen will have him on their radio. Now hit it, for Chrissakes!'

Will's gloved finger hovered for a split second over the stubby silver switch.

'Here goes nothin'…' He flicked the switch.

Joe, about to inform Mother Hen that 'she had control', stared down at the black box, frowning.

Will looked up anxiously.

'Is that it?' Joe demanded.

Will shrugged. 'Nope. We should be getting a green.' His finger tapped the small green bulb that remained unlit. 'Hey… wait a minute…' His gloved fingers pincered the tiny bulb delicately and screwed it tightly into its socket. 'Loose bulb, I guess.'

'Try it again,' Joe urged.

Will complied, rapidly flicking the switch off, then on again. The green light winked fitfully, stayed on for five seconds then died.

'Oh, shit,' Will cursed softly as Joe hastily told the mother-ship what was happening.

Will tapped the bulb gently. When he flicked the switch once more, the green light gleamed steadily.

They both laughed in their relief.

Joe reported back to the mother-ship. 'T-11 to Mother Hen. T-11 to Mother-Hen. Spade Flush. I repeat, Spade Flush. Over.'

His call was acknowledged. With his gloved hands resting on his lap – with Will watching on in silence – Joe saw the joy-stick moving slightly in obedience to the remote-control guidance signal radioed in from Mother Hen. The Liberator banked gently to port, turning its nose eastwards.

'Jeez, Joe. It works,' Will whispered in awe.

'Look, Ma! No hands!' Joe laughed, breaking the tension. His voice was light – but his eyes remained serious and his jaw-line tense.

At 18.20 hours, after a test-run of several minutes, Will switched off the remote-control and Joe resumed command of the bomber, putting it back on course for their target just as the Project Anvil formation closed up at 1500 feet over Blythburgh.

Looking down, Joe saw the hedgerows quartering the fields into a patchwork of green, stubble and fallow. Suddenly, in the lengthening shadow of a fleetingly glimpsed tree, he saw a cluster of children – their dog scampering at their heels – waving and cheering up at the airborne armada. Grinning, he waved down briefly to their upturned faces, knowing that they would not see the gesture... and then they were gone.

The flight-group tightened formation as it crossed the coastline, climbing up to 2000 feet. 'Ace of Spades' flew below the rest, with Mother Hen and the back-up plane a thousand feet above. Mustang fighter cover criss-crossed two thousand feet above the bombers.

Will tapped Joe's shoulder lightly, jerking his thumb up at the planes above. They saw the observer plane, a Mosquito, closing in behind the mother-ship and back-up plane.

'That's Roosevelt's son up there,' Will shouted above the noise in the cockpit.

Joe pursed his lips. With his father's political blood flowing through his veins – and the President's son riding shotgun up above in the Mosquito – Project Anvil was turning more into a diplomatic mission than a raid. Joe shrugged the notion aside, consoling himself with the thought that they were bearing Torpex not a treaty. The knowledge gave Joe a grim satisfaction.

They flew along the North Sea coast and turned towards the English Channel. Joe peered down into the sparkle of the sea below. He spotted a steady line of small, dark ships in convoy, their smoke stacks smudging the air. A convoy of supply and support ships, heading for the approaching coastline of France. Raising his gaze up and staring dead ahead through the Perspex, Joe experienced a sharp thrill at the thought that somewhere over the horizon down in Normandy, Allied tanks were engaging German defences.

'Can't see the Cat,' Will broke in, peering about the sky around them.

Joe radioed the mother-ship. 'T-11 to Mother Hen. T-11 to Mother Hen. Any sign of our Catalina? Over.'

'Mother Hen to T-11. Mother Hen to T-11. Sorry, boys. Negative on the Cat. Contact lost but we're still sending. Over.'

'You hear that?' Joe shouted.

Will shrugged. 'What about the boats?'

'T-11 to Mother Hen. T-11 to Mother Hen. Keep sending. I repeat. Keep sending. We sure as hell need that Catalina. Getting close to abandon. What about the MTBs. Over.'

'Mother Hen to T-11. Mother Hen to T-11. Affirmative. Three MTBs are on their way but ETA revised. I repeat. ETA revised. Over.'

Joe was quick to respond, demanding details. Mother Hen advised him of the swell in the Channel which was delaying the small flotilla of rescue boats.

'Shit,' he cursed. 'And we've got a tail wind behind us pushing us ahead of schedule.'

'While they're battling through choppy waters down there,' Will broke in gloomily. 'Hey, wish we could do a 360,' he said, swivelling his finger in a circular shape.

A harsh crackle of static prevented Joe from replying.

'Mother Hen to T-11. Mother Hen to T-11. Stand-by to switch to remote-control. Over.'

'Standing-by. Over,'

'No going back now,' Will grinned.

'Ready, Will?' Joe demanded.

Will nodded.

Joe gazed down at the flickering dials. 'Twelve seconds.'

Will flexed his fingers in anticipation as he silently counted down the seconds.

'Do it,' Joe grunted.

Will flicked the switch on the black control box. The green light came on instantly, gleaming steadily.

'T-11 to Mother Hen. T-11 to Mother Hen. Spade Flush,' Joe cried, unable to keep the excitement out of his voice. 'I repeat. Spade Flush. Over.'

'Acknowledged. Over.' The reply was terse. Unemotional.

'OK Will. Time to jump.'

'Let's get the hell outa here.'

Will made his way along the fuselage and opened the enlarged escape hatch. He launched himself feet first out of the belly of the bomber, escaping the whistling slip-stream and, rolling over as instructed in training, hurtled face-down towards the sea below. His main chute opened smoothly, the ballooning canopy above braking his descent, jerking his body upright into suspension. He didn't need to deploy his reserve chute. Dangling, his body was caught and buffeted in the strong cross-wind that then slapped him into the waves. He gulped for air, coughing as the cold water stung his face and forced its way into his mouth.

Joe, following a few seconds later, made a less adroit exit from 'Ace of Spades,' which left him tumbling for a few seconds in the bomber's turbulent slip-stream. Twisting and rolling in free-fall, Joe snatched at the ripcord of his chest chute. The silk flapped uselessly as the strings twisted and entangled. He continued to fall. Still tumbling, he located the ripcord of his reserve chute and yanked it. His second chute opened, billowing slightly off-centre, causing him to spiral and drift away from Will.

Joe looked down into the dazzle of the sea below. The cold wind made his eyes water and he had to struggle to breathe evenly. He knew that he was still falling too fast. He braced himself, flexing his knees slightly and keeping his feet together. He entered the waves cleanly, submerging briefly before emerging, spluttering and gasping for air, thanking God for his life-jacket.

Out of the corner of his eye Joe saw the small dark shape slicing a silver curve in the sea about two miles away. He felt a huge wave of relief surge over him. The pick-up MTB was right on time.

His boots and legs felt heavy and awkward. He resisted the urge to struggle as the waves tried to claim him. Joe felt their sucking, implacable pull at his helpless body – but the billowing chute continued to drag him sideways through the heaving swell. His fist sought and found the release catches. He punched fiercely. The failed chute dragged in the water while his reserve chute ballooned defiantly in the strong wind. Soaked and exhausted, Joe was pulled through the water as he struggled desperately to release himself.

Despite his impact with the waves still ringing in his ears, he heard a deep, dull thump echoing across the sea from the distant shoreline. He strained to twist his face around but could not manage to see if it was the explosion of 'Ace of Spades' crash-landing, but the thought of it thrilled him. He hoped it had found its target.

His sodden uniform was growing heavier by the second, threatening to submerge him. Knife – he knew that he must locate his knife and cut himself free before being pulled under. And the strong wind was taking him towards the shore: if he didn't drown he would be dragged within range of enemy fire. Joe could not locate his knife. His tired arms moved slowly in the water, his hands becoming increasingly clumsy and useless in their sodden gloves. He made one final, supreme effort to rid himself of the chute. The release clasp responded at last. The result was immediate – and terrifying. Despite his life-jacket, as soon as the reserve chute's cords fell away, the waves began to swamp him. Gulping, he struggled to keep his head above the surface. Where were the MTBs? Where the hell were those rescue boats?

He was answered by the sound of chugging engines. A grey hull loomed up. The wash broke over him, catching him unawares. Once more, his eyes and lungs were stung by the cold, salt water. He splashed back up to the surface. Spluttering and coughing, he stretched out an aching arm. The rope lay just out of reach. He was helpless and grateful for the hands reaching out for him, grateful for the pinching fingers plucking at his skin through his wet uniform. He was hauled aboard, face down. After another fit of coughing, Joe groaned and rolled over onto his back.

'Hey,' he managed, joking grimly. 'What kept you guys? Have you got Will?'

Struggling up on one elbow, Joe blinked. Blearily, he opened his stinging eyes. 'What the...?'

The words froze on his salt-rimed lips. The men who had just plucked him from the Channel were wearing German naval uniforms.

'Pistol. Pistol,' the E-boat Captain demanded harshly.

Joe rolled slightly and pawed at his holster with a sodden glove. The holster was empty, his .45 somewhere down in the depths. He peeled the leather flap back to show the empty holster.

The E-boat Captain nodded then suddenly crouched, squatting on the wet deck alongside Joe as the air was filled with the snarl of a Mustang coming in low and fast. The American P-51 fighter buzzed the E-boat but did not open fire. Joe strained to catch a glimpse of the fighter streaking away in a steep climb. He sank back down, exhausted.

Spitting out his contempt at the retreating plane, the Captain regained his feet and a little of his dignity. He straightened his crumpled uniform.

'Your friends cannot help you now,' he sneered. 'Perhaps you are connected with that explosion we heard some minutes before pulling you out of the sea, eh?'

Joe did not even shake his head in response. Name, rank and number. Nothing else, he thought resolutely. Nothing else.

'Take him below.'

Joe was dragged up onto his feet, his arms pinioned painfully by two crewmen. The E-boat's engine opened up with a roar. Joe swayed as he felt the deck beneath his feet dip as the sleek craft, nose up, sliced through the glinting waves.

A strong hand pushed his head down as he was frog-marched swiftly along the slippery deck and then forcefully propelled down a short flight of steel steps.

The Captain, a man no older than his captive, lit up a foul-smelling cigarette and sat down at the narrow table directly opposite Joe. The cabin was cramped, dimly lit and reeked of oil and sweat. The cigarette smoke curled across the table. Joe, already shivering, started to cough. The Captain took in a long, slow lungful of smoke then deliberately blew it into Joe's face.

'What was wrong with your plane? The Liberator bomber. We saw no sign of damage. There was no smoke.'

Joe, coughing less violently now, did not answer.

'And yet, you abandoned it. And there were only two parachutes.'

Joe, desperate to find out Will's fate, was almost tempted but did not fall into the verbal trap.

Joe gave his name, rank and number.

'So, Lieutenant, were you the co-pilot? Who flew your plane after you baled out? Answer me.'

The questioning continued. It was repetitive and relentless. Joe felt a huge wave of weariness break over him. He slumped in his chair. Across the narrow table, the E-boat Captain's eyes flickered up a fraction. One of the crew standing behind Joe grabbed a handful of the captive airman's wet hair, forcing Joe's head up. Joe's grunt of pain could be heard despite the noisy engine.

'Who flew the Liberator after you baled out? Who was the other crew member who used his parachute?'

The hull of the E-boat trembled as it sped through the waves at full throttle. The dull roar of the engine filled the cramped confines of the cabin. Joe suddenly felt sick. Achingly, stomach-churningly sick. He had swallowed a lot of sea water. His shoulders hunched as he gagged. The sound of his vomitless spasm brought a cruel smile to the German's face.

'A poor airman and now a poor sailor, eh, American?'

The crewmen laughed. The E-boat, bouncing and pitching as it raced across the heaving swell, buffeted those crowded down in the cabin.

The questioning continued, the monotonous catechism repeating itself as the Captain ignored Joe's wretched discomfort. Joe calculated that they would be onshore within another five minutes or so. If he could just hold on... Name, rank and number.

'A pity, Lieutenant.' The Captain's tone was mocking.

Joe looked across the narrow table. The E-boat Captain was stubbing out his second cigarette in a tin ashtray.

'A pity you have chosen to remain silent, Lieutenant. I would have appreciated your co-operation. Now you will have to answer questions put to you by the Gestapo.'

Joe stiffened. He had hoped to be treated as just another unlucky airman. An ordinary POW.

The engine throttled back. The E-boat slowed down. Joe was bundled up onto the deck. He saw two other E-boats heaving to alongside. There was no sign of Will. Ahead, he could just make out the concrete block-houses of the German coastal defences. Soon the E-boats had reached a green-slimed harbour wall and were nudging at the worn lorry-tyres slung down against the granite.

A dark blue Kubelwagen drew up. Jackboots clattered on the cobblestones. Joe just caught a glimpse of Will, blindfolded, being manhandled ashore, before he too was blindfolded. Then his hands were tied securely behind his back. The sensation of being frog-marched across the cobblestones made him feel queasy. His feet squelched in his soaking boots. He heard the door of the Kubelwagen being yanked open. A soft thud and muffled curse told him that Will was aboard. A violent push propelled him head first inside on top of Will.

'Silence,' a stern voice barked.

* * *

'What do you mean, Goddam it. You must...'

'Information is sketchy just now. I've told you all we know,' Colonel Forrest replied wearily.

'Well that ain't much and it sure as hell ain't good enough. And where the hell was that Catalina, huh?'

'I can't go into any operational details...' Forrest murmured.

'Bullshit, Colonel. I got you that fucking flying boat like I said I would, so where the hell…?'

Forrest, his face reddening as he endured a further tirade of abuse from Joe Kennedy Senior, managed to keep his voice under control.

'I assure you everything possible has been…'

'Has been? Has been? What do you mean, has been?'

'Will be… done. We had a Mustang on the spot within minutes and a Mosquito maintained aerial surveillance…'

'I don't want fucking photographs. I want my son back, Forrest, do you hear me? Get me my son.'

The phone clicked abruptly. Colonel Forrest replaced his receiver and exhaled slowly through clenched teeth.

'Oh God. Oh God… er… there's something called the Geneva Convention. Daddy says if you are wearing a uniform you have to be looked after properly…' Jane blurted out.

'Yes, and treated fairly,' Liz added quickly. 'And there's the Red Cross…'

Jane nodded. 'Anyway it'll all be over in a few weeks so they're bound to be home soon… won't they? They will, won't they?'

The girls could not look at each other. Liz was smoking and Jane was nursing a long-cold cup of tea as they sat at the kitchen table in the darkness of the Norfolk night.

'Missing in action. That's the official position. That's all Mummy could manage to get out of Colonel Forrest on the phone.' Jane's voice rose in shrill desperation.

'Oh, Jane darling, don't. They'll be alright. They had two parachutes each. Will told me. To be doubly sure. We'll hear from them, or somebody, soon. They may not even have been…'

'Captured? Or do you mean injured? Jane said quietly,

'No, Jane, don't. Poor Will.'

'But surely…'

'Let's not assume anything. Not now. Let's just wait and see. There will be some news in the morning. And there's Lou. I'll go down to the gates and ask to speak with him. He'll know something.'

'It's the waiting I can't bear. I simply can't bear it. Sitting here. Not knowing. Not knowing if…'

'I know,' Liz murmured, putting down her cigarette and coming round the kitchen table to comfort Jane with a hug. 'But we must be strong.'

Jane turned her face up to accept Liz's kiss. Liz saw Jane's tears sparkling down her cheeks in the darkness.

'Darling… you mustn't cry so much… you'll make yourself ill.'

'I don't care. I don't…' Jane sniffled, her words lost in a choking sob.

Gestapo HQ
The Citadel, Arras
Northern France
14th August 1944

Joe woke up with a start. Despite the sleep, he felt exhausted. His body ached. Instinctively, he tried to raise his arms up to stretch. His wrists suddenly burned. Then he remembered why: both hands remained stubbornly on the wooden bench to which his wrists had been securely bound. When he tried to shuffle his feet, he found that his ankles had been shackled to the legs of the bench. He was still blindfolded and had no sense of whether it was night or day. The air around him felt dank and clammy.

A door, heavy by the sound of its hinges, opened slowly. Joe tensed as boots clumped across a stone flag floor. There was another sound. It puzzled Joe before he was able to identify it as that of a trolley, rattling and bumping, being pushed into the room. The squeak of unoiled wheels set his teeth on edge. The door clanged shut.

THE HAMMER AND THE ANVIL

Despite his overwhelming exhaustion, Joe stiffened alertly, his heart beginning to hammer. His mouth dried, making it difficult for him to swallow. He knew that within a few seconds his blindfold would be removed. Would his captors be the Wehrmacht – in the olive-green uniform of the German army – or the Gestapo. Would he be in the spartan out-house of some bombed out farm, or in a cold, stone-walled cell. And would, Joe wondered, Will be there beside him when the blindfold was removed.

But the blindfold remained firmly in place. Leather-gloved fingers checked it roughly, ensuring that Joe saw nothing. There were no preliminaries. No introductions. A voice hissed into Joe's right ear, informing him curtly that he had obviously been on some secret mission against the Third Reich and so would be interrogated without the protection of the Geneva Convention protocols. Joe's nose wrinkled at the smell of the unexpectedly sweet, cloying scented soap used by his captor. A promise of leniency, the voice at his ear purred, could be considered in exchange for Joe's complete co-operation.

Swallowing with some difficulty, Joe took a deep breath and in a slow, deliberate voice, gave his name, rank and number. His statement was received in silence. The trolley rattled as it was brought closer to the bench to which he was bound. A soft scraping sound then the chink of metal broke the momentary quiet. Joe shouted – first in surprise then in protest – as gloved hands unfastened his trousers and dragged them below his knees. The stretch of the damp fabric at his shackled limbs dragged at his skin. Tightly bound to the bench, Joe struggled in vain to resist the knife cutting away his underpants. Twice he felt the blade nicking his flesh. Joe was alarmed at the warmth from the tiny trickles of blood over his exposed skin. The sound of ripping cotton filled him with a sudden horror. Joe's next cries were ones of pain as metal clips were clamped to his exposed genitals: the first biting into his scrotum, the second searing into the tip of his penis. Fear flooded his veins.

A curt order was rasped out. Joe's breath came rapidly. He started to repeat his name, rank and ...

The voice suddenly at his ear once more hissed viciously, demanding mission details. The target. The payload. The base he had flown from, the number of crew on the Liberator. Joe shook his head, refusing to speak.

In response to a command, a switch was clicked. A loud humming filled the air. Joe raised his head, inquisitively. There was a sharp crackling...Joe's back arched as a scream was torn from his throat. A peculiarly thin, piercing scream.

Sweating and trembling, Joe slumped, his head lolling down. The voice returned to his right ear, demanding details of his mission. Joe managed to whisper out, his voice thick and stumbling, his name, rank and number. The metal click of the switch heralded the loud humming, then the brief crackle, and another high-pitched scream from Joe. Seconds later, he slumped into unconsciousness.

'Bring him round.'

'Jawohl, Hauptmann Eigner.'

Joe's pain-clogged brain registered the words before the acrid smelling salts jolted him into full consciousness.

He tested his wrists and ankles. He was still shackled. His eyes were still sheathed by the tight blindfold, making his head throb. The region between his belly and his knees was a numbed void filled with palpable memories of indescribable pain.

The smelling salts were thrust under his nose once more. Joe coughed violently, twisting his face away from the searing ammonia. Cold water was dashed across his face. Harsh laughter greeted Joe's desperate attempts to catch the stray droplets on his parched lips with a straining tongue-tip.

'He is awake? Fully awake?' a voice demanded. The note of cruel anticipation made Joe flinch.

'Ja. He is all yours, Hauptmann Eigner.'

'Very good. So, Lieutenant Kennedy. Are you determined to persist with this unnecessary foolishness or are you going to be reasonable? By reasonable, I mean, of course...sensible.'

The metallic click of the switch sounded in the darkness beyond Joe's blindfold. He gasped, tensing up and bracing himself for the searing pain.

'No, no, Lieutenant. You seem almost anxious for your pain. That is not sensible. You will suffer, if you insist, but only when I say so. Do you understand?'

Joe swore aloud. His profanity was greeted with a cold chuckle.

'Let me, as one officer to another, help you, hmm? I already know all I need to know. I only seek your full co-operation by your readiness to confirm a few minor details. Mere details, you understand.'

Joe's head rose up in response to this unexpected gambit.

'Oh, yes, Lieutenant. I know all I need to know, now. Your fellow crewman was... most obliging. How is it you say in your Hollywood gangster movies? Ah, yes. He sang like the canary... before he died.'

'You piece of fucking Nazi shit...' The stream of abuse broke from Joe's parched lips as he cursed his tormentor.

The switch clicked, the humming grew louder. A bolt of lightning seemed to tear up through Joe, forcing the air out of his lungs through his throat in a long, terrible cry of desolation. Joe's scream collapsed into spluttering tears as he sobbed his sorrow for Will.

'How touching, but far too decadent for my tastes,' the voice of Hauptmann Eigner mocked. 'Now, stop wasting my time. You must confirm all details of your futile mission, Herr Kennedy. Your target. Your payload...'

Joe, in a surging wave of anger, cursed his interrogator savagely.

'You need to be taught some manners, Lieutenant. Servants of the glorious Reich deserve more respect than...'

'Servants?' Joe's anger was interrupted by a spluttering cough. 'More like asshole...' Again, the rupturing coughing. '...robots...'

The click. The hum. The scream of pain. Then, the blissful release into unconsciousness once more.

The Rectory, Fersfield.
15th August, 1944

'No, no, of course not, Colonel Forrest. I quite understand. Yes. Quite understand.'

There was a pause in her flow as Jane's mother changed the receiver from her right ear to her left.

'Next of kin? Oh, goodness me, no. No… just what you might call a social connection. Hmm. Yes, I see. Of course, I quite understand.'

Jane's mother drummed her fingers impatiently down upon the polished surface of the circular pear-wood table. Torn between propriety – her daughter's 'friendship' must be seen as nothing , absolutely nothing but perfectly above board – and her desire to learn the fate of a potential son-in-law with highly satisfactory credentials, she was finding Colonel Forrest singularly difficult to manage. It was most annoying, especially for one who prided herself at being able to bully sweetly the most recalcitrant official at fetes or County Shows.

'Application in writing? Oh, now my dear Colonel Forrest that sounds most awfully formal… Hmm? Classified, you say? I see…'

Another pause.

'Well now you see it seems such a shame… yes… the young things seemed to have taken-up with one-another during the summer… yes… tennis and so forth…'

Her fingers twisted the telephone cord angrily.

'Well, if you are quite unable to say…thank you. Goodbye.'

She replaced the receiver, her hand remaining on it. Now who did she know who could be useful, she mused to herself. Johnny Lewis-Allen? No… he was Navy. Surely there was someone among the circle she had so carefully cultivated across the county in order to help secure her husband's ecclesiastical advancement – someone who would be able to find out what Colonel Forrest seemed so reluctant to divulge. Lady Austin's youngest, Rollo? Yes, of course. He was in something hush-hush. Bound to be able to pull a few strings.

Her husband entered the drawing room.

'Who was that? On the telephone?'

'Nothing important, dear. Just the fishmonger. Apparently there's been an unexpected landing of herring at Lowestoft this morning and would we like to be remembered on his rounds.'

'Herring? Little silver darlings,' he murmured, his voice softening momentarily. 'Excellent.' His voice was brisk again. A rising tone usually reserved for the conclusion of a bracing homily. 'The sea lanes are opening up. Why, my dear, I do believe the tide is turning at last.'

V

White House. Washington D.C.
DATELINE: Monday 22 October 1962

The blue haze of cigarette smoke hung like an LA freeway smog over the heads of the men seated at the table in the briefing room. Ties had been unknotted and jackets discarded. Only the military remained firmly buttoned up.

Despite the urgency of the situation, a tinge of weariness was creeping into the voices slugging out each bout of contention. Several rounds had gone to the doves, slightly more to the hawks. Stalemate threatened to congeal the contest, and the president knew that a clear cut decision was imperative.

'OK. So let's say...' Joe broke into the bickering incisively. 'Let's say we go for an air strike.'

General Taylor's head shot up expectantly. A responsive glint lit up his dark eyes. Joe avoided Taylor's gaze and addressed the table, his hands spread expansively.

'Give me a close up of what we think... no, damn it, what we know for sure... what happens next.'

The president's gaze focused on Paul Nitze, inviting him to reply.

Nitze (Assistant Secretary of Defence) stubbed out a half-smoked cigarette.

'Pin-point, Sir. We gotta go in with pin-point strikes.'

'Precision bombing, Mr President,' General Taylor supplied. 'Knock the eye out of a jack-rabbit from 800 feet.'

Joe Kennedy nodded impatiently.

Nitze continued. 'Restrict the bombing to the nuclear sites. Limit the collateral to the absolute minimum. Priority one is to disable the nuclear capability ...'

'Wasps' nest,' the EX-COMM team heard General Taylor mutter.

Nitze blinked, continuing, 'Then a limited incursion. Our tactical ground forces overwhelm and secure...'

'Limited?' Joe queried, frowning.

'Temporary invasion, Mr President. Thirty-six, maybe forty-eight hours, tops. We're talking short-term occupation for a search and destroy, not a duration, get me? Before the UN starts to bleat, our guys get in there, do the business and get out. No comeback, no mess. So we'll bomb, go in hard, tidy up and then get out. Pronto.'

'Pronto?' a voice asked. 'How realistic is your pronto, time-wise?'

If there was irony in the question Nitze missed the barb.

'Forty-eight hours, tops. Like I say,' Nitze continued, his voice drawling, 'we tell the UN - after the pin-point bombing - that our ground forces are only there to check that the nuclear threat, and by that I mean escalation, has been removed.'

'Escalation?'

Sure,' Nitze grinned. 'Look at it from the UN's point of view. We tell them we've done them a fucking favour, get it? Saved their sorry arses by taking conventional pre-emptive action.'

General Taylor chuckled.

Nitze appealed directly to the President. 'Fast action, Sir. That's our game plan. Jeez, we could go in like greased lightning and knock 'em out. Take them off guard. Only thing left for them to do then is climb down. Climb down and scuttle away like crabs...'

'Blitzkreig,' General Taylor nodded.

Joe Kennedy winced at the word, but before he could frame his response, George Ball broke in.

Several heads turned in unison towards Ball.

'Hold on, now, you guys. We hit Cuba, they hit back – maybe wiping out our strategic capability in, say, Turkey. Likewise,' the Under-Secretary of State reasoned, 'we follow up a strike on Cuba with ground forces, why, hell, the Russkies'll cross into our sector in Berlin. And don't you guys forget...'

'Well?' grunted General Taylor. 'What were we forgetting?'

Ball's voice slowed and softened, like a nurse soothing a fractious patient. 'We suspect…'

'Suspect?' a voice derided.

'OK,' Ball snapped. 'We goddam know that Soviet forces on Cuba have tactical battlefield nuclear weapons…'

Someone whispered 'Fighting dirty.'

'… we can't be sure of taking those babies out completely in our first strike,' Ball argued. 'And what if they just use a couple, huh? Or maybe play cat-and-mouse and tease us with just the one mobile warhead? Our response? How the hell do we reply? How hard are we prepared to hit back? And with what?'

LeMay intervened. 'That's classified information…'

'Goddam helpful,' a voice murmured with heavy sarcasm.

Ball echoed LeMay's interruption pointedly. 'So, we hit them with something out of the classified cookie jar… hell, guys, we'd be wiping Cuba off the map by sundown.'

Joe nodded. Down the table, shrugging off the burden of such consequences, the military men clenched their fists in collective frustration.

'Sir?'

Joe looked across the table at Douglas Dillon. Secretary of the Treasury, Dillon would have no such tactical imperatives to resolve. Joe, sensing that his Treasury man would lay down a more strategic line, allowed Dillon the floor.

To Joe's surprise, Dillon echoed Nitze's proposition, implying deftly that George Ball's prognosis was alarmist – without actually shaming the Under-Secretary of State for being defeatist.

His contribution was applauded by the hawks. Emboldened, he concluded, 'NATO can punch its weight, Mr President. We've got Berlin covered.'

Adlai Stevenson, silent for the last few minutes, challenged the Nitze-Dillon line. He cleared his throat before speaking judiciously. 'Like George Ball said, Sir. Too risky. Can't cover it all. Maybe NATO will hold the line in Berlin. Maybe. But do the Soviets think that? Do they believe that? Because, Mr President, if we misread the Soviet mind – get their thinking on this wrong

– we've got ourselves another conventional confrontation in Europe. For Chrissakes, gentlemen,' he appealed to those around the table, his measured tones replaced by urgency, 'are we actually prepared to contemplate firing the first shots of World War III?'

George Ball brought his hand down emphatically. 'Exactly. And what about their subs? Eh? Nuclear capability torpedo-wise? Do we respond? Maybe lose Miami? New Orleans?'

His words were drowned as raised voices raged across the table. Nobody heard the polite tap-tapping at the door. The repeated knocking caught Joe's ear. Using his spoon against the side of his coffee cup, he brought EX-COMM to order. General Taylor, who had been remonstrating with Sorensen, responded to the third knock at the door.

'I'll get that.'

Opening the door briskly, he revealed a breakfast-laden trolley.

'Your breakfasts, Sirs,' the pretty young woman murmured, propelling the trolley into the briefing room.

As she bent to the task of pouring coffee she drew appreciative glances from several of those seated around the table.

The rattling trolley, its silver frame glinting under the neon lighting, broke into Joe Kennedy's consciousness. For a split second, something ugly stirred in the deepest recesses of his mind, causing a flicker of half-forgotten fear.

The sudden lurch from power politics to the mundane munching of cinnamon toast brought a sullen silence to the EX-COMM team. Joe ate nothing but signalled his desire for fresh coffee. Feeling self-conscious, and sensing the tension in the room, the waitress rattled the trolley nervously. Joe managed to swallow down his impatience.

'That's OK, we'll just help ourselves.'

Smiling her relief, the young woman withdrew.

Down along the table, Douglas Dillon resumed his attack on George Ball. Ball swallowed his mouthful of waffle in readiness to reply but was prevented from doing so when Joe raised his hand.

'OK, that's enough. We're taking a time-out here. Let's just all simmer down. Enjoy your breakfast in silence, gentlemen, and give yourselves time for a little reflection.'

Most of those assembled nodded their assent. General Taylor muttered resentfully that they were all capable of eating and talking at the same time.

'Let's try the silence, OK?' Joe asked assertively.

Taylor bit into a doughnut, smothering his reply.

When his coffee cup had been drained for the second time, Joe glanced at his watch, looked down the table and called EX-COMM to order.

He spoke deliberately, determined to remain in control of the volatile meeting. He advised them that each must come to a decision and be prepared to vote openly when backing their favoured response to the crisis.

His audience nodded.

'But I tell you, gentlemen, each and every one of you. This is the moment to look into your hearts. Consider the consequences of your decision wisely. What did someone say about rushing into marriage? It must be entered into soberly, not rashly…'

'Or else we're really fucked …'

Grunts of laughter greeted Douglas Dillon's aside as the tension eased around the table.

Joe waited for a few seconds before continuing. 'We will not be able to hold the heavy weight of World War III on our shoulders alone, so we must not make enemies of those we will need to count on soon as allies and friends.'

Around the table, the hawks and the doves all saw the stark truth in their president's words.

'And,' Joe concluded, 'while the court of world opinion will find us guilty should we get this wrong, the American people will prove utterly unforgiving. They will not tolerate any miscalculation. Any mistake.'

Nobody responded, even if the military men suspected that the president was covering his butt, politically.

The solemnity of Joe's words settled over EX-COMM, silencing their irritability and impatience. Joe seized his advantage and nodded to his brother. Robert broke the silence, easing into his role as decision-making broker.

'Gentlemen, as I see it, we have ourselves three deals on the table...'

'As you see it?' General Taylor growled, resenting Bobby Kennedy's assumed authority.

'Three,' Bobby repeated firmly. 'Option One. We do not respond. Nothing direct, no military strike – but,' he added hastily, cutting across Taylor's groan, 'we complain, and we complain bitterly, through the offices of the UN. And we open up a covert communication channel for secret negotiations. The deal would be along these lines: they withdraw their missiles from Cuba, we withdraw US capability from Turkey.'

'Hell, no,' a voice objected. 'Our bases in Turkey protect the Gulf, securing Persian and Saudi oil...'

'And the soft underbelly of Europe...'

The President raised his hand for silence.

'Option Two,' Bobby continued doggedly, 'is the tactical response. A two-part military intervention. Pre-emptive air strikes with immediate land invasion follow-up.'

Those around the table wearing uniform nodded vigorously. Despite Joe's warning look, General Taylor spoke, affirming that military action was the only option they had.

'Option Three,' Bobby concluded, 'is where we play cat-and-mouse. We impose a tough naval blockade. Nothing gets in. Nothing comes out. And we show them we mean business if we have to. A blockade gentlemen, coupled with an even tougher negotiating stance.'

'OK, thanks Bobby. I guess that lays it on the line pretty neatly. Everyone in agreement that those are our options?' the president asked.

All agreed.

'Then I need your decisions. As members of EX-COMM, you each get one vote. And remember, each option from the choice must be weighed carefully before you make your decision.'

After a few minutes, a soft rustling of unrest began to disturb the quiet of concentration, telling Joe that it was time for the voting.

'All ready?'

All nodded their readiness to vote.

'Let's do it.'

One by one, the members of EX-COMM voted. Starting from his left, Joe invited their responses. 'So,' he summed up. 'Option One gets no votes. Options Two and Three get nine apiece. We're looking at a split decision, gentlemen.'

'That leaves you with the casting vote, Sir,' George Ball prompted.

Joe Kennedy sat motionlessly at the table, his hands palms-down into the smoothness of the wood. Suddenly, Joe realized that he would have to leave his hands resting on the table, reluctant to raise them in case EX-COMM saw his sweat cloud the polished surface.

Option Two or Option Three? The decision, despite all the heated discussion of the morning, felt like it was his alone.

An emboldened knocking at the door broke the intense silence in the briefing room.

'Mr President?' General Taylor asked, rising from his chair to answer.

Joe nodded. It could be Richardson, bringing an urgent update. Perhaps Joe would never get the opportunity to choose between the two options. Maybe events had overtaken EX-COMM. Could the crisis have broken?

'Yes?' Taylor barked after yanking the door open violently.

The spasm running down Joe's jaw-line fluttered.

It was Richardson, with the pretty waitress. Her hands joined together momentarily as if in prayer then fluttered nervously down to smooth the tight material of her blouse above her hips. The action caused a collective exhalation.

'Can I get you anything else, gentlemen?'

Joe, gritting his teeth, waved them away without reply.

The Citadel, Arras.
16th August, 1944.

Joe heard the slapping as a far away noise before he felt the stinging blows and – breaking through the surface of consciousness – realized that his own face was being slowly, methodically slapped.

Shaking his head as he coughed and spluttered, Joe felt his cheeks being captured and squeezed within the grip of leather-gloved fingers, as his blindfold was wrenched away.

'Welcome back, Lieutenant,' Eigner mocked. 'So glad you were able to re-join our little party.'

He felt so exhausted and wanted to let his chin loll down onto his chest but his tormentor's controlling hand forced and kept Joe's head up.

Out of the corner of his eye, Joe glimpsed the trolley. Trailing down from the upper tray were two snaking coils of wire. The wires, thick electrical flex, disappeared out of his range of vision at his feet below. Joe could feel the numbing pain of the bulldog clips biting into his scrotum. He groaned. Behind his back, his bound hands writhed, his fingers flexing and splaying in agony.

'Are you prepared to answer my questions, Lieutenant? I do hope so,' Eigner purred. 'Or do you,' he whispered, 'propose to continue with your stubborn foolishness, hmm?'

Joe closed his eyes. Eigner squeezed Joe's face with his gloved hand, forcing the eyes of his captive to open.

'Give him some more treatment,' Eigner rasped to an assistant in the shadows.

Joe tried to shout a response but the fingers squeezing his cheeks so fiercely distorted his mouth. The trolley rattled ominously as Eigner's accomplice bent over it.

The cell door crashed open. The gloved fingers at Joe's face relaxed their grip. Eigner turned, cursing, to see two Schmeisser-bearing soldiers enter, peel aside and, face to face, draw their polished jack-boots smartly together. A Senior SS Officer strode between them into the dingy cell. Through his haze of pain, Joe could see fury etched on the newcomer's face.

Brusque commands were shouted. Seconds later, Eigner's assistant was kneeling to remove the clips from Joe's genitals. Soon Joe was rubbing the blood-flow back into his hands after his wrists had been untied. Testing his feet and legs, Joe half rose from the wooden bench – only to slither down immediately and collapse on the stone floor.

Peering up, Joe watched as the soldiers lowered the snouts of their Schmeissers and, both Eigner and his assistant begrudgingly allowed themselves to be marched out of the cell.

A medical orderly entered. After swathing Joe's nakedness in a soft blanket, he helped Joe regain his seat on the bench. As Joe steadied himself, his hands planted down at either side, the medical orderly hurriedly bundled the trolley away.

'My name, Herr Kennedy, is Oberst Kettner,' the Officer informed Joe. To Joe's surprise, a respectful apology for the recent mistreatment was proffered.

The medical orderly returned. After assisting Joe to some sips of brandy – and a half glass of water – he knelt down and began to dress Joe's wounds.

'First, we must repair any damage, Lieutenant. An unfortunate misunderstanding, I assure you. Most unfortunate,'

Joe groaned. Even the slightest touch of a swab at his genitals was agony.

Kettner winced, continuing hurriedly, 'Food. Yes, food, then a hot bath for you. A saline bath to speed your recovery. Clean, dry clothing, of course. And what could seem better to you right now than, my dear Lieutenant, a sound night's sleep in a comfortable bed?'

Joe nodded, calculating that a nod was giving nothing away. His nod was merely the acknowledgement of Kettner's decency.

'I shall return to talk with you after you are fully rested, Herr Kennedy.'

Talk? Fancy word for a grilling, Joe mused. Mr Nasty had wheeled in that trolley full of tricks to loosen Joe's tongue. Now, he suspected, Mr Nice was going to try soft beds and warm food. Masking his suspicions with an agreeable nod, Joe stood up – teetering on unsteady feet – to allow the medical orderly access to his wounds.

'Barbarous,' Oberst Kettner snorted, shaking his head in disapproval. 'What must you think of...some of us. The lower orders really have no idea. My apologies. That damn fool Eigner should have known that he was interrogating the most important American airman we have ever taken into captivity.'

Joe stiffened at these words.

Noting the reaction, Kettner smiled, continuing suavely, 'I remember listening to many of your father's speeches. Yes. Speeches he made when he was the American Ambassador to Britain. He is, I believe, a Republican at heart, and a Republican by instinct …'

Joe concealed a wry grimace.

'– but a Democrat by political pragmatism. We in the Third Reich are of the same opinion, I believe, as your father on many important issues... communism... trade unionists... the Jewish question... oh, yes, I heard his speeches, and of course we have had access to the contents of so many cables he sent to Roosevelt. Yes,' Kettner assured Joe, who had reacted with surprise, 'your father advocated American neutrality, recommending non-involvement in the European theatre. France and Italy were, he thought, corrupted and Britain was about to be led into conflict by a drunkard... oh, yes... we have read the cables, Lieutenant... but of course, I am telling you things you already know...'

Joe remained silent as inwardly he struggled to come to terms with what Kettner had said. What Kettner had told Joe had left an opening for a response. Joe said nothing, swallowing down his anger.

'We have friends in England, of course. Perhaps not on the terraces of the football stadia, but certainly on the playing fields of Eton. Not in the backstreets or at the factory gates or in the shipyards, but we ignore the views of such *untermenschen*, just as we disregard the Poles and Slavs...'

Joe's thoughts flew back to Fersfield. He pictured Jane's father's verger along with a mere handful of elderly comrades hurrying across the fields, pitchforks in hand, perhaps only one rifle between them, towards a crashed German bomber. Joe smiled inwardly as he relished the image of the verger, leading the Home Guard unit in his best black Sunday suit, converging on the crew of a downed Dornier.

Kettner's voice broke into Joe's thoughts. 'Not supporters in large numbers but support where it counts. Where it most matters. Among the aristocracy. Among financiers hit hard by the General Strike and then by the Slump. Why,' Kettner reasoned expansively, 'even their one-time King saluted the Fuehrer in 1938.'

Joe, caught between anger and revulsion, smothered his feelings of disgust with a groan.

Solicitously, Kettner cautioned the medical orderly to be more gentle in the task of smearing Joe's groin with antiseptic cream.

'Now, my dear Lieutenant, it may be of some interest to you to learn that many of us here feel that the Fuehrer has served Germany and the third Reich well... but has served his purpose. A strong man to lead us through the thirties. A bold man. Our initial military successes were compromised, I fear, by a series of errors of judgement –'

'Compromised?' Joe inquired, genuinely intrigued.

'We should have taken England in 1940. 1941 by the latest. Yes, that was a big mistake. Operation Sealion should have gone ahead. And,' Kettner spread his hands out, 'the foolishness of attacking Russia when we did'

'Had you a choice?'

'We could have starved them into submission. Much more expedient to bring Stalin to his knees by razing the wheat fields in Georgia. No matter. What is done, is done.' He shrugged. 'But now, you see, my dear Lieutenant, everyone is expendable. We find ourselves still – and perhaps only just – in a position to negotiate for "a peace with honour" settlement that would secure our new borders and leave us as a buffer state against the Soviet hordes. Both Roosevelt and Churchill might well agree to that strategically.'

'You see that as the end-game?' Joe demanded. 'You and your... colleagues... really believe that the Allies will sit down at the conference table and talk peace?'

'If the Fuehrer was not in the picture, but a sensible alternative... why yes. Which of us does not seek to bring to an end the folly of this costly war?'

'Why? Why are you telling me this?'

'I have been in communication with my friends in Berlin since the moment of your capture. There were unfortunate delays, hence Eigner. We see you as perfect for the part of go-between. You, Herr Kennedy, with your credentials, and contacts, will act as our emissary. You will be given safe passage back to London...'

Joe raised his eyebrows.

Kettner smiled. 'We have our methods. Once in London, you will personally deliver our terms to certain...authorities.' He held up his hand. 'But enough of all that, Herr Kennedy. Now, you must rest. Rest, and sleep. Good night, Lieutenant. You will be conducted to new quarters once your wounds have been dressed. I shall visit you there in the morning.'

Fersfield US 8th Air Force Base, Norfolk.
17th August, 1944

'Come in, Father,' Colonel Forrest grimaced. 'There will be a phone call for you any moment now.'

'Colonel? I don't understand.' The chaplain closed the door behind him.

'It'll be put through to this office. I'll... I'd better leave you to it.'

Fuming at being ousted from his own office, Colonel Forrest strode out, banging the door.

The chaplain sat in the chair Forrest had vacated and eyed the black telephone nervously. When it rang, he picked it up and found himself talking to Joe Kennedy Senior.

'Anything? Anything at all?'

'No, Sir,' the chaplain replied. 'Nothing. Even the Red Cross...'

'Fuck the Red Cross. What do they know? You guys... the Church... see and hear everything. Why, the Papal Nuncio has a free hand across Europe.'

'I wouldn't quite say that, Sir. There are difficulties even for an exalted personage such as...'

'Come on, level with me, Padre. Have you actually tapped into the grapevine yet, eh?'

'Well, you see, Sir, as you know I've only been here a couple of weeks and the mission was classified as top secret.'

'There must be some news.'

'Everyone here on the base is in the dark – even your son's friends have been pulling strings...'

'Friends?' came the sharp interruption. 'What friends?'

'They say the girl's mother has been –'

'Girl? What girl?' Joe Senior snapped.

'Can't say, exactly. Seems your son was friendly with a local minister's family hereabouts.'

'Hell,' came the explosive response. 'Now see here. What are your plans for after the war, eh?'

There was a pause.

'Well?' prompted the questioner.

'I'm none too sure... maybe work with displaced orphans...'

'Sure, sure. Now I'm playing golf with the bishop next week. Fix you up with a neat little parish in upstate New York, eh? You interested?'

'Why, yes indeed, but...'

'OK, now this is what I want you to do. First, speak to the boys on the base. Not just the air crews. All of them. Ask about Will Ford and any girl he was seeing. With me so far?'

'Yes.'

'Now this is where you tread softly. Chances are that Ford's girl will know about any girl Joe might have been involved with...

'Yes, I see...'

'And I want you to get the low-down on that girl's family, too. I want everything, understand?'

'I'm not sure that...'

'By the way, I always let the bishop win at golf. Puts him in a sweeter mood at the nineteenth hole,' Joe Senior chuckled. 'You get the picture?'

'An upstate parish sure would be fine...'

'And keep trying out your contacts. Use my name. They know me in the Vatican, for Chrissakes...'

Beads of shining sweat broke out on the chaplain's brow at the mention of the Vatican.

'OK, I'll be in touch,' barked Joe Senior, ringing off abruptly.

Replacing the phone as if in a daze, the chaplain sat motionless in Colonel Forrest's chair.

The Citadel, Arras.
17th August 1944

The sunlight streaming down through the tiny window crept across the pillow onto Joe's face. His eyes flickered as if he was in a troubled dream – then opened. He blinked. Beside his bed, breakfast waited for him on a trolley. Coffee and croissants. The white porcelain cup and plate were eggshell thin. The trolley was the one which had brought in the apparatus used by Eigner's assistant.

Reaching for a croissant, Joe stretched his arm down stiffly, lowering his splayed fingers towards the pastry. As he moved to close them over it, his fraternity ring slipped down from his finger and clattered loudly onto the plate.

Washing down the first delicious mouthful with coffee, Joe reached down to the foot of the bed and dragged out his left boot. Working quickly with the breakfast knife, he forced a split in the boot's heel, gouging out a ragged little hole. Secreting the fraternity ring into the gap he made in the rubber was the work of a moment. When Oberst Kettner knocked, unlocked the door and entered a minute later, Joe was relaxing on his bed enjoying another croissant.

Kettner picked up the third remaining pastry and bit into it.

'You are a very fortunate young man, Herr Kennedy,' he announced, spitting crumbs.

'I'm sure I'll be asked to sing for my supper,' Joe replied drily.

'Perhaps I have a song for you that will not be unpleasing.'

'Music to my ears.'

Kettner smiled. 'May I?' he sat down on the edge of the bed before Joe could respond. 'We spoke last night about the important part you might play in bringing this senseless war to a negotiated settlement.'

'You talked. I listened,' Joe countered.

Kettner, ignoring this, continued by describing how he saw the mission being brought to a successful conclusion. There would be a U-boat to the Irish Free State. A train ride up to Belfast. Once there, the escort would slip away into the shadows – remaining on hand, naturally – leaving Joe to arrange a flight to London.

'But aren't you overlooking one tiny little detail in this plan of yours, Oberst?' Joe challenged.

'Just the one?'

'OK two. First, didn't Hess try something like this a couple of years back?'

Kettner's impassive face darkened with a scowl. He flushed angrily as he stood up from Joe's bed abruptly and paced the floor. Mastering his momentary agitation, he turned, sweeping his flattened hand – palm down – in a dismissive gesture.

'Hess was a maverick playing a lone hand. Forget him.' He paused. 'And the second little detail?'

Joe shrugged. 'I ditch your papers in the River Liffey, give your goons the slip and hop on a boat from Dublin to Liverpool. Easy enough. Get back to... my base... climb into a bomber and high tail it across the Channel after that shit Eigner...'

Disconcertingly, Joe watched as Kettner chuckled and clapped his hands delightedly.

'Well?' Joe demanded. 'That little detail enough for you?'

'I have every confidence in the escort which will accompany you to Belfast. I have every confidence in you, my dear Lieutenant, and in the fact that you will agree to act as our emissary – bringing our message to General Eisenhower.'

'Eisenhower? Joe echoed. 'You mean...'

'My people will deal with the general directly once contact has been established. But,' Kettner's tone hardened, 'if you choose not to co-operate we will find someone else who will... while you rot in some wretched POW camp.'

Joe shook his head slowly.

'Stalag VI, I believe, is particularly inhospitable when the winter arrives... and American fliers there receive special attention from the guards, many of whom I am informed lost family and friends during your raids on the Ruhr.'

Joe told Oberst Kettner to go and fuck himself, adding that the only time Kettner would get to sit at a table with General Eisenhower would be at the surrender of Berlin.

'You disappoint me, Lieutenant, Yes. I had thought that politics would flow in your veins along with your father's blood. But I still may yet be able to... persuade you...'

Kettner's foot kicked the trolley by Joe's bedside. The rattle brought back a momentary horror to Joe's mind.

'You'll never make me...'

Kettner turned, approached the door and pulled it open. There, slumped in the fierce grip of two guards, stood Will. His swollen face bore the testament to recent brutality, as did his bloodstained shirt. Joe's delight turned instantly to dismay.

'Will – Christ!' Joe shouted, struggling up off the bed.

Will's head jerked up but his heavily bruised eyes remained shut.

'Take him away,' Oberst Kettner ordered, slamming the door shut. 'Sit down, Lieutenant. Now, as you can clearly see, I have more cards in my hand than you thought. Is that not so? No, do not get excited. I will make sure that Eigner keeps his eager hands well away from your compatriot. For now.'

Joe slumped back down onto the bed, his fists clenched in impotent rage.

'It is decided, then. Tomorrow, we drive to Berlin.'

Fersfield Air Force base.
17th August, 1944

'They've got him. That's all we know. And young Ford. No, they haven't. No, they're still – What? I don't know why not,' Colonel Forrest snapped down the phone.

'Guys who go down end up in a goddam Stalag within forty-eight hours, Colonel. You know that as well as I do. Damn it, why the hell is my son still stuck in some...'

'Who knows? Maybe the trains are out of action...'

'Bullshit...'

'Now hold on...'

'No. you hold it right there, Forrest. I'm totally disgusted with the way you fellahs have handled this. Word's reached me the goddam Catalina was late – the pick-up boats too. Seems to me you guys couldn't organise a poke in a whorehouse...'

Forrest broke in angrily. 'Seems to me if you hadn't been so goddam anxious to push him for a mission…'

Outside Colonel Forrest's office door, an airman stood uncertainly, a mug of coffee on a tray. The raised voice coming from inside stayed his hand from knocking on the door.

'And how the hell should I know that?' the Colonel's angry bark sang through the door. 'Some local parson, I guess. The dame chews my ear off twice a day and the girl hangs around the gatehouse asking for news – What?'

During the ominous silence that followed, the airman hovered irresolutely at the door.

'Oh you think so, do you? Well it seems to me maybe you needed to cut your son a little slack. He might still be your boy but he was out over here doing a man's job…'

It was a brief silence this time for the listening airman. A brief silence ruptured by a furious response.

'And fuck you too…'

The airman crept away, coffee slopping the tray.

The White House, Washington D.C.
Monday 23rd. October 1962
10.47 am Eastern Standard Time

The President sat hunched forward, his elbows on the table, his hands across his eyes. All the members of EX-COMM maintained a respectful silence as their Chief weighed up the options as he struggled to decide.

Joe wiped his eyes and planted his hands down on the table. He pushed himself upright and looked directly at Nitze.

'Go through it again. Tell me why you are so confident in our pre-emptive strike capability. Tell me how you can be so sure that such a strike or series of strikes will force them to climb down, and not,' Joe paused for a second, 'lead directly into escalation.'

Nitze answered promptly in the tone of a man absolutely sure of his facts. US intelligence, he stressed, was quite certain that their assessment of the situation was accurate.

'Our boys tell us that they have a full appreciation of both positions, Mr President. We have military dominance over the Soviets in both the immediate and adjacent theatres.'

That dominance, he emphasized, was asserted not only through US nuclear capability but in like-for-like conventional strengths in the air and at sea.

Stevenson shook his head. After seeking and receiving Joe's permission, he interrupted Nitze.

'We'd better not underestimate the Soviets. What they may or may not lack in hardware they sure as hell make up for in…'

'Guts and grit?' a sardonic voice asked.

'Spirit and resolve, gentlemen. And numbers. Those tanks racing for Berlin back in 1945 had little more than ideology under the hood…'

Several heads nodded appreciatively. Stevenson had scored an important point.

'Stalingrad,' a voice murmured. 'Those Nazi bastards sure caught the tiger by the tail there…'

Joe, forcing down a flood of personal memories from those days seventeen years ago, merely acknowledged the Red Army's undoubted valour. His comment drew a speculative glance from General Taylor.

It was acknowledged that the Soviets had huge land forces massed up along their European borders.

'Those Russkies could sure pack a punch…'

Joe redirected the discussion back onto the effectiveness of pre-emptive air strikes, asking General Le May if such strikes could be certain of taking out all of the Cuban missiles.

'Yes, Sir, Mr President,' Le May replied. There was a slight pause, during which Le May fingered his chin. 'Leastways, all the ones we know about…'

'What the hell - ?'

'For Chrissakes…'

Joe held up his hand for silence. 'Thanks, general,' Joe nodded. 'You see gentlemen,' he addressed EX-COMM. 'It's time for clear thinking and straight talking. We've been evaluating the potential of a pre-emptive air strike for hours and we've just found out that we don't even know what the Soviets might have buried under the sand down there in Cuba.'

Taylor expostulated with Le May, threatening to bring rancour back to the table. Bobby asked for EX-COMM's attention.

'OK, let's see what we've got here…'

Bobby amplified Le May's recent caveat, explored the implications and ended with a direct appeal against precipitate action which could trigger unforeseen consequences.

'We've got to stay on top of this. We've got to call the shots…' Bobby insisted.

EX-COMM listened to him patiently.

'… You're gonna kill an awful lot of people,' Bobby concluded, 'and we're gonna get the heat for it…'

After Bobby had spoken, a gloom descended over the meeting, propelling EX-COMM from fractiousness to weariness. To the surprise of all those seated at the table, Joe was the first to break the silence.

'Gentlemen…' President Kennedy announced, his voice hardening with resolve. 'Option Three. Minimum risks for maximum effect – and it keeps us on-side with the UN. I'm going to give the executive order. Agreed? The naval blockade will be put into effect…'

'But, Mr President…'

'The naval blockade will be our initial response. I have made my decision,' Joe pronounced, folding his arms resolutely.

The Citadel, Arras.
18th August, 1944

Joe woke up with a start. He thought he had heard a short, single scream. Will? He struggled to sit up in the bed – then sank back down wearily. Awake until the first flush of dawn, he had been wrestling all night with the options – the two stark choices – given to him by Kettner. To comply or to refuse. To refuse, he knew, would be to sign Will's painful death warrant.

Joe knew, deep down, even before his emotions had resolved into reasons, that he had come to a decision. Shifting the uneasy weight from his mind, Joe anticipated breakfast. The flakey croissants were delicious, but Joe had a belly-longing for ham and eggs.

The minutes passed slowly. Outside, Joe could just catch the sounds of activity. Muted orders being barked, the dull clump of boots marching in unison, an engine being revved into life.

The sound of a key scraping in the lock brought a flicker of a smile to Joe. Even if he had to endure more of Kettner's posturing, the coffee would be good.

But it was not coffee, croissants or Kettner that met Joe's gaze as the door swung open. It was Eigner. Joe's faint smile vanished – Eigner's leer broadened. Joe instinctively took a step back. Eigner, remaining at the open door, curled his fore-finger in a beckoning gesture. Joe remained rooted to the spot, his heart beating rapidly, his mouth dry and sour.

Eigner swore, snapped his fingers twice and stood aside. Two guards entered and, flanking Joe, seized him roughly before frog-marching him through the door and down along a dank, echoing corridor.

Still in the grip of his guards, Joe was led through an open wooden door and out into the bright sunshine. Squinting into the brightness, he saw that he was standing in a courtyard enclosed by a high stone wall.

Great-coated soldiers, their rifles leveled, were guarding a line of eight disheveled-looking prisoners. Each prisoner faced the wall, their arms spread out like the espaliered pear-trees that splayed against the white washed bricks. Joe recognized Will standing third in line.

Eigner stepped up softly to Joe and, capturing Joe's face in his gloved hand, slowly forced Joe's attention over towards the south facing wall. A walnut tree spread its branches up against the pale blue sky. Joe thought it was a ragged blanket – no, it must be a bundle of rags – spindling from the lowest branch.

Eigner, chuckling darkly, propelled Joe by the scruff of his neck towards the walnut tree. Then – unable to smother his grunt of surprised disgust – Joe saw that what was dangling and twisting from the branch of the walnut tree was the body of Oberst Kettner. The dead man's once pristine uniform was torn into tatters and his lolling neck all but severed by piano wire. Piano wire so thin it was almost invisible as it suspended Kettner's corpse. Joe looked down. The once immaculate boots were scuffed and soiled. Soiled, inevitably, by the urine voided from the dead man's bladder.

'A word with you, Herr Kennedy,' a soft voice whispered in Joe's ear. 'Be careful of the friends you make during your visit to the Third Reich. See? That is what we do to traitors. That is a fitting end for treason.'

Joe felt his knees buckle as he saw that Oberst Kettner's tongue had been cut out. A slender, fair haired man in a leather trench coat walked past Joe and strode right up to the walnut tree. Raising a 35mm cine camera, he recorded the terrible scene in careful detail.

'A surprise for the Fuehrer. He has a private cinema,' Eigner confided.

Joe gazed stupidly at the dark hole of the dead Oberst's mouth. The missing tongue lay beneath the corpse. Had that been the single, stifled scream Joe had heard earlier? Or had the sharp cry of anguish that had awoken Joe been when the piano wire sliced into Kettner's throat.

'You have been lucky... perhaps...' Eigner hissed. 'The Luftwaffe seem eager to have you. Just pray that we do not ever meet again, Lieutenant.'

Spitting deliberately at Joe's feet, Eigner wheeled away and joined the man with the cine-camera. The guards pushed Joe roughly into line against the white washed wall between the other prisoners and the espaliered pear-trees. A large wooden gate creaked as it was unbolted and then dragged open, allowing a lorry to reverse into the courtyard. The tail-gate crashed down noisily and, one by one, the guards singled out each prisoner, binding their hands and applying blindfolds, before bundling them up into the back of the lorry.

The tail-gate was slammed into place and secured. The gears crashed and with a jolt, Joe and Will's journey to the prison camp began.

Fersfield Air Force base.
19th August 1944

'You gonna talk to her or what?'

Walt Irwin pretended to ignore the question and tackled the obstinate wheel nut with his spanner.

'Gal's been at the fence there every day ever since...'

Walt tossed his spanner down angrily. 'OK, lay off me, huh? I'll go talk to her.'

At the perimeter fence, Jane stood up on tiptoe against the wire.

'It's Walt, isn't it? You're Walt Irwin. I'm Jane...'

'Yeh, so Joe said. Look – Jane – there ain't no use you comin' here like this or goin' up to the gatehouse neither. It's kinda early days for... I'm sure we'll get word soon...'

'But they were both rescued from the sea. The Germans picked both of them out of the water and took... and took them away...' Jane's tears overwhelmed her.

Walt snatched off his forage cap and reddened.

'But that's good, eh?' he cajoled unconvincingly. 'They were both, like you say, rescued...'

Despite her tears, Jane had fire in her angry eyes. 'You know something, don't you? Oh, you men with your top secret this and your restricted that... just tell me, tell me please... everything you know.'

Jane's angry outburst left Walt Irwin floundering miserably.

From beneath the wing of a Liberator parked nearby, Colonel Forrest witnessed these exchanges through the perimeter fence of his air base. He strode rapidly towards the couple separated by the meshed wire.

'Irwin?'

'Sir, yes, Sir.' Walt saluted snappily.

'Back to your duties.'

'Sir, yes, Sir,' Walt replied, transparently relieved to be dismissed.

'Oh, Colonel,' Jane implored.

'Now look, little lady...' Colonel Forrest sighed, unequal to her tears of rage and grief.

Lille, Occupied France.
22nd August 1944

Joe managed to shuffle along the line until he was standing directly behind Will. It was chilly. The railway station had been bombed the previous night. A thin film of concrete dust covered everything. Underfoot, the platform still sparkled with shards of splintered glass. The stench of cordite – mixed with doused, charred timber – hung in the air.

All conversation was forbidden. Those risking a surreptitious whispered exchange were rewarded with a rifle-butt clubbing. Several dozen POWs – mostly air crew – waited in the enforced silence until their transport arrived.

Two-and-a-half hours later, their train – a wheezing engine dragging a line of rattling cattle trucks – pulled in. Rifle butts were used brutally to drive the POWs aboard. Slatted wooden doors were slid shut and padlocked. The engine expressed a huge cloud of steam and the whistle shrilled – but an air raid siren sounded. The German soldiers and the train crew abandoned the POWs to their fate, leaving them locked in the cattle trucks as the station was evacuated. The POWs crouched in the darkness of the cattle trucks as the drone of the approaching bombers grew louder. Joe braced himself for the explosions as the first wave roared directly overhead – but the aircraft passed over in pursuit of some other, more vital target.

The 'all clear' was sounded twenty minutes later. The German soldiers and the train crew returned. Through the wooden slats, the hungry captives saw their guards staggering under looted bottles of wine, sausage, cheese, fruit and white bread loaves.

Six hours later, when they were eventually fed, the POWs were given hard, grey bread meanly scraped with oily margarine. The *erstatz* coffee, made from acorns, was bitter, sugarless and tepid. It loosened the bowels of the prisoners for the duration of their exhausting train journey. A journey punctuated by inexplicable delays in sidings and tunnels.

Some forty hours after being herded on board, the POWs left their cattle trucks under close guard in cold, driving rain close to a Luftwaffe base – night fighters, Joe guessed – on the outskirts of Cologne.

There was no hot food. The prisoners were allowed five minutes to shit in a ditch before being forced to march in double-time to the main railway station. The streets of Cologne were almost deserted, the mood of the few civilians sullen and subdued. A few of them hurled stones at the POWs in revenge for recent Allied bombing raids.

The train journey to Frankfurt was a thirty hour nightmare devoid of food, water, sleep, warmth or sanitation. The forced march over twelve kilometres brought the miserable prisoners to the gates of the Oberursel Interrogation Centre.

Oberursel provided a bleak, comfortless existence. Joe, who had lost contact with Wil, was routinely interrogated every morning for a full two hours and then returned to his blanketless, unheated solitary confinement for the remaining twenty-two.

Sometimes, the metal bucket of thin soup did not stop at Joe's cell door to dispense the regulation ration. He lost track of time and count of the passing days. He did not know if it was on his seventh or seventeenth day at Oberursel that he caught a cockroach.

It scuttled around within his closed fist as Joe was contemplating the impending mouthful. He heard its faint rasp – just like the sound of the cigars his father would twirl between expectant fingers. Then, closing his eyes, Joe squeezed the cockroach between his filthy, black-nailed fingers, retching immediately his palm felt the ooze. Joe concentrated hard. The cockroach meant protein. Vital protein. His training manuals had stressed how important protein was to a pilot's eyesight. The sticky substance in his cupped hand was protein – just like a rib-eye steak, only from a smaller animal.

The minutes filled with revulsion. Suddenly, his mouth firmly shut, Joe used the squashed cockroach – now held like a stub of chalk between his fingers – to scrawl a name on the nearest brick wall. Jane.

The White House, Washington D.C.
Late morning, Wednesday 24th October, 1962

Bobby sought out Joe in the president's private office. 'You OK?' he asked his older brother.

Joe, looking strained and tired, seemed to be staring vacantly at the model of the Liberator suspended over his desk.

'Huh?'

'You OK?'

'Yeah. Sure. I'm fine. Grab a seat. We need to talk.'

Bobby drew up an ornate gilt chair and joined Joe behind the desk. They were both wearing knotted ties but in shirt-sleeves, jacketless.

Bobby cracked a gag about General Taylor's reaction to Option Three. Joe didn't catch it. Bobby was about to explain the gag when his eyes alighted on the picture Joe was taking out of the desk drawer and placing down before him. It was the snap-shot of Jane. The shadow of the Liberator's starboard wingtip fell down across her upturned face.

'Jeez, Joe. Is that... wise?'

'Huh?'

'Come on, Joe. Ted'll be in here any second.'

'Damn Sorensen... maybe you're right.' Joe picked up the picture of Jane and returned it carefully to the darkness of the desk drawer.

'Ted'll want to brief you on what you are going to tell the people...Oh, word came in just now. The leader of the Senate is calling for air strikes, Joe. You've gotta convince them about the blockade strategy.'

Richardson ushered Ted Sorensen in and withdrew. Sorensen bustled about in front of the desk, struggling with a sheaf of papers. The three men got down to their task immediately – agreeing to, altering and then tearing up draft statements.

'We're doing this all wrong,' Joe snapped testily.

'You'll need one for the press, another for the TV cameras...'

'And all the time I'm not speaking to the one audience I should be...'

'Wall Street?'

'Capitol Hill?'

Joe looked up at them. 'The Kremlin,' he growled.

Bobby was momentarily speechless.

'Holy shit,' Sorensen managed.

'Bobby.'

'Yes, Joe?'

'Fix me up with a back-channel. Push it all the way. I'm prepared to go face-to-face in Moscow if need be.'

'I'm on it,' Bobby replied.

VI

The outskirts of Wetzlar, Germany.
28th August, 1944.

It was an unseasonably cold, grey dawn. The relentless rain drenched the canvas covering the Wehrmacht Opel transport lorry, steadily dripping down upon the prisoners huddled in the gloom. As the truck lurched from pot-hole to pot-hole, each bump punctuated the grim silence with groans of protest from the POWs.

Joe, unwell and in pain, was crushed up against the side. He knew that Will was somewhere in the foetid shadows. They had not spoken much for the last few hours. As the mud-spattered vehicle laboured onwards, Joe pressed his face against the dank canvas, inching his left eye towards a gleam of light. The cold air made it water. He blinked and tried to focus, struggling against the jolting of the truck. Through the small gash he caught the occasional glimpse of bomb damaged buildings. He saw factory chimneys – many of them toppled or fractured, none of them smoking. Closing his eye against the chill, he quietly acknowledged the precious detail. Allied bombing was silencing the Nazi industrial machine here in central Germany just as it had done in the Ruhr. He opened his eye again as the truck slowed and stopped at a checkpoint. The red and white barrier rose up. As they lumbered through, Joe glimpsed the huddle of civilians standing aside. Weary-looking and bedraggled, they stood in sullen silence with their prams and handcarts. One of the check-point guards was an elderly man draped in a shabby overcoat. Joe spotted the silver lettering of the Deutsche Volkssturm on the black armband. The man leaned wearily on his rifle. The other two guards were mere boys. Fourteen? Sixteen at the most, Joe guessed, squinting through the small tear in the canvas at the pale young faces beneath their ill-fitting steel helmets.

'What daya see?' a Bronx voice whispered softly in the darkness.

Joe paused, unable to choose between two words: 'victory' and 'defeat'.

At that moment, swerving to avoid a bomb crater, the truck mounted the muddy verge. Slewing and skidding, it jolted the prisoners on board.

'Ah, Jeez,' swore a voice in the darkness. The sudden lurch had caused the unseen blasphemer to empty his bowels, filling his ragged uniform with diarrhoea and the gloomy interior of the lorry with a sweet, fecal stench. Joe, suppressing the urge to vomit, placed his mouth to the rent in the canvas and sucked at the clear air.

Passing through the miserable outskirts of the town, the lorry nosed through the shabby suburbs, slowing down to crawl over several railway lines before pulling up at a tall, black wrought-iron gate. Joe saw the wire-mesh with the coils of barbed wire clustered above. The sign across the gate read: DULAG LUFT. They passed through and the lorry pulled up in the mud beyond as the gate was closed and chained. Guards, unshouldering their rifles, tumbled out of a wooden hut and surrounded the truck. The canvas was unfastened from the outside and the tail-gate was dropped with a crash. Rubbing their eyes and stretching from their crouched positions, the prisoners were slow to move. Sharp commands and the impatient use of rifle butts soon emptied the lorry. Joe, slipping on the mud, burned with anger and wounded pride as he watched his compatriots slither and stagger like drunkards to the jeers of their captors. Many of the POWs could not stand properly, and struggled to regain their balance and their dignity. Joe did not understand the ribald comments of the guards, but he caught the words 'Messerschmitt' and 'flak'.

Half in defiance, half against the chill, Joe dug his hands down into his pockets as the guards barked out their commands, ordering the POWs to form into two ragged lines. His fingertips found the touch of something unrecognisable in the lining. Stealthily, he pinched the tiny morsel and withdrew it to examine it in the grey light. He smiled weakly as he gazed down at the palm of his hand. In it lay the withered but unmistakable fragment of *Primula elatior*. The tiny oxlip Jane had entrusted to his safe-keeping.

Northern Line, London.
2nd October, 1944.

The crowded underground train braked to a halt for the third time since Baker Street. The dull yellow light bulbs flickered, brightened and then died. Only the tiny emergency lights studding the curved roof of the carriage remained to tinge the overwhelming darkness with their faint bluish glow.

Liz sighed. Wriggling slightly, she eased herself away from the fat man sitting next to her. His gas mask, boxed and carefully strapped, had been digging into her back. The carriage was full of tired faces.

Nobody spoke – except three sailors in uniform unselfconsciously describing how they planned to pass the next couple of days with their sweethearts. Five years ago, such frank discussion would have been terminated by the summoning of a policeman, Liz mused. Now, it seemed natural. Natural and life affirming. One of the sailors, a Welshman by accent and teasingly called 'Jock' by his pals, was likening his girl's lips to a toffee apple.

The fat man next to Liz rattled his newspaper and huffed disapprovingly. Liz's thoughts drifted back to the summer colours of the countryside around Fersfield. London was so gritty and grey. Liz had been shocked at the bomb damage – though heartened by the 'Open For Business' signs behind the sand bags and boarded glass windows of damaged shops and offices. She had smiled at the sight of a customer sitting in a salvaged leather chair on the pavement having his hair cut outside the train station while ARP workers and AFS firemen picked through the still smouldering rubble of the barber's shop.

The yellow light bulbs flickered, dimmed then glowed to full strength. The steel wheels screeched as the tube train gathered speed and rumbled along the narrow darkness of the tunnel. With the return of the carriage lighting, the sailors' voices dropped to a conspiratorial murmur, but they signaled their intentions clearly with suggestive mime and vigorous gestures. Liz, blushing to herself, remembered Will's eagerness and tender lust. She then recalled the brief but fruitless encounter with the chaplain from the airbase at Fersfield. Ambushing him as he had cycled past the rectory, she had questioned him anxiously for news of Will and Joe. Able to tell her nothing, the young priest had asked her about her friendship with Will, touching on the beauty of youthful alliances – and appearing keen to discover the nature of young Joe Kennedy's attachments. Liz closed her eyes. At least there had been no dreaded telegram delivered to the rectory. With every week that passed, Liz and Jane grew in their confidence that their lovers had survived.

Alighting at Finchley Road, Liz surrendered her ticket at the barrier. 'Is your journey really necessary?' the poster at the exit demanded. Her brief trip down to London, before recommencing her studies at Cambridge, was to visit her aunt who was recuperating after a recent illness.

Walking down along the Finchley Road, Liz was appalled by the damage to the houses. In places, as many as four homes stood half gutted or wholly demolished where bombs had fallen. She picked her way carefully through the teetering piles of furniture that were blocking the pavement – much of it scorched or water damaged.

Her aunt's house remained habitable. The house next door had no windows. Liz stepped up to the front door and knocked. Her aunt received her with a smothering hug, almost pulling her in over the doorstep. Inside, sitting at the kitchen table while the kettle slowly laboured to the boil on a glimmering gas ring, Liz noted the disarray in the house she had always known to be spick and span. Her aunt, carefully measuring leveled spoonfuls of tea from the caddy into the brown pot, shrugged her shoulders and smiled ruefully.

'No sooner you dust and clear up it's all to do again after a raid', she explained. 'Jerry's after the railway lines, most probably. If it's not the bombing it's the doodlebugs.'

Liz nodded. Bending down, she delved into her bag, unearthing the carefully wrapped eggs and jar of honey she had brought down from Jane's mother at Fersfield.

DULAG LUFT
Wetzlar, Germany.
Early October, 1944.

It had been some weeks since their arrival at Dulag Luft – weeks filled with boredom and frustration. It was so crowded in the low-roofed wooden hut that some of the more able prisoners slept on the floor-boards between the double bunks. Will, still suffering from his interrogation and subsequent beatings, had been allocated a bunk by his fellow POWs. Joe, whose wounds were less visible, had been given a single, smelly blanket and a couple of feet of dirty planking.

For the fifth night running, the wail of an air raid siren disturbed their sleep. Joe, bleary eyed, propped himself up on one elbow. The single blanket slid from his shoulder. He yawned and shivered. Dulag Luft was situated only a mile and a half from Wetzlar, exposing the captive POWs to the risk of allied bombing. Joe heard the sound of approaching planes just seconds after the siren. Soon the bombers were overhead. The low drone had increased to a thundering roar – then the crump-crump of exploding bombs echoed as the first wave flew over their target zone.

Some of the prisoners groaned weary protests and rolled over in their bunks, others jumped down to find shelter beneath. Joe, Will and four others staggered out through the door and were instantly silhouetted against the searing flashes of silver, orange and yellow from exploding bombs. The bombs were falling so thickly their deafening explosions were almost continuous. Steadying himself against the wall of the wooden hut, Joe gazed up into the night sky. Tracer fire flickered up into the void. A search-light stabbed its thick finger upwards, raking the belly of the cloud-base to pin-point the bombers for the anti-aircraft flak batteries defending the few industrial sites remaining in Wetzlar. As the bombing intensified and the fires took hold, Joe recalled from briefings that Wetzlar was the centre for production of cameras and optical instrumentation. Wiping out Wetzlar, he mused, would leave the Luftwaffe blind. He craned to see the ground defences in action. The search-lights were not deployed effectively and the flak was fitful and impotent. A huge silver flash caused the watching POWs to duck. Red and orange flames shot up hundreds of feet into the air in an instant fireball.

'Oil or petrol storage depot,' a voice rang out. 'Give it to them, boys. Give the bastards a licking.'

Joe exchanged a grin with Will.

More prisoners emerged, jostling through the doorway and spilling out onto the muddy area surrounding the hut. Another huge explosion ripped through the night about half a mile away. A ragged cheer echoed throughout the Dulag. Two prisoners linked arms and danced a jig – slipping and sliding in the wet mud. Dogs barked and whistles blew. The shouts of the approaching guards broke up the dancing but the POWs stood their ground, pointing to the flames leaping in the distance and cheering. The guards formed a semi-circle around their captives. Vicious Alsatians, straining on metal chains, snapped at the prisoners as they retreated back towards their huts. There was another huge explosion – and once again a loud cheer rang out. Their response infuriated the guards, who levelled their rifles and aimed above the POWs' heads.

'Jesus,' Will shouted. 'They mean it, Joe.'

'Get everyone back inside,' Joe warned. 'Get everyone back inside the fucking huts.'

A volley of shots whistled over the prisoners' heads.

Joe braced himself at the door, pulling and shoving frantically until the last of the POWs jostled into safety. Joe had not seen Will get inside. He glanced out into the darkness. To his horror, he saw three of the guards rolling over a dead body with their muddy jack boots. An Alsatian savaged the dead man's throat. Joe felt hot and suddenly sick.

'Christ, that was close. Too fucking close.'

Joe spun round and stared into the face of Will. Swallowing his surge of relief, he nodded curtly.

A convoy of trucks came two days later, a little after six in the morning. The prisoners were roused and marshalled into the covered lorries without any warning. They shivered in the gloom – once more covered in canvas – without benefit of breakfast or the toilet. As the convoy trundled out of Dulag Luft, Joe prised the flap apart slightly. Through it, he could appreciate just how badly the town had been damaged by the recent raids.

The trucks changed down to bottom gear as they hauled themselves up the road leading away from the ruined town. Beneath the dank canvas, the prisoners huddled for warmth.

That night, the POWs were herded into filthy railway cattle-trucks. Joe strained to catch any clue to their destination from the guards but was unsuccessful. The train, dragging sixty trucks behind it, pulled out from the unlit sidings and crawled along the line in a cloud of steam. The wagons clattered across the points, jolting those inside mercilessly. Steel squealed against steel as the train took a long stretch of curved track. Progress was slow, with frequent stops. Will crawled across to where Joe crouched against the cattle-truck's wooden slatted side.

'Let the dog see the rabbit,' he whispered, nudging Joe aside.

'What the hell do you mean? Dog? Rabbit?' Joe hissed.

'Liz used to say it. Never mind,' Will grunted. 'Any stars out?'

Joe nodded. 'Take a butchers.'

Will chuckled softly. 'Butchers? One of Jane's?'

Straining to peer up through the slats while he steadied himself with outstretched arms, Will read the night sky.

'If my reckoning is right, we're heading east.'

'Poland?' Joe wondered aloud, scratching at the fleas buried in the damp warmth of his armpit.

Finchley, North London.
3rd October, 1944 2.16 am

Liz had slept fitfully after retiring to bed earlier than her accustomed hour. She was wide awake and surreptitiously smoking while her aunt snored softly beside her. In the darkness of the bedroom, the tiny red point of light glowed brightly each time she drew on the cigarette.

In an effort to spare her aunt the tiresome struggle with linen and blackouts, Liz had happily suggested sharing her aunt's bed. She had shown the three snapshots of Will she carried with her to her aunt and placed the largest of these by her bedside. Leaning towards the snapshot carefully, so as not to disturb her aunt, she dragged heavily on her cigarette. In the fleeting red glow, Will grinned out at her – then vanished.

Suddenly, an air raid siren echoed across the roof tops. The single, thin wail was joined by several others until the night was filled with noise.

Incredibly, Liz had to shake her aunt quite roughly. The fear tightening her throat made speech difficult. Her aunt struggled into wakefulness, a stray hair-curler dangling drunkenly over her left eye.

'Now don't be alarmed, my dear. No need to panic. This your first, hmm? I thought so.'

Liz snatched up a dressing gown but her fingers fumbled uselessly at the buttons and belt.

'Just follow me downstairs. We'll shelter in the cellar. We'll be quite safe there. No,' her aunt gestured impatiently as Liz returned to snatch up the snapshot of Will. 'Leave him there. He'll be perfectly safe.'

Liz followed her aunt swiftly down the staircase in the darkness, feeling her way gingerly along the banisters. At the entrance to the cellar door, Liz paused. Her face tilted up as she listened intently.

'Quickly now, my dear. Come along, don't dawdle.'

'But I can't hear any planes, Auntie. No... wait... I think I can hear it. It's a doodlebug!'

There was a low pulsing buzz. The windows started to rattle as the doodlebug approached. The buzzing drone ceased abruptly and for a few seconds all was eerily silent.

Suddenly, Liz heard a thin whistling sound...

Fersfield Rectory.
7th October, 1944.

Jane was gazing down into the border of Michaelmas daisies. She would have preferred to have remained up in her bedroom but her mother had badgered her over the breakfast table.

'And you simply must stop moping upstairs all day, my dear. It just isn't healthy. Are you quite sure you are well? I don't think you are...'

'I'm fine, Mummy. Please don't fuss so.'

'All the same, perhaps Dr Elliot should take a look at you...'

'No, Mummy. There's really no need...'

In order to placate her mother, Jane was in the rectory garden. Perhaps, she thought, she had better show willing and make an attempt at dead-heading the roses after lunch. Anything to avoid Dr Elliot. Thank goodness she would be back up at Cambridge next week...

'Jane?'

She heard her mother calling from the kitchen door. Jane looked and caught a glimpse of the telegram-envelope in her mother's raised hand.

'Jane, darling. It's for you.'

Joe. It must be Joe. At last. She shrieked with delight as she bounded down along the cinder path towards the kitchen door, sure that at last news of Joe had come. Skidding to an inelegant stop, she hugged her mother and snatched up the brown envelope. Tearing it open, she began to read the telegram inside.

'Well, darling?' her mother demanded impatiently.

Jane froze, her pale face expressionless. She seemed to shake her head as if bewildered. A dry sob broke from her lips.

'Jane! Whatever is the matter?'

Jane shook her head then buried her face in her hands, weeping uncontrollably. Her mother, concern increasing to alarm, stooped down and recovered the scrunched up telegram. Smoothing it out gently, she read in horror of Liz's death in the V-1 raid on Finchley.

'Oh my poor darling,' she murmured, kneeling down – and flinching as the cinders stung her knees – to comfort her sobbing daughter.

Sagan, Poland.
Mid-October, 1944

It was a dull afternoon. It had been raining heavily all morning. As the POWs disembarked from their cattle-trucks onto the wet concrete of the platform next to Stalag Luft III a cold wind from the east nipped their numbed limbs.

'Jeez,' Will murmured, falling into line next to Joe.

Joe inclined his head in acknowledgement. Will's reaction mirrored his own response to the vast sprawl of the Stalag. Joe's gaze carefully took in the machine gun nests perched up on the towers, the double lines of barbed wire fencing and the flood lighting around the perimeter. The Stalag seemed to be run on ruthlessly organised and secure lines. Dozens of POWs were gathering up against the inner perimeter to witness the new arrivals, keen, Joe guessed, to glean the latest news.

Joe and Will became separated and were marched away to different huts. Joe stepped into his billet and was surprised to find that the low, dark interior was crowded with rows of bunks. They were, he discovered on closer inspection, triple-tiered wooden bunks, the mattresses filled with straw or wood chips. There was a stove but Joe doubted its capacity to sustain its function of heating and cooking during the coming winter months.

The grey days passed slowly. Chief of all the discomforts was the boredom. Joe soon realised that had it not been for the International Red Cross parcels, food would have been a serious problem. Issued with little more than starvation rations by the Germans, food parcels – despite being regularly pilfered by the many hands through which they passed – kept the prisoners alive. Both Joe and Will had already lost several pounds in weight during their period of captivity.

In his hut, Joe grew to know his fellow captives. These were the unfortunate few RAF and Fleet Air Arm servicemen who had been shot down in the early months of the war and were in their fourth year of captivity. They had a resigned and morose air, and Joe did his best to cheer them up, pointing out that with the successful campaign on the Second Front – and the westward movement of Russian forces – the end of the war and freedom could only be a matter of months away.

The White House, Washington D.C.
Thursday 25th October 1962 09.06 am

Despite the overnight use of sickly-sweet aerosol air fresheners, the briefing room remained heavy with the smell of stale cigarette smoke and perspiration. The carefully polished surface of the vast table was already dulled with the imprints of sweating palms. The EX-COMM meeting had been reconvened. With the addition of three new faces – team players recommended by Bobby Kennedy and brought in by Joe to counter Adlai

Stevenson's forceful yet unpopular views – there were now sixteen men around the conference table.

General Taylor's manner was brisk.

'We got these from a low level pass.'

'Wasn't that... provocative?' George Ball challenged.

'High risk strategy,' Nitze shrugged, 'but it had to be done.'

General Taylor dismissed the matter brusquely as he circulated the latest reconnaissance photos. The black and white shots were stunningly crisp and clear, and were received with soft whistles of amazement around the table.

'Missiles. Ready to launch. There's no doubt about it, gentlemen,' the general grunted.

His words were received in silence. Almost to a man, EX-COMM nodded in agreement. The tension was broken when someone swore softly.

General Taylor followed up the psychological advantage swiftly. 'We knew they had them and I guess we knew where they were. What nobody could have known is that the bastards have them primed for launch. Those babies are ready to fly.'

A voice of caution asked for a more detailed technical appraisal.

'You've got eyes, haven't you? Goddamit, what more 'appraisal' do you need?'

General Taylor grew red-faced in his mounting agitation. Angrily dismissing the need for further analysis or assessment, he continued impatiently. 'You guys were wrong to veto the use of pre-emptive air-strikes...'

Joe Kennedy's head rose up sharply but Taylor refused to defer.

'We need to go in hard and we need to do it now,' he barked, 'and the Senate leaders are with me. At least they've got their heads screwed on. They know what needs to be done.'

Gasoline on a wasps' nest, Joe reflected despairingly as all around the table, EX-COMM broke into brief but blistering dispute.

Voices rose in anger – then in counter-protest. Joe let them vent for thirty seconds or so before firmly bringing them all back to order.

Fifteen faces turned to him, some of them in sullen silence, others in anxious expectation.

'Mr President.'

–It was getting too close to call. Taylor had LeMay, Nitze, Bundy and Ball on-side. The hawks were increasing towards a majority that he might find hard to deflect.

'Mr President.' It was McGeorge Bundy.

'Go ahead,' Joe responded unenthusiastically.

'I say we stick to our agreed position.'

Joe tried to conceal his surprise. Taylor and the other hawks could not conceal their dismay. Nitze shot a withering glance across the table at Bundy.

'What the fuck?' Curtis LeMay growled.

'Like I say,' Bundy continued quickly, 'we stick to what we agreed. Hell and tarnation,' he turned angrily on the hawks, 'we've got the unanimous backing of the Organization of American States for a naval blockade…'

'The OAS?' General Taylor snapped contemptuously. 'What the hell do that truck-load of fucking Latinos know?'

Bobby Kennedy grinned briefly as he glimpsed Theodore Sorensen reddening in diplomatic outrage.

'Cut it out,' the President warned. 'Go on, McGeorge.'

As General Taylor scowled in suppressed rage, McGeorge Bundy continued.

'Despite these reconnaissance shots, I say we stick to our decision for a blockade. I know… I know…' he protested against the angry faces around him. 'Sure, I voted against the blockade yesterday, but, well, I guess I've changed my mind. A guy can change his mind,' he reasoned, spreading his hands out expansively. 'I think we should stick with the quarantine or we'll lose the support of our own people.'

The phrase brought Joe's train of thought to an abrupt halt. Roosevelt had gone into World War II with seventy two per cent of the nation dead against it, he remembered suddenly, according to Randolph Hearst's newspaper polls.

Joe nodded as he thanked Bundy for his frankness, adding that it was not a weakness or a failure of strategy to have a change of heart – or mind. To be able to alter direction or intention was a sign of tactical and political strength. They must hold a line, of course. A firm line. But a firm line could be flexible. Taylor, Nitze and LeMay looked unconvinced. Joe saw the resentment in their eyes.

As a comforter to the hawks among EX-COMM, he concluded, 'If a pre-emptive air-strike proves both expedient and essential, then, gentlemen, as the general says, we will go in fast. Very fast, and very hard.'

General Taylor beamed his satisfaction, rubbing his large hands appreciatively. Joe noted the gesture, and wondered if the general had rubbed his hands like that in the hours before Hiroshima and Nagasaki.

At his side, Bobby coughed pointedly, signaling to his brother to move on.

Joe smiled fleetingly and pressed on adroitly, consolidating his position.

'Staffort? Where are your boys now, exactly?'

Admiral Staffort bristled with importance, replying that by 1700 hours Eastern Standard Time all of the ships in the blockade deployment would be in position along the quarantine line.

'Nothing in, nothing out. Understood?' Joe countered.

'My boys have their mission orders, Mr President. The US Navy will not let you down, sir. They'll be ready to intervene…'

'Interdict,' Bobby Kennedy broke in.

Sorensen nodded sagely. 'That's what we gave out to the UN.'

General Taylor almost snarled. 'Intervene. Interdict. Who gives a shit.' He rounded on the admiral. 'They will open fire? They will destroy…actually sink any commie ship trying to break through?'

Admiral Staffort was quick to reply. 'They will, General.' There was no mistaking the grim resolve of his tone.

Joe interrupted, eager to curtail Taylor. 'That about wraps things up for the moment, gentlemen. Say,' his voice was suddenly bleak and weary, 'I could use some coffee. Will someone get some in here, fast?'

A little after 11.27 pm the President closed his eyes on the long day but did not fall asleep. Still nothing from the Kremlin and up in New York, their Ambassador, Zorin, was stone-walling the UN. Nothing unofficial through the CIA. The press and TV were camped out on the White House lawns and over on Capitol Hill, Bobby's 'interdict' was causing problems.

Joe kept his eyes closed and tried to relax, but sleep eluded his racing thoughts. Why now, he wanted to understand. Why was Moscow pushing this brinkmanship to the very limit? To smoke screen some internal crisis, some impending economic disaster? Was the crisis in the Kremlin itself? Was Khrushchev facing a coup, Joe wondered?

Suddenly his eyes snapped open and glittered in the darkness. His hand shot out and found the bedside lamp switch and then the telephone.

'Get me Dean Rusk.'

A few minutes later Joe was once more in the darkness, seeing Khrushchev's game behind closed eyes. Rusk had had it all at his fingertips. The anniversary of the October Revolution. Yes. That must be it. Rusk had qualified the details. The actual dates. He had explained to Joe that with the change to the calendar, the actual anniversary date now came in November. Joe brushed aside such detail. It must be it, he thought. It must be. Moscow was building up its game to coincide with Revolution Day. So was this just the beginning of something really big?

The next morning Joe was in the briefing room by 08.15 am. Bobby, drinking coffee from a mug, joined him.

'Did you manage to get them?'

'Sure did, Joe. They'll be here in time.'

At 09.05 am, Ex-COMM was assembled around the table with Joe at their head. He felt tense and raw. He intercepted a wink between Nitze and General Taylor. The muscle in his jaw twitched. He quickly counted those around the table. Good. Bobby had drafted two more non-hawks into the team, making EX-COMM now eighteen in all. Joe suddenly wondered if it was such a good idea after all. The hawks, he reflected, could be right in their judgement. He decided he should keep that in mind.

'Give me an update on the blockade,' Joe demanded, getting straight down to business.

Bobby looked at his brother, slightly concerned by the urgency in the president's voice.

Admiral Staffort replied promptly, without consulting his notes, that several Soviet ships were still on course and closing down on the quarantine line.

'Stubborn bastards,' someone murmured.

'And we know for sure that they are Cuba-bound?' Nitze interjected.

'Cuba-bound,' the admiral confirmed.

Sorensen speculated aloud whether Moscow had had enough time to instruct the Soviet ships' captains. His point was lost, swallowed up by Staffort's bombshell.

'The thing is, Mr President, there's been a development overnight.'

'A development? Well?'

'We guess that there are at least four Soviet submarines...'

'You guess? Jesus Christ, don't you know? Can't you be sure?' Curtis LeMay exploded.

'I was speaking figuratively,' the admiral snapped primly. 'When I say I guess I mean I know for certain that...'

'Stop horseshitting with the facts, Staffort, and spit it out,' LeMay countered. 'You guess... You know...'

'Cut it out,' Joe barked.

Bobby shot his brother another keen glance.

Staffort struggled on, his dignity dented by LeMay's onslaught. 'We've got four Soviet submarines now within the theatre, Mr President.'

'For Christ's sake,' Joe rasped. 'Where did those bastards come from?'

'It's a developing situation we've got ourselves here, sir.'

'Capability?' Joe demanded.

'All four may be armed with nuclear missiles, or at least nuclear torpedoes.'

Nitze was heard to curse vehemently.

Joe's heart grew suddenly heavy and cold. As he mechanically asked for an update on Staffort's sub-hunting capabilities in the zone, his mind rapidly calculated the rising stakes. Moscow meant business. Maybe the hawks would get their way. When Staffort stopped speaking, Joe thanked him and then paused, taking a deep, decisive breath.

'In the light of this latest development, this meeting is suspended, gentlemen.'

After their working lunch of fried chicken and chilled beer (Joe stuck to an iced Coke), Bundy and Sorensen joined Joe in his private office. A television was on but the volume had been turned down to a murmur.

They sat in silence for several minutes, waiting. A polite tap on the door announced the arrival of Dean Rusk. The door opened and Richardson ushered Rusk in. Joe waited for the door to close behind his aide before asking Rusk for the latest on the blockade with a simple 'Well?'

'We were eyeball to eyeball, sir, and the other guy's just blinked.'

The door opened and Bobby came in, waving back Richardson and shutting the door firmly.

'What have we got?' he demanded.

Rusk shared his crucial news of the Soviet climb down – right on the quarantine line – with Joe and the others. The sense of relief in the private office was tangible.

Bundy did not smile. He cautioned them against celebrating too soon.

'What do you mean?' Sorensen queried. 'They pulled back, didn't they?'

'It isn't over yet. It isn't over at all. In fact, Mr President,' he addressed Joe directly, 'I believe this is where it really begins.'

Bobby looked puzzled. Joe nodded slowly.

'I think I know exactly what you mean, Theo.' Then, turning to Bobby, he asked if any contact had been established with Moscow.

Bobby answered quickly. 'It's all fixed up, Joe. A back-channel, just like you wanted, straight through to Khrushchev.'

Sorensen and Rusk looked up simultaneously, the frown of doubt knitting both their brows.

Dean Rusk voiced their thoughts aloud. 'Straight through, Bobby? You really mean that?'

'Via Dobrynin,' Bobby clarified.

'Ah, I see. That old fox,' Rusk smiled.

'Alexander Dobrynin, Soviet Ambassador to the United States,' Sorensen added. 'And five gets you ten they'll keep poor Zorin up in New York out of that little loop.'

Cambridge.
14th November 1944.

The fifth of November came and went, bonfireless for the fifth year in succession. There would have been plenty of fireworks – bangs and flashes – lighting up last night's darkness, Jane thought morosely. Her mind immediately turned to Liz and her eyes welled up with tears.

Jane slipped out of her bed and padded across her small college hall of residence room towards the sink to rinse her face.

Bending to splash the cold water, she suddenly started to retch. Cold perspiration pricked her forehead as she gripped the sides of the sink, shivering in the chill autumn early morning until the spasms ceased.

She slumped down in a shabby armchair, her groping hand reaching out in the gloom to pick up the small brown envelope. It had arrived three days ago, confirming her worst fears. Jane felt forlorn and frightened. Liz. Liz would have known what to do. She drew her knees up as she curled into the armchair. The castors squeaked. They had spotted the chair in a second-hand shop in Peas Hill six months ago coming back to Halls from a debate in Gonville and Caius – laughing helplessly as it refused the cobbles along Sidney Street. Liz had got a young policeman to stop the traffic and then to give them a hand. Liz had been like that.

The brown envelope contained confirmation of her pregnancy. Jane crumpled it in her fist as tears returned to her eyes. There was no Liz now to confide in, no Liz to share her shameful secret with – a secret she was determined to keep from her parents.

Skipping breakfast in the communal refectory, Jane made the lecture theatre just in time. Two hours later, her head aching, she stood listlessly in the long line stretching back from a huge tea urn. She felt a gentle tap at her elbow. Turning, her eyes met the grave stare of the girl who had taken Liz's room next door to Jane in halls.

'Are you... are you OK?'

'Mmm,' Jane smiled weakly.

'It's just that... well... I've heard you... in the mornings... being sick. Do you need...?'

'I'm perfectly fine, thanks,' Jane retorted brusquely, her face crimsoning.

'I'm sorry. Look, I know it's none of my business,' the girl with the grave eyes met the rising challenge in Jane's '... but take this. It could be useful... should you need it. And don't, oh please don't take this the wrong way, don't feel quite so alone. I mean, after losing your friend like that and everything...?' she ended lamely.

Jane felt the folded piece of paper being pressed into her hand. When she had secured a cup of tea and a secluded corner, she opened it discreetly. She saw it was an address just off Hills Road, close to the railway station.

'Be with you in just a tick,' the young woman in the brown pullover, brown shirt and red tie muttered as she struggled with an ancient typewriter. Her words were all but lost under the rumbling thunder of the loose shunting in the adjacent marshalling yards.

Jane took the only seat – a rickety wooden chair with an alarming wobble – and waited. The office was cramped and dreary. The girl's ARP tin hat partially covered a teapot at the edge of her desk.

'Minutes from our last meeting,' the voice behind the typewriter explained, 'but the damn 's' is missing from the keyboard. Bloody nui-ance.'

Jane smiled wanly.

'Anybody follow you?'

Jane looked up in surprise, shrugged and shook her head in response. 'Why should anyone follow me?' she inquired.

'Buggers are out to get us all the time. We've had to move office twice already this year.' She spoke indistinctly due to the pencil clamped between her small white teeth.

Jane frowned. This was not what she expected at all. The sudden sound of paper being ripped out of the typewriter made Jane wince.

'So how did you find us?' As the girl behind the desk raised her head to ask the question, her spectacles flashed beneath the single light bulb above.

'How? Oh, I see. A girl in Halls – she has the room next to mine – suggested...'

'Jolly good. That's fine. Best not to mix town and gown, never know where you are. We have to be...careful. If we get a raid, we stick to our guns. 'Advice' is the name of our game. We hide the contraceptives in the cistern in the outside loo, though what with spivs and racketeers, you'd think the police would have other fish to fry.'

Jane, who found the young woman's hearty tone irritating, grew perplexed.

'Bloody ridiculous, really, but there it is. What we do is actually against the law, you see. As the law stands. Men make damn stupid laws. But after the war...'

Jane listened as the earnest young woman with the red tie outlined her manifesto for 'after the war'.

'By gosh yes,' she concluded, taking her spectacles off and polishing them feverishly, 'there are going to be real changes. None of your soft Fabian tit-bits to keep the masses quiet but real changes.'

Some of those changes were laid bare. My God, Jane thought, are we really going to see people like this in power after peace is declared.

'But we'll need the right people. Women. Our sort. And we'll put an end to laws for men passed by men. The future will be women – mind you,' she added contemptuously, 'some women and girls are their own worst enemy. The way these factory girls and land girls have been behaving. Nothing short of traitors to the cause.'

Jane shifted uneasily in her chair. It creaked ominously.

'Type?' The spectacles gleamed interrogatively.

Jane did not understand.

'Never mind, we'll put you to good use. Plenty of filing to be done. Need all the help we can muster.' Before Jane could interrupt the flow, the woman continued. 'What I've seen in the blackout doing my ARP stints. How can women possibly assume influence and political power when so many of them seem to simply lose their heads. Alley-cats. No better than alley-cats…losing their heads – and more – for some damn Spitfire jockey or a Yank with nylons in his pocket…'

Jane frowned, then blushed.

The young woman laughed harshly. 'We've had sluts in here who don't even remember the name of the chap they dropped their knickers for.'

Jane flushed furiously.

'So you've come to join us, eh? Jolly good. Thank God some of us know how to behave ourselves. Still, I suppose we must do what we can for our less fortunate sisters however simple or stupid they are…Marx of course would say that they are no better than they should be because of socio-economic suppression…'

The young woman gasped and fell silent as Jane rose abruptly and strode out of the dingy room.

Jane read the letter she had written earlier while sitting on the sandbags marking the entrance to the shelter, by the ornamental lake in Emmanuel College gardens. Liz and Jane had bathed their sore feet in the lake in the early dawn after the May Ball in the first week of last June. Partially but not completely satisfied – letters never managed to say what you really meant – she folded it carefully before putting it in the envelope neatly addressed to Joseph Kennedy Senior. In it she had expressed, without giving specific or explicit details, why it was absolutely imperative (underlined) that she was informed of Joe's whereabouts and well-being.

With the letter to Joe's father sealed and stamped, Jane attempted no less than three times to explain in a letter to her own father her predicament. She carefully avoided direct mention of her actual condition. All attempts failed and she knew that she could not put down on paper what she was in truth ashamed to say to him directly. She put on her raincoat then checked to make sure that she had small change in her purse. Out in the settling fog of the November night, she found a post box and then a telephone kiosk. It was difficult dialling in the blackout but her reluctant fingers found the well known numbers.

Her mother answered.

'Hello, Mummy...'

Crying gently, Jane replaced the phone and bumped her bottom against the kiosk door. Outside, her tear-stained face burning with shame, a sense of desolation swallowed her up as completely as the swirling fog.

Joe's father replied – or at least a letter from his office, no doubt dictated, reached Jane several weeks later. The signature was there: florid and assured, but Jane's sense was of a cautiously crafted letter which, in cold yet polite terms, expressed little spontaneity, less warmth and no immediacy. Nor was there the slightest evidence of a paternal overture to a filial alliance.

News of Joe, she was advised, was scant, communications being both sporadic and unreliable. The letter noted Liz's death but distanced itself from the tragedy by observing how terribly tragic war indeed was. On a second reading, Jane noted the disclaimer to Joe's friendship with Will. Jane's acquaintance (Jane was not unaware of the avoidance of the term friendship) with Joe was a surprise to his father. Even reading between the lines, Jane could glean nothing but polite indifference.

Tearfully, she responded, expressing all her fears for Joe's well-being, her ardent hopes for their eventual reunion – and their mutual love for each other. Her letter outlined their shared hopes and plans for a future together. Conscious that Joe had revealed nothing about her to his father, Jane included a somewhat prim autobiography, just as she had when writing the letter of application to the Master of her college. She brought her letter to an unambiguous conclusion: she was in love with Joe and he with her. Their futures were intertwined.

With a sense of fragile triumph in her achievement, she sealed and posted the letter then turned her mind to the ordeal ahead. Christmas at Fersfield.

'We will simply say you have a chill. A severe chill.'

Her mother was forcing sage and onion stuffing with unnecessary violence into a plucked goose. After the storm, a deadly calm reigned over the rectory. Jane's mother had indulged in tears and sherry, after her initial anger, but had lapsed into a cold disdain Jane was finding insufferable.

Her father's dismay had turned into fastidious aloofness. He avoided Jane, retreating to his study to take what little solace he could from his butterfly collection.

The pudding simmered slowly on the Aga, infusing the Rectory with the spices of Christmastide but Jane knew that nothing could ever be the same again. She had no appetite or energy, only a dull, grey sense of desolation.

'Yes,' her mother snapped, wrestling the trussed goose into the roasting pan. 'That should do it. A severe chill. Stop any idle speculation. You will not attend any of the services and we will not be receiving any visitors…'

'I haven't got the plague!' Jane protested.

'Be quiet, you wicked, selfish girl. You may quite possibly have entirely ruined all my hopes for… I mean your father's chances of advancement. The scandal. The shame of it.'

Jane heard the sparse congregation tackling 'O Come All Ye Faithful' with ragged fervour from her bedroom on Christmas morning. No presents or cards were exchanged. An unnatural, almost hysterical silence grew throughout the afternoon. Jane retired to her bed before tea time, tired by her pregnancy. When she heard the roar of three Liberators taking off from the neighbouring airfield, she thought of Joe in the darkness before crying herself to sleep.

Boxing Day was a wet, desultory event. The meagre coals in the drawing room failed to warm those sitting in silence around them. The chimney smoked, forcing Jane's father to retreat – gratefully – to his cold study, pleading a weak chest. Jane's mother approached the matter of a termination. It would have been the best solution, she said. The matter would be put to Dr Elliot over a quiet supper. Perhaps it was still not too late. He might know what could be done.

The following morning, Jane stole out into the frost glistening darkness before her parents had risen. The milk train would take her to Ely where she would have to change for Cambridge. Turning in the lane, she buttoned up her coat to her chin and gripped her suitcase, leaving the rectory without a second glance.

* * *

Joseph Kennedy Senior's hand-written letter came at the end of February when the ice on Sheeps Green pond behind Peterhouse had already cracked and thawed. The letter to Jane urged both caution and hope. Acknowledging Joe's friendship – but admitting to nothing more than friendship – the advice given in it was avuncular. Do nothing intemperate or injudicious was the essence of Joe Senior's response; advice larded with the piety of prayerful hope for Joe's deliverance.

The letter failed to either comfort or console Jane, its contents leaving her peculiarly unsatisfied. The one solid fact buried in the bland sentimental tract was that Joseph Kennedy Senior planned to arrive in England in March and he would, the last paragraph assured her, endeavour to arrange a meeting with her, at which the best interests of his son and his son's friend could be resolved.

Jane sensed that if Joe's father had felt any dismay or disappointment in his son's affair, Joseph Kennedy Senior had concealed such feelings with consummate discretion.

VII

STALAG LUFT III, POLAND
Late February, 1945

Will's toecap caught the furrow of frozen mud. Tripping, he stumbled. Joe caught him and steadied his balance.

'Better put more water in it, old man,' Mitch – RAF Pilot Officer Mike Mitchell – chuckled.

Will grinned. He and Joe had both grown to like and respect Mitch. Not so much a British bulldog type, more a wire-haired terrier with an irrepressible sense of humour.

They trudged across the rutted, hard earth towards the first of two perimeter fences. The snow had stopped and above them the Polish sky was cloudless and ice-blue. Daytime temperatures never climbed much above freezing, and at night they dropped to minus ten.

Mitch looked up into the blue. 'Bloody perfect flying weather,' he sighed.

Joe nodded.

'Wish to God I was back in my old crate.'

'Spitfire or Hurricane?' Will asked.

'Spit. Hello…what the hell's that?'

They stood rooted to the spot. Will cupped his hand to his ear.

'Bombing?' Mitch wondered aloud. 'There's precious little around these parts to waste good bombs on.'

Joe, his eyes closed, motioned for silence. 'Artillery,' he suggested.

'Who the hell is Jerry shooting at?' Mitch demanded.

'And who the hell is shooting back?' Will responded.

'Russians,' Joe grinned. 'I bet it's the fucking Russians. I bet they're breaking through.'

The three men hugged and embraced one-another then Mitch broke away to execute a triumphant jig. His boots trod the ground rhythmically as he whooped his delight. Forty yards away, a grey-coated guard unslung his rifle and took aim.

Mitch risked a swift 'V' sign then fell in with Joe and Will.

'Howitzers against the Russians' field guns. Soon it will be tank rounds we'll be hearing – and they won't be Nazi Tigers but Uncle Joe Stalin's babies.'

'How long have we got... three weeks?' pondered Will.

'Depends,' Joe shrugged. 'They could take a detour around Sagan or park right up against the wire.'

'Good God,' Mitch exclaimed. 'I dread to think what Jerry will do with us if the war rolls up on the bloody doorstep!'

Joe and Mitch exchanged anxious glances. Will broke the pause in their banter with a shout.

'Hey, look, you guys! Ten o'clock. Ten o'clock and closing fast. Jeez, look at that mother go!'

They sprawled down as an RAF Mosquito reconnaissance plane screamed over the tree line and drowned the air with the roar of its twin Merlin engines. A klaxon snarled, then another. Guards tumbled out of their huts and raised their Schmeissers.

A little under two miles away the twin-engined fighter-bomber turned, climbed and then dipped down to a hundred feet. In seconds it had swooped over the Stalag. Scores of prisoners ran out to shout and wave at the plane. A couple of futile rounds were fired off at the Mosquito as it screamed overhead.

They heard it turn over the tree line and make a third approach. As it passed low over the Stalag, leaflets spilled out from its belly like feathers from a burst pillow – and like feathers, they floated in the air, drifting down to settle on the mud below. More impotent shots rang out after the retreating plane – then the guns were lowered and pointed at the prisoners. Orders were barked: return to your huts immediately. Several prisoners attempted to snatch up some of the wind-whipped leaflets that were cart-wheeling around their feet. Again, the Schmeissers crackled, and a man twenty yards from Will keeled over, dropping down onto his knees and clutching his belly.

'Bloody Nazi swine!' Mitch spat out. 'Shooting an unarmed chap like that...'

'Sure ain't fuckin' cricket,' gasped Will with a nod to Mitch as they dashed with the others for the shelter of their huts.

Two hours later all the prisoners were ordered outside and herded in a shivering huddle. There were, Joe estimated, a couple of thousand men. He also detected a nervousness in the guards, who encircled their captives, Schmeissers at the ready.

The camp Kommandant addressed them curtly. 'You may think that the war is nearly over, but I assure you that it is not. I have received orders to shoot you all...'

The prisoners stirred uneasily. The guards aimed their guns ominously.

'... but you are lucky... I observe the Geneva Convention... and anyway, it would be a waste of ammunition. So, you will be marching, instead. Westwards to Germany. Tomorrow morning. But be warned. It will not take much to make me change my mind. Do not try my patience, gentlemen, or you will quickly suffer my wrath.'

It was still dark the next morning when the prisoners were forced to line up, five abreast, and begin the long march. It was bitterly cold, and most of the men had managed to stuff their sparse clothing with the contents of torn-up mattresses.

'Like a regiment of bloody scare-crows,' Mitch muttered. 'Could have managed a spot of breakfast. Long trek ahead on an empty stomach.'

Joe, who was scanning the ranks of pale-faced men for a glimpse of Will, nodded grimly.

The long line of prisoners snaked out through the open gates, breaking the silence of the crisp air with the crunch of their boots upon the frozen ground.

THE HAMMER AND THE ANVIL

The White House, Washington D.C.
Thursday morning, 25 October, 1962

There were nineteen members of EX-COMM seated around the table in the briefing room.

'Stevenson's just got into New York,' Bobby advised Joe.

The president nodded, concealing from those around him his private doubts about Adlai Stevenson's effectiveness before the UN Security Council. His Russian counter-part Zorin would probably ride-out any minor storm Stevenson might manage to whip up quite easily, suspected Joe.

General Taylor expressed aloud what Joe was privately thinking by confirming that the Military Alert Status had been increased to DEFCON 2.

Clever bastard, Joe mused, eyeing Taylor across the polished table. There had been no direct criticism of Adlai Stevenson by the general but he had left EX-COMM in no doubt of his concerns by immediately stating the DEFCON 2 status. Joe made his move instantly, cutting across Taylor.

'As Commander-in-Chief I personally authorized DEFCON 2. I am fully aware, gentlemen, that this places us at the highest level of military preparedness since World War II.'

'What cards do we have left, now...? We sure need to be holding a winning hand,' LeMay queried.

Joe nodded. 'Let's be absolutely clear about this. DEFCON 2 enables the military to launch an outright attack on Cuba...'

'And the Soviet Union?' General Taylor challenged.

'And the Soviet Union. Her territories, military assets or operational capabilities,' the president said distinctly.

His words were received in silence. Joe paused before continuing, 'An outright attack which will not happen without my say-so.' He gave each military member of EX-COMM a significant glance. Taylor expressed his feelings with a scowl.

Up in New York, just as Joe was clarifying the DEFCON 2 status to EX-COMM, Adlai Stevenson was taking on Soviet Ambassador Zorin at the UN.

The tension in the Security Council chamber was palpable – confrontation was expected. Interpreters, accustomed to the task of translating the dry dialogues of diplomacy, became acutely alert to the change in both mood and tone as Stevenson began to spar openly with Zorin.

Adlai Stevenson's normally courteous tones had been replaced with undisguised anger. 'You have yet to answer my question, Mr Ambassador.'

Zorin, visibly taken aback by Stevenson's sudden vehemence, took refuge in formulaic prevarication. His response was brusquely interrupted by Stevenson's impatient outburst.

'Yes or no? Do you deny the presence of missiles and launch-sites in Cuba? Don't wait for the translation. *Yes* or *no?*'

Audible gasps around the Security Council chamber greeted this unprecedented directness.

Zorin, flustered, spread his hands out. 'I am not in an American court-room, sir, and I do not wish to answer a question put to me in the manner in which a prosecutor does...'

'You are in the court-room of world opinion, right now, and you can answer yes or no,' Stevenson barked. 'I am prepared to wait for my answer until hell freezes over, if that's your decision, and I am also prepared to present the evidence to this room.'

Zorin remained sullenly silent. All around the Security Council chamber, council members were peeling off their head phones and craning from their desks to witness the undiplomatic skirmish.

At the Soviet desk, heads bent down in hurried conference.

'Very well,' Stevenson's voice rang out. 'Let's all take a good look at the evidence.'

The chamber received the reconnaissance photographs in stunned silence. One of Zorin's aides scrambled out of the chamber, desperate for a secure line to Moscow.

THE HAMMER AND THE ANVIL

Western Poland.
End of February, 1945

The footsteps of the long line of prisoners left a dark scar across the Polish snow-scape. Starving, numb from their continuous exposure to the extreme cold and close to exhaustion, the POWs stumbled to a halt at the River Oder – the border with Germany. With only handfuls of snow for sustenance, many had grown weak during the forced march. Those that had faltered or stumbled had been beaten and kicked by the guards. Those whom such encouragement had failed to motivate had been dragged into roadside ditches and shot.

Joe and Mitch had managed to find Will. Will's frost-bitten toes caused him to limp badly. Joe and Mitch saved Will from a grave in the ditch by shouldering him and supporting him at either side. The three men struggled on determinedly, their breath clouding the frozen air, but months of meagre rations and the fatigue of their several days of marching soon told. Will lapsed into semi-consciousness, leaving Joe and Mitch to shoulder his dead weight. With their stamina spent, only their courage spurred them on. Ahead and behind them, the occasional bark of a rifle shot told them of another fallen comrade.

They came to a stretch of road where waste from a ruptured sewer had frozen to form a treacherous sheen of soiled ice. Mitch slithered then stumbled, losing his supporting grip on Will. Groaning, Will slumped down on his knees. As Joe and Mitch struggled to get him standing again, a guard approached and prodded Will in the back with the tip of his gleaming bayonet. Mitch turned and reached out to sweep the bayonet away. Snarling, the guard stepped back and raised his rifle.

'Raus! Raus!' he bellowed.

'For God's sake don't rile him,' Joe warned.

Between them, they managed to haul Will onto his feet, but as they struggled to support him, the guard deliberately tripped

Mitch and laughed as all three men sprawled face down into the frozen sewage.

'Scheissen-kopf!' Mitch muttered, but his curse was smothered by the crunch of the rifle butt into his face.

They managed to struggle back up onto their feet again, Mitch wiping the blood from his mouth and spitting out two broken teeth.

On the evening of the ninth day of forced marching, having crossed the River Oder, the prisoners were herded by their guards into the ruined town of Lamsfeld. Few of the deserted buildings remained intact. The town centre had been reduced to rubble and so the prisoners were forced to take shelter, in small groups, in the rows of abandoned houses. Doors and windows had been blown out leaving little shelter from the freezing rain. The sounds of heavy artillery booming in the distance became increasingly drowned by tank cannon and machine gun fire reverberating closer at hand as the approaching Soviets punctured the German lines.

Joe, Will and Mitch huddled together for warmth, in what had once been a living room, under the watchful eye and leveled rifle of their guard. The hearth was empty except for a smashed picture of the Fuhrer. Wallpaper hung limply from the remaining portion of wall. Shells had punched their way through the shattered roof. A search of both the kitchen and the cellar had proved useless beyond the discovery of a few stinking cabbages and a few rat-gnawed potatoes. Half starved, they ate them raw.

'No bloody water from the tap!' Mitch murmured. 'Some glorious bloody Reich this is.'

Will smiled and was about to wisecrack when Joe held up his hand, his head tilted attentively.

'What?' Will whispered.

The growling engines of Tiger tanks approached then the squeaking of their tracks filled the darkness. A straggle of German infantrymen, shouting as they ran, followed.

'Christ,' Joe whispered. 'They're in retreat…'

Incoming shell rounds exploded in the next street, drowning his words. The last of the three Tiger tanks squealed to a halt at the corner of their street. Mitch strained to listen to the orders being shouted by the officer from the top of the tank-turret.

'He's telling the guards to shoot us… He says the Russians are coming. They're only a few minutes away…'

'Jesus Christ!' Joe cursed. 'Let's get going…'

Will struggled up onto his feet, supported by Joe and Mitch. The guard who had been assigned to their group dashed through the gaping hole in the wall and disappeared into the darkness. The rest of the prisoners ran to the rear of the house, leaving Mitch and Joe supporting Will.

'Fuck this darkness,' Will cursed, stumbling.

'Easy, fellah. We've got you,' Joe soothed.

The sound of firing from the house next door shattered the momentary lull. Heavy foot-steps, running and crunching over the rubble, approached the gap that had been the front door. Joe and Mitch exchanged glances, nodded, and dumped Will unceremoniously down.

'Jeez, you guys…'

A grey-coated guard appeared in the doorway, his rifle at the ready. It was their tormentor on the forced march. Joe and Mitch flung themselves at him. His gun fell to the ground. Mitch snatched it up and jabbed the butt into the guard's face. Joe stepped back as Mitch turned the gun deftly in his grip and put two bullets into the guard. 'Scheissen-kopf', he pronounced, turning the dead body over with his foot.

Sporadic gunfire rattled in the street outside. Red and gold tracer shells zipped over the broken roof-tops as machine guns stuttered their response. Bullets smacked into the side of the house forcing the three men to crouch behind the body of the dead guard.

A hail of bullets spattered around them, splintering the wooden floor boards. Mitch yelled and clasped his leg. 'Oh God, I've stopped one!'

'Let's get the hell out of here,' Joe shouted. 'Come on, you guys. Move it.'

Joe dragged Will towards the back of the house and Mitch limped behind. Kicking open the back door, Joe bundled Will out into the courtyard. The sound of the encircling battle was deafening. Joe, turning, mimed to Mitch that they should take shelter in a hut next to a high brick wall. They staggered down the path towards the out-building. It had no roof or door but would give them temporary cover. Shots rang out from next door. Mitch joined Joe in the darkness of the shed.

'You keep the gun?' Joe hissed.

'Shit, no...' Mitch groaned. 'I dropped it... lost it when I was hit'

'Here,' Joe whispered, 'let me take a look at that leg.'

Will moaned as Joe eased him back against the wall of the hut and then felt in the darkness for Mitch's blood-soaked thigh.

'No exit wound. Bullet's still in... or else it's shrapnel.'

A Schmeisser snarled from the darkness of the garden, spraying the hut with zinging bullets. Joe grunted and slumped across Mitch, a wound at the side of his head oozing blood.

'Christ, Joe,' Will hissed. 'Are you... Is he...?'

'Can't tell,' Mitch's muffled voice whispered. 'Blighter's on top of me...'

'Joe.' Will almost choked on the word.

'Help me,' Mitch pleaded.

Between them, Will and Mitch managed to roll Joe over onto his back. Will felt the warm blood on his friend's face as he cradled Joe's head. More bullets smashed into the wall of the hut. Mitch and Will crouched in the darkness. A German soldier loomed in the doorway, rifle at the ready. Mitch groaned and sank back against the wall. Will covered Joe protectively as the German infantryman swung the rifle from one to the other as if savouring the moment before the kill. Will jerked his head up defiantly. Seeing the movement in the gloom, the German clubbed Will with the rifle. Will, stunned, sprawled across Joe's unconscious form. Mitch stared up balefully into the tiny mouth of the rifle and closed his eyes – and opened them in both alarm and astonishment as the high wall opposite suddenly burst open and collapsed as a Soviet tank crashed through it. The German turned, raised his rifle instinctively, then fell dead – brought down by two pistol shots fired by the Soviet Officer in the turret. Crushing the fallen masonry, the tank ground to a halt in a cloud of stinking smoke. The rest of the wall collapsed onto the outbuilding which buckled and sagged – exposing the huddled forms of Will, Mitch and Joe.

Later that night, as the Russian infantry dealt with the last of the German soldiers who had been defending Lamsfeld, Will and Joe warmed themselves next to a fire for the first time in months. Other POWs from the forced march had been drawn from their shadows and cellars by the flickering flames and the smell of warm food. Mitch slept under the blanket of morphine while Will lay propped against Joe as the Russian medic tended their wounds. Will rescued and pocketed the bullet taken from Mitch's thigh before himself succumbing to the morphine. Joe's ear had been badly torn by a ricocheting bullet, but stitching and a bandage was all that was required.

Orders were barked out in Russian to distribute blankets.

Joe, his head swimming from exhaustion and pain, peered up into the face of the speaker.

'Da, it is me, eh? I save your... how do you say... hides... no?'

Joe grinned weakly. It was the Soviet Tank Commander who had come to their rescue just in time.

More orders were issued to give soup to those still awake and more blankets for those sleeping.

Joe noticed that the Officer himself was carrying blankets, and helped the medics make the wounded comfortable.

'Skins,' Joe murmured as a blanket was wrapped around him with care.

The Russian bent down, his face inches away from Joe's. 'Sins? You want to confess, American? I have no priest for you. Just soup and blankets...'

'Skins,' Joe grinned. 'Not hides. You saved our skins.'

'Da, it is good what I do, eh? Me, Captain Anatoly Melnyev. Me, a good Soviet, I save the skins of the Yankees. Big favour, no?'

The White House, Washington D.C.
Friday morning, 26 October, 1962

The president called EX-COMM to order. 'What's the word from London?' he asked his brother.

Bobby's response was encouraging. 'It's not just London, it's nearly the whole world...'

'Except the Soviet bloc and China,' LeMay voiced drily.

'After Adlai's performance yesterday – Christ, the way he handled Zorin in front of the Security Council – we've got everyone on-side.'

'Sure did a helluva good job,' LeMay observed.

General Taylor said grudgingly that words were no use against the commie bastards. Joe Kennedy ignored this and steered EX-COMM back to business.

'Even Canada...' Bobby continued.

'Canada?' queried Taylor with heavy sarcasm.

'Will offer every measure of assistance...'

'Short of actual help,' LeMay interrupted derisively.

President Kennedy observed that Adlai Stevenson had shamed the Soviets not only in the Security Council but before the court of world opinion, adding that he had been both surprised and satisfied with the performance of his Ambassador to the UN.

'Those aerial photos sure hit Zorin out of the ball park. No doubt he'll be recalled to Moscow. Guess I wouldn't like to be in that guy's shoes,' General Taylor chuckled.

'So what's new?' the President asked, briefly scanning the faces around the table.

'We stopped and searched a Soviet ship we didn't like the look of, but they weren't carrying anything. Nothing of interest to us. Bits and pieces of tractors, some medical supplies and paper for printing presses. We let her go.'

'No munitions?' Bobby Kennedy asked.

'We know what we are looking for,' Staffort rebuked the President's brother haughtily.

'Communications equipment?' Bobby Kennedy pressed, ignoring Staffort's snub.

'Nothing.' Staffort was emphatic – this time his voice held an edge of anger.

Joe intervened. He invited Curtis LeMay to give EX-COMM an update.

LeMay's report was crisp and to the point. The black and white aerial shots of camouflaged missiles at various sites on Cuba proved more eloquent than the many words he could have spoken.

'U-2?' Joe demanded, tapping the photos that were spread out on the table before him.

LeMay, beaming proudly, nodded.

'I want you to evaluate every mission, LeMay. I want you to keep a tight rein on things. No barn-storming, understand? U-2's must only be deployed when there is a major development or a significant threat.'

'Understood, Mr President.'

'For God's sake, we've just got ourselves a huge pile of chips at the UN. Don't let's go and blow them away while the cards are falling our way. I don't want some joker fucking this game up, understood?'

'Yessir.'

'O.K. Bobby? What have you got?'

Robert Kennedy tabled copies of a letter from Khruschev received through the back-channel he had established on Joe's authority. The next hour was taken up in a detailed evaluation of its contents, but the discussion was inconclusive, leaving EX-COMM deeply divided.

The following morning EX-COMM reconvened. Joe Kennedy was the last to arrive. He sensed, as he assumed his seat at the table, a tension in the air. Glancing around the table, he wondered if the hawks had been meeting together to hammer out a strategy – a strategy to railroad their agenda through the diplomatic stance.

'So what have we got? Give me an update.'

Nobody seemed anxious to answer the President. Joe sensed that there had been developments – if not difficulties.

'Well?' he demanded. 'Staffort? What have you got?'

'It's this way, Mr President. A Soviet ship approached the quarantine line –'

Joe Kennedy looked up quickly from his briefing notes. The muscle in his jaw spasmed. 'Approached? How close did she get to the exclusion zone?'

Staffort reddened. 'She crossed the line, Mr President. Crossed it and pressed on. Wouldn't stop …'

'What the hell? What do you mean, wouldn't stop? Where is she now?'

'We turned her, Sir. We …'

'You turned her? What in God's name do you mean, Staffort?'

Staffort cleared his throat uncomfortably. 'Star-flares were deployed across the Soviet ship's bows, Mr President. The ship hove-to then turned back.'

Bobby Kennedy whistled softly. Blasphemous mutterings echoed around the table.

'What the hell is all this?' Joe almost shouted. 'When was this? Why wasn't I informed?'

Staffort began a lame account of the incident. Joe silenced him with a raised hand.

'I thought I made it perfectly clear, perfectly clear,' he repeated softly, 'that there was to be no engagement, no firing, without my authorization.'

His words were greeted with silence.

'Do I make myself clear? No firing without my say-so. Is that understood?'

'Yessir, Mr President.'

Joe's voice resumed a tone of cool authority as he asked for details of the incident. Staffort, still slightly flustered, explained that the Soviet ship had ignored all attempts to communicate with it and had crossed the line into the exclusion zone on a steady course at about eighteen knots. A U.S. destroyer (The John R. Pierce) had been deployed immediately and had overhauled the intruder. Five star- flares had been fired across her bows and then radio traffic with a Soviet sub had been intercepted. Fourteen minutes later, the Soviet ship had turned tail and retreated.

Joe received the account impassively and nodded curtly when Staffort's report ended.

'Anything else?' Joe demanded, taking in the EX-COMM team in a sweeping glance around the table.

LeMay took a deep breath before blurting out that a U-2 had "accidently" flown over what he coyly termed "hostile" air space.

'*Hostile* air space? What the fuck do you mean?'

LeMay swallowed. 'Russia, Sir. The U-2 overflew Russia. It was in Soviet air space for forty-six minutes.'

'Jesus,' Bobby whispered, his eyes on his brother's pale, angry face.

'Did the Soviets scramble?' Joe Kennedy snapped. 'Did they send their MIGs up or use ground-to-air?'

'The Soviets didn't intercept, Sir. Or if they did we didn't get any of it on our radar. We got away with it…'

'Got away with it?' The President made no attempt to conceal his anger in the almost contemptuous retort.

EX-COMM fell silent. Bobby glanced anxiously across at his brother's scowling face.

'Talk me through it. I want all the details.'

LeMay struggled to brief his president on the incident of the U-2. It was a routine mission, he stressed. It had been Pentagon approved. Joe barked that nothing was 'routine' in the present situation, and demanded to know who exactly had approved the mission.

'I can get you that information, Sir,' LeMay replied, scribbling something down on his pad.

It seemed to Joe that LeMay was avoiding eye-contact. Addressing him directly, Joe demanded: 'What else, general? What happened?'

LeMay grew red above the shirt collar. He cleared his throat and swallowed.

'We lost a U-2 over Cuba late last night, Sir.'

Joe's harsh curse was almost drowned by the grunts of alarm around the table.

The next few minutes were spent in a detailed update on how the U-2 was downed. Joe took firm control of the debate, insisting that the press were kept in the dark and there were to be no leaks.

'Pilot's family?' Bobby murmured.

Joe nodded.

'Kept on base, Sir.'

'Keep it that way. Jesus, you cowboys...I can't believe...'

A restrained knock at the door disturbed the tense lull. The presidential aide, Richardson, entered and motioned to Bobby. Joe waved Bobby leave of absence. When the door had closed behind Bobby, Joe drew a short breath and then spoke, with a curbed vehemence that was all the more disturbing for its restraint.

'I want it absolutely understood that no, I repeat no, military response, either offensive or defensive, is to be instigated without my knowledge, approval and authorization. Do I make myself clear, gentlemen?'

As the military chiefs assembled around the conference table gave their terse assurances, Joe still had the uneasy feeling that he had not been informed of everything. Taylor was returning his gaze with an unflinching stare. Joe knew that look, a bluff that should be called.

'What else don't you want to tell me?' Joe said, speaking softly.

Taylor cleared his throat, flustered by the President's prescience.

'The pilots didn't know, Sir, neither did the top brass…'

'Didn't know what, exactly?'

'The F105s… the F105s we scrambled when the U-2 was brought down over Cuba.'

'What about them?' Joe snapped, losing his patience.

'They were fully armed, Sir. I mean… with nuclear capability.'

Curtis LeMay twisted in his chair. 'You mean those babies went in with air-to-ground nukes?' he whispered almost reverentially.

Joe slammed his hand down on the table, silencing the excited murmuring around him.

Robert Kennedy returned and immediately sensed the escalating tension in the conference room – and was alert to his brother's barely suppressed rage.

'Well?' Joe demanded.

'Another letter from Khrushchev.' He passed copies of the letter around to the EX-COMM team and resumed his seat as, around the silenced table, all heads were bowed in scrutiny.

They read Khrushchev's detailed rationale for the Soviet Union's installation of intermediate-range nuclear missiles in Cuba. Such missiles, it was argued, were necessary as a counter to the incremental strategic superiority the United States had achieved by their installation of missiles in Turkey. The ghost of the failed 1961 *Bay of Pigs* fiasco was raised in the concluding paragraph, with Khruschev asserting that the Cuban-based missiles were essential to deter any further US-sponsored invasions.

Faces reddened and loud objections were raised. Joe silenced the angry voices around the table with a firm statement on the US missiles located in Turkey.

'Anything else?' Joe continued.

'Seems we've got a line on the guy running things in Cuba. Our U-2 was brought down on his personal orders, not Moscow's. Looks like he's calling the shots from Havana as communication between Cuba and Moscow is poor. Very little radio traffic for us to intercept but Dobrynin confirms the set-up. A top Soviet General. Military Intelligence and the CIA don't have much on him...'

Northern Germany
18th March, 1945

Six days after their liberation, and beginning to recover from their ordeal, Joe, Will and Mitch – together with a column of Russian soldiers and cheerful Allied POWs – were trudging along in the rain. Mitch, limping gamely, was leading the singing then pausing to allow the ragged chorus to reply in several languages.

Where they could not join in, the Soviet infantrymen laughed, clapped their free hand against their sides in time to the tune or hummed a rich deep bass accompaniment. The marching line frequently slowed and edged to the side of the road to allow convoy after convoy of trucks to pass. Each lorry had the Red Star emblazoned on side of its canvas cover.

Will nudged Joe 'Heading for Berlin. Lucky bastards. They'll be in at the kill.'

Joe replied softly. 'Want to know something? Those trucks are empty.'

'Empty?' Will was astonished.

'It's been puzzling me. I can't quite figure it. Look, this one's slowing down. See?'

Will glimpsed daylight through the flapping canvas.

'Trucks drop off their supplies... food... munitions...but continue heading West instead of turning back...'

'I don't get it,' Will said simply.

'Maybe they... say, don't I know that guy?'

A Soviet tank pulled over and scrunched to a halt alongside them. A grinning face looked down at them from the turret.

'Hey, Americans. It's me. I save your skins, remember?'

Will and Joe waved up to the smiling Russian.

'What are the odds of his turning up and finding us?' Joe whispered.

Will caught the speculative tone in Joe's soft aside.

'Jeez, Joe. You think that guy was looking for us?'

Melnyev thumped the side of his tank with a gloved fist. The driver's head poked up alongside him.

'We will stop here.'

The driver snatched the headphones away and cupped his left ear. Melnyev, laughing, repeated his order and, pulling off his gloves, climbed out of the turret and jumped down alongside Joe.

'Now, American, I give you vodka to keep out the cold and you teach me English, maybe too good to play better the game of poker, no?'

They ate rye bread, a soapy tasting sausage cut with Melnyev's knife and some strong, tinned cheese, which Mitch ate with gusto, using the armour covering the tank's caterpillar track as a table. Melnyev good-naturedly passed the vodka back to Joe and Will, urging them to drink. Joe noticed that this courtesy was not extended to the tank driver. The drink hit Mitch hard. Hauling himself up onto the tank, he curled up over the warmth of the rear engine cowling and dozed.

'Now we play cards,' Melnyev pronounced, using his gloves to flick away the crumbs of rye bread from the armour plate. 'I deal.'

The game attracted a circle of onlookers. Will joined Melnyev and advised him on his hand. The cards were dog-eared and frequently kept sliding off the smooth surface of the armour plating – causing Melynev to laugh raucously and take another swig of vodka. Under Will's tutelage and with Joe happy to humour their saviour, Melnyev won the first three hands – rewarding himself with a hefty swig of vodka with each gleeful shout of 'I win.'

Joe won the fourth hand – a straight running flush.

'Spade flush,' Joe murmured.

Will whistled and was about to speak when Joe's imperceptible look silenced him.

'You win a drink, Mr Kennedy. May I congratulate you on your win…how did you call it…your spade flush.'

Joe's expression remained impassive.

'What's the Russian for "Good Health"?' Joe inquired, the bottle at his lips.

Melnyev grinned. 'Na zdorovie!'

Joe repeated the salute and drank, aware of Melnyev's close scrutiny.

'You are curious, no?' the Russian bantered. 'You ask yourself, I think, how does this Tank officer know my name, no?'

Joe returned the vodka with a bow. 'Me,' he shrugged, 'I'm curious about nothing. Let's play.'

'For the son of such an important American polit-bureau member… I mean, how do you say, politician… you betray very little curiosity.'

'Curiosity killed the cat,' Joe said pleasantly, gathering up his cards.

'Now that one I did not know. About the cat.'

Joe played two more hands, losing both to Melnyev.

'I win again.'

'Jeez, Joe, he's good. He's done this before, I guess. Say, aren't you guys in a hurry to get to Berlin?'

Melynev shrugged off Will's question. 'No hurry, American. It is already settled. All is settled.' His eyes met Joe's cool gaze. 'Stalin came back from his poker game at Yalta a very happy man. Big prize.'

Joe would not be drawn. 'Speaking of winnings,' he grunted, tugging off his boot and examining the worn sole, 'I guess it's time I paid up.'

Reaching across for the knife they had used to cut their sausage and cheese, he prised open the heel and extracted his signet ring.

The Russian raised a quizzical eyebrow.

Joe shrugged his shoulders. 'It's all I have.'

Blowing on it and wiping it on his sleeve, he inspected it fondly before reaching over and dropping it in Melnyev's open palm.

'All debts paid,' Joe said softly.

The Soviet grinned and shrugged, delighted with his prize.

'But I have one more duty to discharge,'

Joe looked up quickly.

'I want to get you home, or, in direction of home, we can say, immediately.'

The Dorchester Hotel, London
22 March 1945

Jane looked up expectantly at each arrival, hoping to spot Joe's resemblance in his father. She felt slightly self-conscious sitting in the reception area in her shabby coat as well-groomed men escorted their elegant partners into the afternoon tea lounge. A piano was being played softly, its tinkling notes adding to Jane's apprehension. Large glass doors kept the noise of the traffic outside. Impeccable waiters glided by, flicking suspicious glances at her. Jane felt the flame rise up in her cheeks. She should not have arrived so early – unescorted girls in hotels could only be regarded with suspicion.

A newspaper rustled as it was lowered by a middle-aged man sitting behind the fringe of a large potted palm. The revealed face was somewhat florid and a little heavily set. The man, now openly looking directly across at Jane, managed something between a grimace and a smile. Jane's heart quickened and she flushed angrily. It was Joe's father – the likeness was immediately obvious – and he had been appraising Jane from his concealment for the last ten minutes.

He rose, tossed the newspaper aside and walked towards her.

'Joseph Kennedy,' he spoke briskly. 'I guess you must be...'

Jane gave her name quickly, refusing to be intimidated by this man with a bullying air.

They reached out awkwardly and shook hands without warmth. Jane felt the flame rekindling in her cheeks as Joe Kennedy Senior took in her obvious pregnancy with his shrewd gaze.

'I think it only fair to tell you...'

He held up a peremptory hand. 'I've booked us a table. In a quiet corner. We don't go in for afternoon tea back home. Shall we order some scones with Devonshire clotted cream?'

As Jane suppressed a fleeting smirk at his pronunciation of Devonshire she noticed his curt nod to a nearby waiter. In an instant, they were being ushered into the sumptuous tea lounge.

Jane found herself being deftly steered to a secluded alcove table. She saw the folded ten shilling note being quickly passed, and even more swiftly pocketed by the waiter.

'Sir?' came the respectful inquiry when they had been seated.

'I understand the cream tea is the thing to have here.'

The waiter inclined his head a fraction and scribbled on his pad.

'And for madam?'

'Make that two.' Joe Kennedy spoke with a note of finality. The waiter glided away.

Across the table, Jane simmered resentfully. What had been youthful and beguiling confidence in the son had hardened to a coarse arrogance in the father. Jane glimpsed the same sensuality in the Kennedy lips, but her Joe's had been so quick to break into a smile. The lips of the mouth she studied were resolute.

Joe's father was perturbed by Jane's frankness. Yes, the baby is your grandchild she had affirmed. Joe Senior nodded.

'And your folks? Did you ever discuss the possibility of...?'

Jane's fists thumped the smooth white table cloth. The silver cutlery rattled. For a brief moment, the tinkling piano faltered but recovered almost immediately. Heads turned towards the alcove. Joe Kennedy flushed angrily. 'OK. OK. Don't make a scene for Christ's sake.'

Avoiding painful details of her father's wounded silence and her mother's harsh anger, Jane explained that there had been certain difficulties at home and that though she was virtually on her own, she was determined to keep the child and manage somehow, as best as she could until Joe returned from the war.

Kennedy looked up and was about to speak when the waiter appeared silently at their table and performed the elaborate ceremonies of serving the cream teas. Joe Senior loaded a scone up with jam and cream, bit into it, grunted his displeasure and wiped his mouth with a napkin.

'You were about to say...?' Jane prompted.

The man sitting across the table from her paused. The napkin in his right hand shriveled within the squeezing fist. Jane felt the pulse at her throat quicken as Joe's father raised the napkin up uncertainly – wavering between dabbing it at his mouth or eyes.

'You know something, don't you? Jane demanded. 'Is he...is Joe hurt? Is he badly injured?'

'Look, I guess you should know something. Word got back to me that Joe is gone... and his Radio Operator.'

'Gone?' Jane felt stupid as she looked up and echoed his word.

Then her lip trembled and tears pricked her eyes.

'You mean... you mean they're dead, don't you?'

Suppressing the delight he had experienced when the cable had come confirming Joe's rescue by the Soviets, Kennedy remained silent and simply nodded his lie.

His attempts to console the weeping girl were futile. Her sobbing silenced the piano and drew concerned glances from around the tea lounge. Reaching across the table he gathered up her hand in a pretended communion of shared grief. The waiter, hesitant and then suddenly emboldened, approached.

'Is... is everything all right, Sir?'

Joe Kennedy shunted the cream tea aside impatiently

'Get me a decent cup of coffee and some ham sandwiches.'

'Now listen to me,' he said gruffly as Jane dabbed her eyes, her shoulders still convulsed by dry sobs. 'I'm going to take care of you. Of you both, see? My son's girl and my... grandchild.'

Four days later, Jane received a letter from Joe Kennedy Senior. No mention was made of his son in the letter nor was there any concern for Jane's grief in her bereavement. In a dry, matter-of-fact tone, details of the arrangements to be made were set down. The child would be adopted immediately after the birth by a childless American couple of good Christian standing. Joe Senior knew of just such a couple.

Jane, the letter instructed, would be provided with a monthly allowance for twenty-one years. In almost contractual terms, it was stipulated that Jane was to forego any further or future claim on the child or on the Kennedy family. A telephone number was included for her to contact closer to her confinement. Jane was instructed to communicate her acceptance of all the terms entailed in writing by return.

As she mounted the basement area steps of her Parsonage Street digs, her letter of acceptance in her hand, a bicycle bell jingled and a voice called out her name.

'Hello, stranger. We are beginning to miss you at the Union, you know.'

It was a girl that Jane rather liked, but the exchange was brief and the girl did not press Jane any further. It had been like that ever since she had started to show her condition. The averted, embarrassed eyes of the male undergrads. The pursed lips of disapproving female students. The slow trickle of invitations to tea, or for an evening glass of sherry, had dried up, until every evening was spent alone in her basement flat. Two weeks after meeting Joseph Kennedy Senior, Jane stopped attending her lectures, seminars and tutorials. The rather lame inquiry from her personal tutor remained unanswered. The silence from her parents in Fersfield continued.

On the fourteenth of April, a day of bright sunshine and sharp showers, Jane awoke in considerable discomfort. The ache in her back had eased overnight but there was a more ominous pain in her lower abdomen. She struggled into her overcoat and, panting slightly with exertion, mounted the basement steps up into Parsonage Street. There was a telephone kiosk at the corner of her street and The Causeway. Jane dialled the number Joseph Kennedy Senior had given her. A cool, clinical voice responded. Jane had to wait to be connected to an extension. She was instructed, after confirming her address, to return directly to her flat. A car would arrive to collect her within the hour.

It was a sleek, black Pontiac. A somewhat ominous sort of ambulance, Jane thought. The driver shepherded her gently into the dark, warm interior of the car. She found herself sitting next to a pale, taciturn nurse. The nurse covered Jane's legs with a thick blanket and signalled to the driver. The plates on the Pontiac drew a few curious glances.

They left Cambridge and drove south-east. Jane drifted in and out of full sentience as the increasing pain dulled her awareness. At last, as the car turned in off the road and bumped gently over a cattle grid, she came to with a start. The Pontiac was heading up along a narrow, straight drive flanked on either side by elm trees. Through the trees Jane caught odd glimpses of men struggling to master crutches or manage wheelchairs across the grass, some with assistance. The Pontiac slowed as two young men approached, each supporting and encouraging the other. One had heavily bandaged legs and hands. The other had been blinded.

'Ah, aint it a cryin' shame,' the driver whispered, respectfully saluting the pair.

Prompted by his bandaged comrade, the blind invalid attempted to salute. Jane felt the tears well up in her eyes.

'What is this place?' she asked the driver. 'A hospital?'

'No, m'am, it's a kinda...'

'Now you mustn't tire yourself talking,' the nurse chipped in, her prim accent devoid of any tenderness. 'Everything is arranged. Look, we're here.'

Jane did not decline the offer of a wheelchair. She was propelled briskly along several brightly lit, antiseptic smelling corridors until, in a wing remote from the main building, she was ushered into a small room.

'Just get undressed and put this robe on,' the nurse instructed. 'The doctor will be along in a few minutes.'

Jane simply nodded. Clutching her belly, she felt grateful that it would be sooner rather than later.

After a painful four and a half hour labour, Jane gave birth without complications at eight fifteen the following morning. There was a silver-haired doctor, a midwife and two nurses also in attendance. The nurse who had arrived to collect Jane in the black Pontiac remained by the bedside throughout the delivery. As the midwife scooped up the infant to slap it gently to clear its airway, Jane struggled up from her pillows and propped herself up unsteadily on one elbow.

'Hey,' the nurse murmured, 'take it easy. You must be exhausted.'

Jane looked up and smiled weakly, grateful for the cool towel being dabbed at her forehead and temples.

The baby spluttered and cried. Craning, Jane saw the little fat legs kicking as the midwife lowered the newborn infant into a bowl of warm water. Gentle splashing sounds filled the room. The doctor gave Jane a curious glance and then withdrew, motioning his two other assistant nurses to join him. Jane, impatient to hold her child, murmured to the midwife, who seemed to be drying and then dressing the child in several warm layers.

'May I see my baby? I want to…'

'Here, my girl,' the cool tones of her nurse soothed. 'Take this. It will… settle you.'

The midwife, keeping her back to Jane, walked slowly towards the door. Jane, a note of alarm in her voice, asked if there was anything wrong with her child.

'Now, now, we don't want any fuss,' her nurse said firmly, putting a glass to Jane's lips. 'Drink this. It'll do you good.'

It tasted very bitter. Jane swallowed at least half of it before she was able to raise her forearm and push the nurse's hand away, spilling the remaining contents on her bedspread.

'My baby…' Jane cried.

The midwife closed the door gently behind her, leaving Jane scrambling to escape her bed as the nurse tried to wrestle her back down onto the mattress.

'Believe me – no, don't bite me - it's much better this way. No, don't be stupid.'

Whatever the sedative had been, it seemed to affect Jane's arms first. They fell heavy and useless by her side. She felt a numbness creeping down her legs.

Jane was in a fitful doze when the trolley-bed transferred her from the delivery room to a side room. The nurse peered intently into her eyes before striding briskly out of the room, turning the light off as she departed. Jane woke up briefly and lay sobbing in the darkness before she succumbed to a deep sleep.

The Kennedy family home,
Boston, Mass.
3rd. May, 1945.

Joseph Kennedy Senior's private secretary brought his employer a letter – unopened, as instructed – in an envelope bearing a postmark from Cambridge, England. The private secretary lingered over the outgoing post but Joe Kennedy Senior contained his excitement and apprehension until he was once more alone in his office. He opened the letter and read it, scrutinizing every word. The child had been safely delivered and the mother had expressed her desire to have it called Joseph Patrick on hearing that it was a little boy. Mother and baby had been separated according to instructions immediately after the birth. The child was in a safe location and would be in America by the end of the month. The mother had been deemed medically fit – though anxious and depressed – and had returned to Cambridge. There were no complications or adverse reactions.

Joseph Kennedy Senior unlocked his humidor and selected a choice Cuban cigar. A Romeo y Julietta. Unconscious of the irony, he carefully cut off its tip and used two matches to warm and then light it. He poured himself out a generous measure of Bourbon and splashed a little soda into the glass.

Joseph Patrick, he mused. No, he suddenly decided. It would be Patrick Joseph. Patrick Joe, he nodded approvingly. Raising his glass, he toasted the latest addition to his dynasty. The alcohol warmed his gut. He drew on the cigar. It had gone out. He struck another match. Drawing deeply, he savoured the pungent tobacco as he put the match to the letter and watched it shrivel to ash in the brass waste-paper bin by his opulent desk.

VIII

15th May, 1945

'How's Mary? Still selling War Bonds?'

Dexter O'Neill tightened his grip on the golf club. He secretly resented Joe Kennedy Senior. He resented being a nephew to this overbearing patriarch just as much as he resented having had to turn to him back in 1938 for help to avoid bankruptcy.

'Yes,' he grunted, bringing the club down in suppressed anger and slicing his shot. He disliked being summoned away from his busy office at such short notice to play golf on a hot afternoon and having to be careful not to win by too large a margin.

'War Bonds,' Joe tutted dismissively. 'Show's over for the Germans and we'll have the Japs all wrapped up before Thanksgiving.'

'You think so?' Dexter looked up.

'I know so,' came the confident reply.

Selling War Bonds. Dexter had not seen his wife for three months. Working out of hotel rooms across the mid-West, she had been working for the US Treasury campaign.

'She'll be coming back soon?'

Dexter shook his head impatiently. He wanted to get this part of the conversation out of the way quickly. Being childless, both he and Mary had always felt Joe Kennedy Senior's tacit censure for not increasing the numbers of the dynastic clan.

'She'll go straight on down to Florida, I guess.'

'You planning on joining her, maybe?'

'I might manage a couple of weeks.'

Joe Senior drove his ball onto the fairway. He stepped back, smiling his satisfaction.

'Let's call that evens. We'll walk back to the clubhouse. Got something to tell you. We'll talk out here, all to ourselves.'

Here it comes, Dexter thought, shouldering his clubs (Joe Kennedy had insisted on their playing without caddies) and falling into step with the older man. Seven years ago, timely intervention had prevented the scandal – now it was payback time. Joe Senior was about to reel in his debt.

'Always thought it sad that you and Mary...'

Dexter nodded. 'We... she... always wanted a kid...'

'You have any tests... medical tests done?'

Dexter was tempted to apportion the blame to Mary but loyally shrugged it off as just bad luck.

'Got a proposition for you. The both of you.'

Dexter shot a quick glance of inquiry but Joe looked straight ahead.

'Well? What's the proposition?' Dexter was the first to break the silence. He knew it was a weakness to do so but the other man's deliberate silence had made it necessary.

'Ever thought about adoption, son?'

'No, sir.' Dexter's tone was more startled than puzzled.

For the next quarter of an hour, Joe outlined to his nephew the story of an American pilot of impeccable credentials who had been killed in action after a brief affair with a young English woman of good standing. The fruit of their union was a beautiful little baby boy. In order to protect the honour of the young American officer and spare the English girl the stigma of raising an illegitimate child, Joe had intervened and was now in a position to place the baby with a decent, God-fearing, professional American couple.

'What do you say? Think Mary would be interested?'

Dexter was so relieved not to be involved in one of Joe's more dubious enterprises he did not reply.

'Look at it this way. She's been out of town for a few months. You join her in Florida. Take a few weeks extra holiday. I arrange all the paperwork and you get a baby boy. Come back into circulation. You can say it is your own or say what you like. Just give yourselves time to adjust. Think of it. Victory in Europe. Great way to celebrate, heh? What do you say, son?'

'Uncle,' he whispered. 'It's terrific.'

Stepping closer, he embraced the older man.

'Mary will be thrilled. Our own little kid. After all this time. Joe, I can't thank you enough…'

After quickly scanning the surrounding fairways for other golfers, Joe Kennedy returned the close embrace, patting Dexter's back with avuncular enthusiasm.

'Say, easy fellah. I'm only doing this for you and Mary. You both deserve the chance. I know you'll make fine parents. Little Patrick…'

'Patrick?' Dexter laughed the named out delightedly.

'The kid's going to a fine family. Fine folks.'

'Tell me all about it,' Dexter urged.

Joe caught the approach of a group of golfers out of the corner of his eye.

'Let's get back. No need to say too much now. In fact, best just forget the past entirely and let the little fellah have a fresh start. Why, there'll never be any need for him to know anything otherwise, huh?'

Two weeks later, in an attorney's office in Miami, Dexter and Mary duly signed the necessary adoption papers. Joe Kennedy Senior was not present, but his instructions were made perfectly clear. The adoption was to be undertaken on the binding agreement that no one must ever be told of the arrangement. Strings had been pulled in Dexter's firm and he had been granted a month's leave. He and Mary would return into circulation after sufficient time as the proud parents of a baby boy. So pleased were they both with their good fortune, that neither gave much thought to the signatures that were required of them, pledging never to reveal to the child its true provenance or parentage.

21st June, 1945

The steady drone of the Dakota's engines lulled Will and Joe to the edge of sleep. Down below, the glint of the North Sea sparkled as they left the coast of Holland behind them.

'Huh?' Will grunted. 'What you say?'

Joe stirred and opened his eyes. They exchanged smiles as, emerging from their doze, they woke up to the fact that they had survived everything and were homeward bound.

'Say, did that Anatoly guy ever explain those empty trucks. You and he seemed to get pretty pally.'

Joe grinned. 'He was too cute to say more than he had to, but he gave me a few clues.'

'Like?'

'Seems the Ruskies had their eyes on a few valuables in Berlin.'

'Gold?'

'Art. Paintings. The Nazis had been quietly confiscating and looting art treasures for years.'

'And Uncle Joe Stalin wants a piece of the action.'

Joe nodded. 'Uncle Sam's got his eye on the rocketry at Peenemunde and the guys who designed them. And I guess Uncle Joe's after them too…but the German POWs would rather use the Geneva Convention now it suits them'

'Shit. You're kidding me…'

'Our guy was also talking about papers. Documents.'

'Huh?'

'Asked me,' Joe lowered his voice, 'did I know how much copper wire went into a Heinkel bomber.'

Will grinned and, raising his index to his temple, rotated it.

'No, he wasn't nuts. Told me it took two miles of wiring to rig up the average medium range Kraut bomber. The Nazis were still getting copper from British companies in Rhodesia as late as March 1939.'

'Holy shit. You mean…'

'So the Soviets want to get into Berlin pronto and find out just what was going on back then. Stalin will get political leverage and use it when they redraw the map of Europe.'

'Jeez, gimme a straight fight anyday. I hate all this political crap. Say, don't you think it weird that he came to our rescue twice, Joe? I mean, once, when he rolled up in that tank was swell but…'

'That was no accident. The second time, when he found us on the road. He was sent to get us. He was looking for us.'

'You mean?'

'We were his babies. His mission. To get us back home.'

'Anatoly Melnyev strikes me as being one helluva guy. Say, how come one Ruskie in a tank knows so much about art and copper wire and who the hell put him onto us?'

'He's a Political Officer. They have one in every brigade. Probably in every damn platoon. Keeps an eye on the boys for Uncle Joe.'

'Like the padre does on you…'

Will bit his lip, silently cursing his smart reply.

Joe scowled his fleeting anger. Will saw the tightening muscle along the jaw-line.

'Jeez, Joe, we're flying North-West. Look. The sun's no longer behind us.'

Joe craned his neck and scanned the sea and sky through the small window. He nodded. Will exhaled, hoping the dangerous moment between them had passed.

Joe bent forward and spoke across Will to a US Navy Captain.

'Prestwick,' came the answer.

Joe eased back into his seat. 'That's way up north. In Scotland.'

'Scotland! Aw, shucks. I wanna be with Liz,' Will grunted, 'not a bunch of sheep up a mountain.'

They talked about the girls. Joe gazed down into the palm of his hand and smiled gently at the little brown scrap of a shrivelled flower. The tiny flower Jane had given him on the eve of their mission to Mimoyecques. His mind drifted back to revisit, almost shyly, Jane's body. Would there be an initial awkwardness when they were reunited?

Joe had decided not to share with Jane any of his experiences in captivity, hoping that their reunion and the imminent end of the war would allow him to forget. He shifted impatiently in his seat, suddenly deciding that he would tell her everything, once and once only, then put the last nine months behind him forever. Will's voice broke into his consciousness.

'Will she understand, eh Joe? Huh?'

Joe frowned. 'Will she understand what?'

'Will Liz be OK about…' Will nodded down to his lap.

'Sure she'll be OK about it. Besides, you can't be sure.'

'Mustang's on the runway but I just can't get her up in the air.'

Joe smiled and threw Will a tender punch. 'You'll be fine. You'll go flying again.'

Will nodded and closed his eyes, leaving Joe to lick his dry lips and swallow as unwanted memories of pain and torture flooded back. Will had confided to him that ever since their interrogation things had not been quite right with his 'Mustang'. Joe felt his own secret fears brimming up to threaten the pleasurable anticipation of being back with Jane. He thought of the way they held each other after they had made love.

The Dakota dipped its port wingtip, banked and started its descent.

'We there?' Will mumbled, rousing himself from sleep.

Joe, peering down as they crossed the coastline, nodded.

'Prestwick,' Will grunted. 'Jeez. You think they have trains hereabouts?'

Joe grinned.

The approach and touchdown was a text-book landing. The Dakota taxied up the runway but stopped someway short of the little cluster of huts around the tower. As Joe and Will rose from their seats, the pilot and co-pilot appeared from the cockpit screen.

'Pleasure to get you guys back,' the pilot grinned, saluting his passengers smartly.

Eagerly crowding the narrow gangway between the rows of seats, the returning POWs thanked him with good-natured abuse and voiced their impatience to disembark.

'OK you guys! Keep it in your pants!' the pilot laughed.

Their response to that was a shower of expletives.

'Not you two,' he murmured, waving Joe and Will back down into their seats.

'Huh?' Will said, puzzled.

Joe looked up interrogatively.

'Tower just radioed. You two guys gotta stay put.'

As they watched the lorry take the other returning servicemen away from the Dakota, both Will and Joe saw the sleek black car advancing steadily towards them across the airfield.

A few minutes later, Joe Senior climbed aboard, exchanged handshakes and a few words with the pilot and co-pilot, and after dismissing them, strode down the gangway and embraced his son.

After the hip flask had been passed around twice between them and the bourbon gratefully swallowed, Will withdrew, leaving father and son locked in an emotional welcome. He ambled up to the cockpit door, passed through it and stood gazing down at the control columns. His gaze swept over the panel of instruments, settling on the familiar dials. Reaching out, he lightly fingered the bank of switches and, exhaling his pent up emotion loudly, sat down in the co-pilot's seat.

Will closed his eyes, reached out and grasped the control column, opening them as he closed both hands around the joystick and squeezed his fingers hard. It felt so good, he thought. So fucking good. He grunted as he scanned the bank of instruments once more, feeling an affectionate contempt for the Dakota – the US forces workhorse – as he thought of the layout in a Liberator.

Out of the corner of his eye, he saw something tucked into the webbing behind the pilot's seat. Reaching across, he prised out a tightly folded magazine. Unfolding it and spreading the pages open on his lap, he found himself gazing down at colourful images of scantily clad young women. Real eye-poppers. He felt his throat constricting as he turned the pages slowly, revealing a parade of near-nudes smiling wantonly up at him. He swallowed and licked his lips. His chest felt tight and heavy as he gazed down at the provocative pictures. Will felt the warm surge in his loins as his body responded to the images. He squirmed happily in his seat, causing the magazine to slip from his lap.

Bursting through the cockpit door he called out to Joe.

'I'm airborne. Honest to God, Joe, I'm flying –'

He froze, his mouth stupidly open and silent. Down along the gangway, hunched in his seat, Joe sat pale and shaking. Will saw the tears trickling down his friend's face. Joe Senior seemed to be embarrassed by his son and was gazing unseeingly out through the window.

'What is it, Joe? Tell me. What's happened?'

Neither of the men responded.

'For Christ's sake, Joe. What is it?' Will demanded, answering his own question almost immediately. 'Is it the girls? Is Liz… are they…?'

Joe Kennedy Senior stood up from his seat and walked slowly along the gangway towards Will.

'Leave him be for a little while, son. Here. Sit down I've got… something to tell you.'

Will slumped down and Joe Senior sat beside him. In silence, he took a folded newspaper clipping out of his wallet and passed it to Will, avoiding eye contact. After reading a brief account of 'an incident' in North London – time and date carefully noted – Will's eyes came to the casualty list.

'What? Both of them?' Will whispered hoarsely.

Returning the newspaper clipping to his wallet, the older man merely nodded.

'But I don't understand. What were they… I mean, how the hell…' Will shouted angrily.

'Easy, son, easy. It was all very sad. Very, very sad.'

In a few considered words, sparing Will the painful details, Joe Kennedy Senior recounted what he knew of the V-1 strike which had caused such devastation.

Will felt dazed.

Joe Senior remained quiet. He was seasoned in the art of letting others answer their own questions.

'V-1. It wasn't that goddam big gun we were going after…'

The other merely shook his head.

'It was a fucking doodle-bug' Will cried, as if suddenly remembering through the shock. 'Say,' he whispered, 'did we… did they take out that goddam gun in France?'

In a quiet voice Joe Senior confirmed that the super-gun at Mimoyecques had been destroyed. Will fixed on this, demanding details. Joe Senior shrugged the questioning away and, after squeezing Will's knee, stood to return to his weeping son.

They changed planes, leaving the Dakota for a four-engine, long range C54 Skymaster. Joe Senior waved them off. Clutching bars of chocolate, packs of cigarettes and paper bags crammed with sandwiches and fresh fruit, Will and Joe sat in miserable silence as their plane headed out over the Atlantic towards America.

Will broke the brooding silence.

'Guess your old man was glad to have you back.'

Joe grunted an unintelligible reply.

Will turned towards him. 'Say, Joe. How did he know about… the girls. I mean, it's a kinda long shot, don't you think?'

Joe remained silent for a full minute before speaking. 'Jane and Liz got to asking after us back at the base when we didn't show up. I guess word got back to him. He has a nose for things. Seemed to know pretty much everything about us since we went down in the Channel last summer. Got a hunch he even pulled a few strings with the Russians.'

'Melnyev?' Will whistled softly. 'Holy shit. You're kiddin' me.'

Joe shrugged.

They lapsed into silence as the plane droned on across the Ocean.

Will ate chocolate gloomily and squeezed the wrapper up into a tight ball in his clenched fist.

'At least we got that fuckin' big gun…'

Joe sighed. His chin sunk down to rest in the palm of his hand.

'Joe?'

Joe did not respond.

'Your old man said…'

'My old man talks bullshit. He can't help it. He's a fucking politician.'

'Whatdya mean?'

'The RAF sent Lancaster bombers over to knock out that super gun about a week or so before our mission. When the army got to Mimoyecques last autumn they found that the gun was useless – couldn't have been fired. The RAF earthquake bombs had damaged it beyond repair.'

After sitting in stunned silence, Will replied. 'Ah, Jeez, Joe. You mean it was all for nothing?'

'Not even a medal for me, for my old man to brag about,' Joe spat out, sourly.

The Kennedy family home, Massachusetts.
Late Fall, 1948.

They were a big family around a big table in the dining room. In any other household in the country, a gathering of this size would have been for Thanksgiving dinner, but for the Kennedy clan, it was just a normal get-together. As the domestics returned to take away the remains of a baked Virginia ham, a sirloin of beef and the carcass of a (once) huge turkey, Joe Kennedy Senior asked, 'Does anybody mind?'

Whether they did or not he never knew because it was a ritual to which no-one dared object. He lit up his cigar and blew the smoke straight up at the ceiling. The domestics brought in the desserts – chocolate cake with vanilla ice cream – and withdrew. Around the table, everyone waited patiently for Joe Senior to enjoy his cigar. It was a custom with him to smoke before dessert.

There was a mounting tension in the dining room. Jack had spoken about segregation and the fragility of the white southern Democrat vote. This had angered his father – probably because Joe Senior saw the political truth behind what he took to be a taunt from his irreverent second son. Teddy was about to speak but saw the anger in Joe Senior's eyes. Bobby – always the appeaser – had intervened, deftly restoring a fragile peace, but Joe Senior remained truculent.

After dessert, the women and girls withdrew and Teddy was told to take the dogs for their last walk of the day, leaving Joe Senior and his other three sons to their brandy.

The father raised his glass in order to toast Joe Junior's recent success – assistant treasurer to the Democratic Senator for Massachusetts. The Senator was an old buddy and ally of Joseph Kennedy Senior.

Joe Junior blushed suddenly as he remembered another toast – four, no, five years back – when Jack's silverware was being celebrated. He responded to the toast as he had then, nursing his glass of brandy, allowing his mind to wander. Some minutes later, he was drawn back abruptly into the company around the dining table – by raised, angry voices.

'And just what the hell d'ya mean by that, you goddam jackass dime-a-word scribbler? Huh? What the hell d'ya mean?'

'I hear it all the time. Everywhere I go. In clubs, in bars… everyone says it. Old Joe Kennedy. Republican by nature but Democrat by default. Come on, admit it. If the Rebulicans would have you you'd…'

Joe Senior had turned a dangerous shade of purple. He spluttered out a string of obscenities. Joe Junior froze, unable to intervene. It was Bobby who once more defused the situation.

'What the hell, eh, Pop? So long as they put a Kennedy in the White House in the next decade, who gives a shit...'

Joe Senior grinned his slow, wide smile of self-satisfaction. 'The boy's right. And here's how it's gonna happen. You're supposed to be a journalist, eh?' he snarled at Jack. 'Well here's something for your damn typewriter and it has nothing to do with poor folk or black folk that you liberal commie-loving bastards...'

Joe Junior retreated into his private thoughts. He heard the abusive shouts of 'Yalta' and 'Berlin blockade' being exchanged across the impeccable white tablecloth. His mind's eye suddenly glimpsed Anatoly Melnyev sitting on the armoured plating of a Soviet tank grinning as a hand of poker was being dealt out. Despite his suspicion of his father's hidden hand behind their rescue and ultimate escape from the war torn chaos of mainland Europe, Joe Junior had believed that Melnyev had taken to both himself and Will and had acted out of pure camaraderie.

'Yalta,' his father barked. 'We were sold down the fuckin' river there, boy.'

'Sure thing, Pop, but at least we know what we're up against,' Bobby appealed.

Joe flinched as he heard his father curse the Russians, his anger evaporating as his voice rose in triumph.

'Little Boy showed them. Amen to the A-bomb, huh, you guys? And when we snatched von Braun from under their goddam noses we got ourselves a sure fire delivery system. Jesus, that Kraut's gonna give us a rocket that can reach Moscow from its stateside launch site...'

Joe closed his eyes. Their talk of rockets hurt him deeply, even though von Braun had been behind the V-2s... not the V-1s.

Bobby saw the muscle tighten in his older brother's face and guessed what was flashing across Joe Junior's mind.

'Say, Joe, what are your plans for the next ten years? Tell us how you're gonna walk into the White House…'

Joe snapped into alertness, shaking off the dullness brought on not by brandy but by weariness and memory. His fleeting reflections on wartime experiences left him raw and resentful. Before he could rally and respond to Bobby's good-natured banter, Joe Senior broke in.

'This is how I see it. First, say in three to four years time, he gets elected to the Senate. Can't start the journey to the White House unless you set off from Capitol Hill. And,' Joe Senior paused to sip from his glass of brandy, 'that journey can't be taken alone. Needs a wife. Matter of fact I know the very girl. Harness the power and influence of Boston's two leading families and you've got a winning team…'

'Gimme a date, Pop. When's it all gonna happen. 58? 59?' Bobby urged, clearly humouring his father.

'It's gonna happen when I say so and when Joe gets some ideas into his head and starts talking turkey.'

His words were drowned in groans of protest but Joe Senior banged the table for silence. When he held their grudging attention, he continued.

'Heard a fellah talking the other night. Private dinner, behind closed doors. Liked what I heard. Name of McCarthy. A Republican. Spoke about the dangers of Communism. Warned about it being like some sort of cancer, spreading quietly and lethally across the globe – why, he even said it could worm its way into the USA if not checked. Liked what I heard. Now, you see, there's a guy with a sound head who talks sense and has a great political future. Senator McCarthy. You should look him up, son,' he said to Joe. 'Look him up and learn from him…'

Joe averted his eyes and groaned inwardly. It had been like this ever since he had returned home from the war. He had been kept on a tight leash by his domineering father. Life had quickly settled into a highly organised routine of political dinners, receptions and 'useful introductions'. Sometimes Joe had felt like a prize steer being hawked around by a Texan ranch-owner.

Even contact with Will had been disturbingly sporadic, with Joe Senior constantly encouraging the two to meet up then frustrating any reunion with last minute demands on Joe's schedule. Joe drained his glass.

What a fuckin' family, Joe thought. Jack with his liberal friends, increasing use of pain-killers and the endless succession of girl friends, rapidly becoming the butt of his father's disdain. Bobby, always smoothing and placating the old man by trying to broker a peace between father and sons. And Joe? He felt himself powerless and unable to swim against the current of his father's political ambitions. Where had all his strength gone? What had happened to his soul? Maybe, he thought, pouring himself another brandy, he had left it behind on the other side of the Atlantic.

One thing Joe Junior had determined: to keep his memories and his understanding of the war unpolluted by his father's version of events. Joe had talked to GIs who had driven into Dachau. He was horror-stricken by what he'd heard. Utterly nauseated. – the millions who had perished in the death camps. Five million Jews. Some said six million. Joe Senior dismissed the notion out of hand. It was pointless discussing the issue. His father would bellow that the 'Limey bastards' had given the Jews Palestine. Joe had learned to keep quiet, refusing to acknowledge what had been confided to him by Hauptmann Eigner in the initial stages of his interrogation. Joe felt contempt towards his father, who swelled up with pride when discussing the Marshall Plan. Politics was a dirty business and Joe Senior always had his snout in some rancid trough. The Marshall Plan and the occupation of Berlin meant nothing to Joe. He had followed the Nuremberg trials but knew in his heart that nothing had really been resolved. He had seen the news-reel footage of girls with shorn heads being jostled to their fate along the streets of Paris. He had received first-hand accounts of pits full of bodies outside villages and of minor officials strung up from lamp posts in Italy. Had the bastards who had tortured Will or himself ever been brought to book? Had the swine who had launched the V-1 that took Jane and Liz away from them ever been punished?

Joe's strategy was to hold his peace and nurture a few contacts in the State Department. The US had some interesting policies related to securing oil supplies from the Middle East. The plan, he had recently learned, was to 'get our guy into power in Persia.'

Yes. That was the political future, Joe had decided. There was a shaken, sick world out there waiting to be healed. Joe Kennedy Senior's days of influence were numbered. All Joe had to do was bide his time.

'No, seriously. You've gotta have an angle.'

'Horseshit.' Joe Senior brought his fist down heavily, rattling the coffee cups.

'Will you just listen to me, Pop,' Bobby pleaded.

Joe looked across the table at his younger brother. Bobby seemed to be talking about flowers. Joe frowned – something stirred uneasily deep down in his brandy-fumed brain.

'Every State has a flower, right?'

Joe Senior and Jack nodded.

'So my brother here,' Bobby gestured to Joe 'learns all these state flowers off by heart…'

'So?' Joe Senior demanded aggressively. 'How the fuck does that get him elected? Tell me that, sonny.'

'So? So every time he's at some college graduation he tells the gal he's giving a prize she is as pretty as the state flower, geddit? It will wow them, Pop.'

As the acrimony broke out once more around the table, Joe sensed a cold, heavy sensation somewhere between his heart and the pit of his belly. He felt like a pawn in a game of chess. He thought of the black and white snap-shot of his beloved Jane, hidden from his father's prying eyes upstairs in his old bedroom. Sellotaped to the back of the photo was the tiny vestige of the flower she had entrusted to his safe-keeping at their final meeting.

❧

'What d'ya say?' his father was bellowing at him. 'You think there's any electoral mileage in Bobby's flower crap? God help me, I think I've got fools for sons. Fools for sons...'

Joe felt weary. It was always like this. The bullying and the bickering. Every dinner ending in confrontation and humiliation for one or other of the Kennedy 'boys'. He felt relieved when he was joined by his mother on the steps outside the front door and grateful for the tenderness in her voice as she bade him goodnight.

Boston.
April, 1950

Will took a taxi uptown. The cab became entangled in the lunchtime crawl.

'Can't you cut loose? Is there another route?' Will demanded, a dollar bill in his hand.

'Relax, bud. I'll getcha there. Hot date, huh?'

Will scowled. The taxi driver, anxious to secure the tip, tossed a newspaper over to the back seat. 'Here, take a read of that.'

Will grunted his thanks and picked up the folded newspaper. Only an hour ago, he had been summoned to a meeting with Joe Kennedy Senior. Being a Director of the biggest insurance company in Boston, Joe Kennedy Senior had secured a well-paid job for Will, but there were strings attached. A discreet phone call to Joe Senior here, a document from the claims department there. As Will sat impatiently in the back of the cab, he suspected that another string was about to be jerked by his close friend's father.

The newspaper ran a photo story on pages four and five. Quite a spread. Boston socialites visit the new arts foundation. Joe Junior's new wife was featured. Will had been to the stag party but as there were over forty guys there including Joe's father, two priests and the top slice of male Boston society, there had been no girl-in-a-cake or anything like the shindig Will had anticipated. Indeed, Joe Junior had been drinking heavily throughout the day and seemed to avoid Will most of the evening. When they did find themselves alone, briefly, Will sensed that Joe resented any understanding or sympathy towards him. Not a word was spoken of the real things that bound them together – the war, the girls, their grief. It was a tense encounter leaving Will feeling confused and angry. He had left early.

Will had been promised an invitation to the actual wedding but the printed card had never arrived. Afterwards, profuse apologies had been forthcoming from Joe Senior's office who had managed the entire event, but Will had guessed the truth behind their excuses. Will returned to the newspaper. The caption repeated the well-worn phrases about the alliance through marriage uniting Boston's two leading families. Leading industrialist my arse, Will thought to himself. Jeez, everyone knows that old crony of Joe Senior made his pile running moonshine during prohibition.

'There y'are.' The taxi had pulled up with a shudder.

Inside, beyond the blaze of polished brass name plates and the quartz stone steps, Will was directed to a luxurious elevator operated by a smartly uniformed young woman. She allowed her gaze to flicker with interest over Will as he asked for the top floor. As he left the elevator, he felt her watching him as he made his way along the thickly carpeted corridor, imagining her raising an eyebrow in 'What's a shmuck like you going to see the Big Man for?' speculation.

Joe Kennedy Senior got straight down to business. Will had only just relaxed into the deep leather chair when he heard the older man tell him that Jane was alive and living in England. Will had heard and understood the words spoken to him but he could not grasp their full meaning.

'What? You mean –'

The older man stood up, poured out two glasses of neat rye and passed one to Will. Will gulped his drink gratefully. Joe Kennedy repeated the words slowly and distinctly, then, rising from his chair once more, he refilled Will's glass and brought it to him. Will felt a comforting squeeze on his shoulder.

'Sorry to have to tell you, son, that Liz was, in fact, a casualty in that raid.'

Will felt the sudden surge of his old grief and anger rise up inside him.

'Not the only casualty, but the press report got a few details wrong. Understandable, I guess. Wartime and all that. But Jane survived. And I mean to … protect my son's interests. Follow me?'

Will did not. He looked up, slightly bewildered and still in a partial state of miserable shock.

'Jane's alive? But Joe's…'

'Married,' the older man growled.

Will looked up over the brim of the glass he was drinking and blinked. He felt suddenly stupid and at a loss for the right words.

'Married,' Joe senior repeated, 'and with the first kid on the way.'

'But when did you… Jane… I don't get it… don't get it at all…'

Joe Kennedy Senior waved Will's questions aside. With a decisive gesture, he strode over to Will and hugged him.

'This must be very difficult for you, son. Sure, sure, I understand. Just take your time. I know how much you think of my son… after all you went through together…'

'You want me to tell Joe, huh? Break it to him easy…'

'No, that's exactly what I don't want. Word of this must not reach his ears, understand?

'But…'

'No, you don't understand, do you? Let me tell you the whole story, son.'

In the next fifteen minutes, Will experienced an emotional roller-coaster ride, as Joe Kennedy Senior unfolded the events of late '44 and the first half of '45.

'For six months I had no idea how you and Joe were, or where you were or what shape you were in…' he shrugged.

'Then on top of all that this dame... I mean Jane... started writing me with questions about my son. Questions I couldn't answer. There was a complication, you see.'

'Her parents? Joe being a Catholic. Jane's pa was a minister...' Will ventured.

The older man shook his head dismissively. 'No, though all of that was bad news, I can tell you. No. You see, there was a child.'

'What?'

'Now do you understand me? Now do you see why I did what I did. Not knowing where Joe was or if he would ever return. Now this girl comes out of the woodwork with a love child. Joe, if he ever came back, would walk right into one hell of a mess. Illegitimacy, the whole damn GI bride syndrome. In-laws who had already shown her the door. For Christ's sake, don't you see? I had to protect Joe from all that... and his future. Mud sticks. With shit like that on him he'd never get off the runway politically.'

'So that's what it came down to, huh...' Will faltered, thinking of Joe's – or more probably Joe Senior's – political hopes being exploded.

'Now listen here and listen good, son. The whole deal cost me plenty. I mean plenty...'

Will shrugged awkwardly, wondering just how much it could have cost to buy Jane's silence.

'Goddamit, I don't mind the money I spent on the girl. I'm talking about me... my grandchild. The little boy is a Kennedy...' Here Joe Senior affected to break down, managing a dry sob or two for Will's benefit.

'Ah, shucks, I didn't mean... Gee, I'm sorry. Hearing all this has kinda left me all shook up...'

'I know, I know,' Joe Senior nodded. 'I'm sorry to hit you with all this but I need you to help me.'

'But you don't want me to talk to Joe?'

'No, not to Joe. To Jane.'

Will sat up in his chair, his mind spinning. Thoughts of writing difficult letters or making painful transatlantic phone calls dismayed him.

'Look at it this way. We've all suffered. But for Joe the loss is over. Now he is married and settled and with a future before him. Liz is at rest although I'm sure she is there in your heart and in your memories.'

Will lowered his head as if receiving a benediction. Joe Kennedy noted the younger man's response and grimaced.

'I took care of Jane from the very first. She got the best and I mean the best. And still received my support for years after. No. We're the sufferers in all of this, son. You lost Liz and you still haven't settled down with another girl. I understand. Does you great credit, son. Great credit. And me,' he added quickly. 'I lost a grandson.'

'Where is the boy now?'

Joe Kennedy shook his head. He tapped his heart. 'Still hurts, son. Still hurts. I've managed to get over it. Somehow. Best leave it all alone now, eh?'

The hell we do, Will thought grimly, but nodded out of compassion for the other's pain.

'But why do you want me to speak to Jane? Surely it's best to…?'

'Let sleeping dogs lie? Look at it from this angle. Joe got married a short while ago. What if the Limey press pick up on it and play the photo coverage. And he's going to be a Senator soon. They won't keep that or the Kennedy name out of their Times of London. Say she cottons on to the fact that Joe is back in business…'

'You're telling me she thinks he's dead?' Will broke in.

Joe Senior shrugged. 'I thought it the best way. Less complicated. Give the girl a fresh start.'

'Jeez, what a fuckin' mess…' Will muttered in angry consternation.

'Exactly. And the shit deepens if she gets a hold on Joe and breaks up his marriage or kills his career…'

'Jane wouldn't do that,' Will retorted hotly.

'No, no, I'm not saying that – she wouldn't. Not intentionally. But one whisper to the press boys and Joe's marriage and the rest are history. You get me? She wouldn't mean to but it would all fall apart so that's why I want you to get across over to England and have a little talk, all nice and friendly like, laying it down for her. Stay away from Joe. You with me, son? You'll find her in some place called Harrogate.'

'But what about the boy? Is he ever to be told the truth?'

'Truth would only hurt him. He's only known one ma and pa from the time he opened his eyes. Why smash up that family, Joe's marriage and everything just for some fuckin' version of the truth. Tell me. Do you want to bring all that misery into people's lives for some damn abstract you can't even wipe your arse with?'

Will did not answer. Will could not answer. His brain was reeling under the avalanche of information – facts that seemed to take new twists and turns every time Joe senior opened his mouth.

Out in the corridor, the pretty elevator operator saw the unprecedented sight of the Big Man shepherding his young visitor down along the corridor. Joe Kennedy had his arm around Will.

'You've taken all this like a real man, son. Give my secretary a call tomorrow afternoon. She'll have your plane tickets ready. Get over there as soon as you can and then report directly back to me. OK? I can't thank you enough for all the good you're about to do for... everyone.'

The older man pressed a fat wad of dollar bills into the younger man's hand. Will took the money and pocketed it with alacrity, in furtive shame.

Will stepped into the elevator after returning Joe Kennedy's affectionate hug. The door closed and the elevator slid quietly downwards. The young woman looked at Will through wide, wondering eyes.

Will sensed her interest. He turned to face her. She jerked her head back and stared straight into the oak panelled door.

'Sure could use a little company right now,' Will murmured.

The girl bridled and patted her hair.

'Fresh!'

'Oh, gee, honey, I'm sorry... I didn't mean... I guess I just felt like having someone to talk with... there's a quart of Bourbon somewhere in a bar out there waiting for me. Join me?'

'Lois,' she grinned, tapping the name badge on her breast. 'If it's talk you want and a quart of Bourbon to wash the words down, I'm your girl...'

Will, grinning, caught the interrogative note. He told her his name.

'Don't get off 'til five. Five-thirty's the best...'

'I'll square that at the desk going out. Get your hat and coat, honey... Lois.'

They found a bar within minutes and the barman found Will's quart of Bourbon, iced water and two glasses.

'OK, friend of the Big Man. Shoot.'

Will closed his eyes. The waves of nausea had been killed off by the first swallow of Bourbon and his newfound friend's encouraging smiles. He didn't know where to begin. Besides, he should be talking to Joe. No. he couldn't...mustn't do that. The tangled web Joe Kennedy Senior had spun earlier that afternoon seemed to close in around him, constricting both his brain and his heart.

'Cat got your tongue?'

Will opened his eyes. Staring into the young woman's inquisitive gaze, he felt a great weight lifting from his shoulders. With sudden clarity, he knew what he must do. He'd go to see Jane and square everything and save Joe and his new bride and the little boy –where ever he was right now – a whole heap of heartache.

Will raised his glass and chinked it against the other raised towards him.

THE HAMMER AND THE ANVIL

A beach, Florida.
The same afternoon.

A little under a hundred yards away the surf was breaking on the curve of hot, golden sand. Dexter O'Neill stood waist high in the water, his hands underneath the chest of the small boy who squealed excitedly in the waves.

'I gotcha, son. I gotcha.'

'Gee, Pop, don't let me go,' the little boy yelled.

Dexter O'Neill plucked the wriggling boy up out of the surf and hugged him tightly.

'Say, son, you know your old man ain't ever gonna let go of you because your poppa loves you *so* much.'

From her tartan rug on the beach, Mary O'Neill called out to the man and the boy romping in the sea.

'Hey, you guys. Coke?'

Dexter lowered the boy gently down into the shallows, steadied him, then 'raced' him onto the beach – allowing the boy to make landfall first.

'I win. I win.' The boy shrieked, delightedly.

Dexter, joining him on the hot sand, knelt down and whispered conspiratorially in the child's ear. Nodding agreement, the child squealed excitedly.

'Say, what are you two guys up to, huh?' Mary demanded, shading her eyes against the Florida sun. 'You coming in for a cold Coke?'

Man and boy loped up the beach, matching stride for stride. A few yards from Mary, they separated in a pincer-movement, and then suddenly swerved in upon her. They captured her sun-lotioned body, in its dry bathing dress, in a double embrace and soaked her with their wet bodies. She shrieked and struggled but they clung on until all three collapsed in happy laughter.

Dexter towelled himself dry while Mary threatened to mock-spank the boy. He pressed himself against her warmth as she towelled his head and arms.

'I've got corned beef, relish and tomato on rye or chicken…'

'Chicken,' both man and boy replied.

Dexter ruffled the boy's head. 'Sure is a chip of the old block,' he grinned.

'Don't drop it in the sand, Patrick,' Mary cautioned, passing the boy a chicken leg from the cool box and wrapping it in a red and white chequered cloth.

They all ate in happy silence.

Later, as Patrick stamped at the edge of the incoming tide, Mary and Dexter opened a bottle of root beer each. The bottles chinked as they made a toast.

'God Bless Uncle Joe Kennedy,' Mary murmured, gazing with affection at their little boy on the beach.

'Uncle Joe,' Dexter echoed.

IX

The White House.
27th October, 1962

The faces around the table were weary. Tired eyes struggled to focus on the latest intelligence updates. The air in the EX-COMM conference room was stale with yesterday's cigarette smoke and charged with frustrated anger. They all had facsimile copies of another letter from Khrushchev to read. President Kennedy gazed down along the table at the bowed heads before him. Hawk. Hawk. Dove. He made a silent tally of how things stood if they had to come to a considered or, God forbid, a sudden decision before noon. It would probably go with the hawks, he concluded grimly. As their President and Commander-in-Chief, he would have the final say. The deciding vote. Would it still go with the hawks after he himself had made up his mind?

McNamara cleared his throat as he looked up and rattled his sheet of paper.

'This guy's digging in. Means to make a stand. It's clear as daylight, Mr President. Khrushchev won't back down now.'

'Guess the guy's in too deep,' General Taylor added. 'Even a commie knows when he's in a hole.'

'Dangerous when in a corner,' Curtis LeMay grunted. 'Like a rattler. Nothing other for it but to strike.'

The mood around much of the rest of the table was expressed in similar terms.

'Could be they've got a gun in his back. Khrushchev is only the Politburo's stooge. It's the hard-liners we are really dealing with here, gentlemen. The nameless, faceless wheels that turn the Party machine. Maybe these are his words, but they will be the Politburo's sentiments.'

As Joe raised his head up to respond to George Ball, several voices murmured their agreement.

'You may well be right,' Joe nodded. 'Either way, it's the same. We've got to respond to this letter.' His voice hardened. 'And when we do…'

'Why respond?' Bobby broke in. 'Must we? It's their mess,' he reasoned. 'Let them sweat as they figure a way out for themselves.'

Bundy, sighing, shook his head. His avuncular voice spoke softly, as if patiently sharing wisdom with a fractious subordinate. 'Like the President says, we've got to respond to this letter. Not to do so allows them a certain psychological advantage and leaves us looking weak and indecisive. We must retain the high ground so that we can tighten the diplomatic screw.'

'Screw the psychological advantage,' Taylor thundered. 'I say it's time we either pissed or got off the pot. Am I right, Mr President?'

It was a direct challenge. Bobby looked anxiously across the table at his brother.

Joe merely smiled and nodded back to the belligerent General. 'I believe I'm with you there, Max. I think we've got the weaponry to piss right in their eye.'

Bobby paled. 'For Christ's sake, Joe…'

The President ignored this interjection, and turned to Bundy. 'Yeh?'

'Forgive me, Mr President, but am I to understand that you are in the process of setting up a framework within which the option of first strike is conceded as being viable?'

'What did he say?' General Taylor growled. 'For fuck's sake talk plain English, can't you, Bundy? You're not with your slippery State Department faggots now!'

Taylor's derisive words caused Bundy to wince and flush angrily. It was McNamara who spoke next, breaking protocol as the floor had been with Bundy before Taylor had pulled the rug from under him.

'First strike is an all or nothing option, Mr President. They'll sure as hell retaliate. Not by choice but by compulsion. And,' his voice rose sternly as others began to interrupt him, 'I can assure you that history will deem it our fault and responsibility. A pre-emptive strike on Cuba would be the same as putting our signature to starting the Third World War.'

'Horse shit!'

'Who said anything about a pre-emptive strike on Cuba?'

Every face around the EX-COMM table stared directly at the President in response to these words.

'I thought you said...' Maxwell Taylor remonstrated.

Bundy spread his hands out wide. 'But you indicated...'

'This,' the president gestured, tapping his facsimile of Khrushchev's letter with angrily drumming fingertips, 'is their way of laying down the gauntlet. It is their opportunity as they see it to pull out a couple of the thorns we've pushed into the bear's paw. Thorns like our bases in Britain and Turkey. Then there is Radio Free Europe beaming into the Soviet bloc satellite states... Poland and Hungary. They hate our U-2 capacity to watch their every move and our listening stations monitoring all their radio traffic. Above all, they fear our nuclear subs prowling under the ice-caps and our underground silo system stacked with ICBMs that could raze them down to rubble from Moscow to Minsk. But I say no deal. No concessions. I want those rockets out of Cuba, period. They have thrown down the gauntlet...' he tapped Khrushchev's letter again '... if I choose to pick it up, I won't be going after Cuba. Khrushchev and his thugs aren't holed-up in Havana.'

The hawks around the table tensed. The sweat of their excitement glistened in the neon light.

'All I am saying, gentlemen, is that if I decide to strike the Soviet system I shall strike hard and I shall strike fast, but most of all, I shall strike them right in the heart.'

The few seconds of stunned silence which greeted these words were shattered by the cacophony of EX-COMM voicing either dismay or delight.

George Ball's voice rose up above the tumult. 'As your Under-Secretary of State, Mr President, I most strongly advise you to...'

Air Force General Curtis LeMay was arranging coffee cups out of their saucers across the smooth wooden surface.

'We've got airborne capability here, in Spain, and here, in the UK. And if we go after Peking, there's Diego Garcia…'

'*Are you serious*? Admiral Staffort gasped. 'Moscow *and* Peking?'

'Damn fine thinking, LeMay! Take out the commie bastards red and yellow…'

'For God's sake, gentlemen,' Robert McNamara pleaded. 'Mr President… please.'

'Say, Admiral. Your subs under the polar ice-cap. They all primed up and ready to go?' LeMay demanded.

Admiral Staffort's voice was primly measured in response. 'When we raised the stakes to DEFCON 2, I had two submarines with nuclear ICBM capability stationed just off the Greenland shelf in accordance with agree…'

Bobby reached across and touched his brother's arm. 'Joe!' he hissed.

The President withdrew his arm from his brother's reach.

'OK, OK Gentlemen. Gentlemen.'

EX-COMM came to order.

'What were my words… my *precise* words… a few moments ago?'

'Strike hard and strike fast,' Admiral Staffort snapped.

'Straight to the heart,' Curtis LeMay enthused.

'Shoot! Are we gonna go after Moscow *and* Peking?' Maxwell Taylor rubbed his hands together in brisk anticipation.

'You said "*If*" Mr President,' chimed McGeorge Bundy and Robert McNamara in unison.

Bobby's face broke into a relieved grin as he saw his brother nodding in response.

'Precisely. And I repeat, for the benefit of those who think it'll be raining hellfire and brimstone on Moscow tonight, that important little word. If.'

'Oh, Christ! Are we on or not?' a voice moaned.

'We will respond to this letter, and it will be a tough response. I don't care who is in control over there. Khrushchev or his goons, it doesn't matter a damn. What concerns me most immediately is that we speak to Havana. What I want is for you two,' he nodded towards his brother Bobby and then across the table at General Taylor, 'to hook up with the Soviet Field Commander... this general they've got here. Jesus, it's only ninety goddam miles away. A couple of dimes would cover it long distance.' Joe's exasperation was evident.

'We'll get a field-radio phone connected within the hour,' Bobby said soothingly.

'Sure thing. I'll get my boys onto it straight away,' General Taylor snapped, unwilling to be outdone.

'And have the CIA boys got us any more information on this guy, yet? I need to be fully briefed,' Joe barked, the strain and tiredness wiping out his usual calm. 'Military intelligence got anything? Photographs?'

'Sweet FA,' a voice replied gloomily.

'My God,' Joe Kennedy fumed. 'As soon as we're out of this fuckin' mess I'm gonna go through every goddam department root and branch. There's gonna be one helluva shake-up, that I promise you. We've been caught in the woods with nowhere to shit, on this, and I'm sure as hell gonna make certain it'll never happen again. OK. Enough. This meeting is now suspended and will resume at noon.'

May, 1950.
London, UK.

The bottled Bass had failed to take the taste of dust out of Will's mouth. Grimacing at the warm beer, Will had left his drink unfinished in the desultory railway station buffet and boarded the train for Harrogate glad to leave London's post-war disrepair behind him.

The carriage lurched as the train rattled over the points. Will's nose wrinkled at the smell of stale cigarette smoke and disinfectant. As the train picked up speed through the suburbs, he glimpsed the old wounds of the bomb damage that still scarred the rows of grey houses. His throat tightened and tears scalded his eyes at the memory of Liz.

Out in the open countryside, Will still found the size of the small fields surprising, just as he had done when flying over them six years ago. How the hell did these guys ever make a dollar farming this way?

London, just an overnight stay in a Paddington hotel, had been hell. Still injured men about – some limbless or blind – and a surprising amount of bricks and masonry where shops and offices, schools and churches had once stood proud, re-building slowly underway. The food had been grim. Will shuddered, remembering his breakfast, his coffee that morning undrinkable.

Lulled by the motion of the train, Will began to doze. He had troubled dreams until he was jolted awake, his mouth tasting sour and his heart heavy with sadness, as the train squealed to a halt in a cloud of steam. Doors slammed and whistles shrilled. Will gathered himself together and steeled himself for the ordeal ahead.

The information supplied by Joe Senior to Will was out of date. Exactly four days out of date. The Headmistress of the private school in Harrogate, where Jane had been teaching English for the last few years, told Will that Jane had returned to Cambridge to take up a Junior Lectureship earlier that week.

He just caught the York to London train at Harrogate and when he surrendered his ticket was advised that he would have to change at Peterborough for Cambridge. It was a slow train, stopping at almost every station. Will grew impatient – then anxious. He hoped to intercept Jane and break things to her gently, knowing that if she found out the truth by herself it would cause her a great deal of misery.

At last his train brought him to Cambridge, and from the station a taxi delivered him to her college. A helpful college porter smiled at Will indulgently and told him that he had just missed her. She had asked for directions to the war graves as the porter had pumped up her bicycle tyre.

He found her at the Madingley War Cemetery. It had just stopped raining. Will walked slowly along the wet path, still groggy from the transatlantic flight and the fretful train journeys. Bright sunshine sparkled on the wet leaves of the dripping laurels. He had no idea where he would find her in the maze of graves, but turning right down another length of pathway he saw Jane a few yards ahead.

Dressed in a drab raincoat and with a head-scarf tightly knotted against the inclement weather, she was standing with her back to him as he approached. He paused, a few feet away, and called out her name gently, or as gently as his gruff and emotional voice would allow, so as not to alarm her.

Jane turned around swiftly. Her eyes widened and her mouth opened in silent astonishment. It seemed to Will that she stepped, almost staggered, back a pace in her utter bewilderment and blanched.

'Will?'

He spread his hands out and shrugged. The tears in his eyes made the image of her blurred.

'Will?' Her voice quavered, full of doubt. 'I don't understand… I thought you were…'

Will retreated in his mind from the raw emotions of the moment in a rage of hatred for Joe Kennedy Senior. The deception – above all, the cunning and the calculation behind those painful lies which had greeted both Will and Joe Junior on their return from the war. His hatred for Joe's father now congealed as a frozen lump of bitter resentment that he knew would remain with him for the rest of his life. Swallowing painfully, Will braced himself for the purpose of his visit. A distasteful mission which he could not abort.

She took an uncertain step towards him. They were a foot apart – then in each others embrace after colliding softly, Will's grip on her, tentative and uncertain, her grip on him fierce with tearful delight. He swallowed hard as he felt her, sobbing uncontrollably, bury her face into his coat.

After several seconds of silence broken only by Jane's gulping sobs, she raised her tear-stained face from his chest and, eyes sparkling, smiled tentatively.

'It's a miracle. Simply a miracle,' she whispered, her voice trailing off hoarsely.

Will squeezed her tightly but remained silent, wondering what his first words to her would be.

'Joe made it through with me,' he heard himself murmuring.

Jane stepped back, a piercing cry escaping her lips. 'Joe? Joe is alive?'

Relieved at having broken his silence, Will nodded sternly.

'Alive? You both survived? But I don't understand, I simply don't understand. I was told…'

'We were all told… things, honey. By the same…' Will stopped abruptly, avoiding the word liar.

'Joe's father. He wrote to me. And then when we met he told me that you had both…' she faltered.

Will gulped and held Jane tightly. Will's mind went swiftly to Joe Junior. He was not ready, yet. 'You say Joe's pa wrote you?'

Jane sighed. 'Yes. I wrote to him when there was no word of either of you. I was… I was carrying Joe's baby. His father met me in London, and a little after that he wrote to me. He arranged for the baby to be adopted. He thought it would be for the best, because Joe was dead.'

Will grew angry as he heard her simple account of Joe Senior's complex manipulations.

'Joe survived. He's…'

'Why isn't he here? Where is he? Is he coming?'

'No. He's in the States.'

'Why? Is he ill? Tell me, Will! Is he happy? Tell me everything! What happened after you took off from Fersfield…'

'Whoa! Take it easy, honey. Gimme a chance and I'll do my best…'

They walked haltingly side by side, sometimes turning to each other, sometimes looking away, along the pathways criss-crossing the maze of pale grave stones and wooden crosses. At first, Will spoke hesitantly, but Jane was by turns eager, sympathetic and angry. As they walked he gently shared his understanding of events.

Jane listened intently. When he explained about their return from captivity, she demanded precise details.

'When we landed, Joe's old man broke the news. About you both being killed in the...'

'But he knew I was alive!' Jane shouted.

Will put a protective arm around her. 'Joe's old man deals in lies. Every card comes from the bottom of the pack, honey. Don't you see? He told Joe you were dead. Joe goes back to the States and so his old man gets his way – no English girl with a baby to foul up his son's career. He tells you Joe's dead, so you give up your child. He gives you an allowance to salve his conscience. It was all about Joe's political future. Don't you see? He's like a damned evil spider in the centre of a web...'

'Puppet-master,' Jane snapped. 'I can't believe he would lie to me like that...' Her voice rose angrily as she began to realize the full extent of Joe Kennedy Senior's duplicity. 'Lie to Joe and... cheat us of each other. The bloody swine.'

'It ain't over, honey.'

Jane looked up tearfully.

'It's like this,' Will began, answering her unspoken question.

'No more. I can't bear any more. My baby...' Jane sobbed uncontrollably.

Will hugged her to his chest, patting her reassuringly.

'Patrick is fine! He's a great kid. Fine fellah. Chip off the old block.'

Wiping tears from her face, Jane quizzed him eagerly for news of her son. Will replied, comforting her with a tender account of Patrick's childhood, loving adoptive parents and happy confidence.

'Just like Joe,' he concluded.

'Just like Joe,' Jane echoed, smiling through her tears.

'But the deal stands,' Will cautioned.

'The deal?'

'Joe knows nothing of you. Your being alive. Or of the baby. Of Patrick. His pa kept all that strictly under wraps.'

Jane held her head in her hands as if dizzy. 'I don't understand any of this, Will. You mean Joe still doesn't know about Patrick!'

'Hasn't got the least idea. Never had, I guess, and never will have, if his pa has any say in it. And he's got a kid on the way.'

Jane stiffened. 'What do you mean?'

'Shit,' Will muttered.

'Tell me, Will. I need to know!'

Will reluctantly told her about the marriage of political convenience arranged between Joe and the daughter of a powerful ally. He said, in simple terms, that it was a functional, loveless union on both sides, with Joe burying himself in his career.

Jane resisted Will's attempts to console her. As he stretched out his comforting arms, she stepped back and pushed him away. Blinded by her tears, she turned and started to run down the pathway, but was brought to an ungainly halt by the collapse of the heel of her left shoe. Will just managed to catch up and support her by the elbow as she swayed and almost collapsed.

'Say, honey, why don't you let me get you a taxi and take you home, huh?'

She allowed him to keep his supporting arm around her as she staggered alongside him. 'Alright,' she murmured, adding mechanically, 'but please don't call me honey!'

They stopped and, turning to look into each other's eyes, smiled bleakly at the memory of their first encounter at the wire mesh perimeter fence at the Fersfield air base all those summers ago. In response to her repeated questioning, he recounted everything that he and Joe had experienced from the commencement of their mission to their eventual liberation – omitting only the darkest moments they had endured.

They met the following evening in the ADC Theatre in Cambridge. Arriving, as planned, just in time for curtain-up, they found themselves enjoying the privacy of the deserted 'crush' bar. Will sipped a blended whiskey – there was no ice available – while Jane nursed her schooner of pale sherry. A shyness settled over them, and they spoke with constraint of post-war shortages and the painfully slow recovery in the UK compared to the boom in America. Nothing intimate was mentioned and Will began to feel tension building up inside him. Gradually, the emptiness around them conspired to draw them together. Leaning across the table, Will's fingertip brushed her wrist. It was like an electric shock. Will suffered a sudden alarm as he realised he had feelings – strong feelings – for the beautiful young woman sitting opposite him in the hushed gloom of the theatre bar. As he struggled to cope with this new complication, Jane drew closer and almost at once they were revisiting the words and feelings – and for Jane, the tears – of yesterday.

'He told me that you and Liz –'

She held his hands and drew him closer for a comforting kiss on the cheek. 'Liz was killed,' she said softly.

Will nodded, remembering with bitter irony the 'faked' newspaper article Joe Senior had shown him.

Jane continued, comforting Will and telling him of the incident, mechanically recounting the facts and circumstances. How Liz had gone down to visit her aunt. The direct hit on the house in North London. Will closed his eyes, picturing once more the piles of rubble glimpsed through the train carriage window.

'She wouldn't have felt a thing,' Will muttered. 'Thank God for that at least.'

'She loved you dearly, William Ford. Thank God for that.'

They spoke of Liz affectionately, both loyal to their memories of the big-hearted, brash, red-headed girl, lover to one, best friend to the other.

Jane shook her head as if trying to clear her mind from its confusion. 'But why?'

Will shrugged. 'Why what?'

'Why are you here? Why? Why now? What made you...?'

Reddening slightly in shame, Will explained how he had been summoned by Joe Senior and required to come to England to see Jane – to protect Joe Junior's burgeoning political career.

'I guess he's determined that you and Joe should never see each other again. He sent me over to sort of... warn you off.'

'Warn me off?'

'Easy, honey. It's just that with Joe going up and up the greasy pole, maybe soon he'll be spread across your newspapers over here and maybe Joe Senior thought you'd get wise...'

Joe Kennedy Senior's duplicity and manipulative lying was examined from every possible angle: Jane repeatedly seeking clarification as if her mind was unequal to the task of taking in the enormity of events; Will confirming the facts in an even, colourless tone which masked his anger and disgust.

Retreating from the discomfort his attraction to Jane caused him, he sat and listened as she struggled to understand Joe Senior's callousness – and was jolted into an awareness that Jane was still madly in love with his dearest friend. When he was asked to describe Joe Junior's marriage again, Will was acutely aware that Jane nodded readily – all too readily – in response to Will's assurances that it was a marriage of political expediency and that he did not love his wife.

They ordered another drink, sitting quietly, immersed in their own thoughts, until the waitress had served them. It was difficult to restart their conversation after her intervention. Will sat in gloomy silence, resenting his flickering flame of desire for Jane. He snuffed it out partially by wondering silently if he had not better get in touch with Joe Junior on his return to the States and tell him the truth. Everything – tell Joe of Jane's survival, the baby and her continuing love. The thought of doing so weighed heavily on Will, almost overwhelming him.

'Not even *he* could do that, surely!' Jane's protesting words broke into his thoughts.

'Huh?' Will managed, dragging himself back into her presence.

'I mean, actually showing fake newspaper clippings to you and Joe when you got back. What an absolute monster. He is truly Machiavellian.'

'Machia- what?'

'It's the Italian for lying, cheating, two-faced bastard.'

Will grinned briefly, slumping over his tepid whiskey and relaxing a little. Now it felt easier to talk.

'You still got the hots for him, eh?'

'If by 'hots' you imply that my affections are still engaged by a certain young American pilot, William Ford, I can only asseverate that you would not be misleading yourself in such perceptions.' There was a coy primness in her tone that excited Will.

'Say, honey, is that a yes or a no?' he bantered.

The interval arrived, filling the bar with theatre-goers noisily in pursuit of a drink. The mood around them lightened. Will suggested that they should move on.

'Is there any good food for a guy to eat hereabouts, maybe?'

Jane grimaced and shrugged sympathetically.

'Say, Joe used to tell me when we were holed up in prison camp together about a night he had fish with chips…'

'Fish and chips,' Jane corrected him absently, her mind returning immediately to a warm night in Norwich six summers ago.

The tension that had risen up between them, unvoiced but almost palpable, returned. As they walked along the pavement, self-consciously not touching, it was as if the shadow of Joe Junior walked between them. Even as he spoke in a distracted manner of his friendship with young Patrick – and the pleasure of taking him sailing – he knew he was saying the wrong thing. Jane's tone grew cold and resentful despite her eager desire for every possible tiny detail. Will cursed inwardly, only too aware that Joe Kennedy Senior's poison had risen up once more to blight everything it touched. Angry and irrational – through the guilt of his growing attraction to Jane and his discovery of her continuing love for his best buddy – he announced that he had decided not to eat, after all.

'But Will...' Jane murmured, her manner suddenly softening.

'Fact is, honey, I guess I'm kinda tired. The trip and all. And to be straight with you, I've no stomach for all of this. I sure didn't mean to upset you talking about Patrick... or Joe...'

'Don't be silly. It's certainly not your fault. None of it is. You've just been caught up in the web of deceit like the rest of us. Oh, for God's sake Will, don't just burst back into my life, drop bombshells, and then disappear again!' There was a rising note of panic in her voice.

Will stood still, appalled at his own selfishness. Relenting, he reached out to catch and hold her hand. 'Gee, I'm a mutt. Sorry, honey... whoops, sorry! I was feeling all riled and fired up at the thought of Joe's pa and what really matters is...'

'What really matters is that from this moment we take control of everything. You, me... Joe.'

'And you and Joe?' Will broke in gently. 'You think there's any future for you there, maybe?'

Jane remained silent. Will squeezed her hand.

'And Patrick?' he murmured softly, drawing her closer to him. 'You think Joe should know?'

Jane remained silent. At first she nodded her head slowly then quickly shook it negatively. She sighed. Will did not break the silence.

Burying her face into his chest, she started to weep.

Will slept fitfully that night. He was awake and brooding an hour before a cup of warm tea was brought in on a tray. Will had specifically asked for early morning coffee. He left it untasted, and stretched out on his bed, smoking one cigarette after another, as he tried to straighten out his feelings. He was only sure of one set of unalterable emotions: the dark ones he felt towards Joe Kennedy Senior. When he forced his mind to reflect on Jane, Joe and Patrick, he prickled with the discomfort of anxiety and shame.

Washed, shaved and resolute, he called Jane on the telephone. After reassuring her that he would not precipitate a crisis on his return to the States – and that he would keep an eye on both Patrick and his father, Joe, for her – he lied.

'Fact is, honey, he's calling the shots. He booked the return ticket and I've gotta get back.'

'Still the puppet-master, isn't he.' Jane's voice held bitterness in it.

Will winced under her contempt, even though her venom was directed at Joe Senior.

'Sorry,' she muttered. 'It's all been a great shock.'

'For me too!' Will protested lamely – instantly regretting his childish response.

Jane laughed softly. 'We should start a club. The Joe Kennedy Senior Puppets.'

Tears stung Will's eyes as he gripped the receiver tightly. His voice was husky as, renewing uncertain promises, he steeled himself to say goodbye.

'I'll write you.'

'Yes. Do, please. Write to me.'

'I'll keep in touch.'

'Promise?'

'I swear.'

Will was as good as his word. After an initial spate of letters between them in which both he and Jane re-examined and resolved their decision not to reveal the fact of Jane or Patrick's existence to Joe Junior, their correspondence settled into a pattern of one letter a year and an exchange of Christmas cards for the next decade. In 1954 Will learned that Jane had been appointed as a Junior Fellow at her Cambridge college and had formed an attachment to a donnish bachelor who lectured on Mesopotamian pottery. Three years later, Will realised that this relationship had evolved into a mutual intellectual respect. He himself – in response to Jane's gentle teasing – recorded the passage of the years as if he were a Trappist monk, carefully omitting to inform her of his occasional amorous adventures.

Joe Junior's progress was acknowledged by them both, and Will faithfully recorded Patrick's success at school and prowess at sports. Not once, after their initial exchanges, did either Will or Jane make any reference to Joseph Kennedy Senior.

The President's Private Office,
The White House.
28th October, 1962 09.45 am

The president sat in his shirt sleeves next to five similarly casually dressed men around the small table. Bobby was passing the coffee jug across to McNamara. Sorensen was arguing a point with Bundy while Ball reread the Krushchev letters.

Joe Kennedy called the meeting to order.

'We could ignore the last letter, put it on hold, and only respond to the previous one,' Sorensen suggested.

Joe rejected the idea firmly. 'No. We'll let the bastards sweat... you with me?'

Ball tapped the letter in question thoughtfully and nodded.

Sorensen was enthusiastic. 'Dammit, Mr President, that's exactly how you should proceed. Don't let them force your hand.'

McNamara murmured that the stakes had been raised too high, too quickly, by these communications. 'Give you more room to manoeuvre. What were you thinking of offering them?'

Bobby looked across at his brother anxiously. 'Gonna leak it to our Press boys or keep it under wraps?'

Joe smiled. 'I see it this way. We'll go public with the response, twelve hours after they've received it. Put the squeeze on them.'

'Neat work, Sir,' Bundy approved.

Joe continued. 'We'll offer a guaranteed hands-off policy on Cuba. No incursions, no more pressure – we'll even lift the blockade with immediate effect – in return for the withdrawal of all nuclear capability from Cuban territory.'

Sorensen turned to Bundy and Ball. They nodded.

'Great idea, Joe. You give them a face saving option like that and they're sure to grab it with both hands,' Bobby broke in, slapping his brother on the back.

'Go easy on the celebrations,' McNamara cautioned. 'Damned Politburo's full of thugs. Khrushchev might buy it but who knows how long he's got after this foul-up? We might be looking down the barrel of an entirely different gun next week. We need to show a strong and united front. Any show of irresolution or appeasement is red meat to a hungry bear.'

'Sure thing, but I think it is worth pulling back from the very edge. Just the once. If it fails, it fails,' Bobby replied. His tone managed to conceal his growing concern for – and sense of distance from – his brother. The president, increasingly perceived as something of a maverick, risked becoming isolated.

'Are we all agreed, then?' Joe demanded, the weariness sounding more like impatience.

The other five men around the table signalled their agreement.

Joe's tone grew crisp and incisive. 'Bobby, get our response down the line as soon as you can.'

'You gonna send it through the back-channel? Do you trust Dobrynin?' Sorensen's voice held a note of anxiety.

Before Bobby could reply, the President interrupted in a soft tone. 'If he fouls up or they pretend it never arrived, we've lost nothing and gained time. Either way, we'll know which way to move.'

'Speaking of moving, Mr President, the CIA have got their butts into gear and come up with some fresh dope on the Soviet's guy in Cuba –'

'What have we got?' Joe demanded.

'Well, for starters,' Sorensen continued, peering through his glasses down at a sheet of paper in front of him, 'he's a seasoned and much decorated veteran of World War II. A tough soldier, apparently. A top general, with political clout. Name something like Antanov – couldn't quite make it out… they're still working on it.'

'Molatov, more like!' McNamara snapped, testily.

Joe clenched and unclenched his fists. He took a deep breath and placed his hands palms down on the polished surface of the table. 'Bobby?'

Bobby, engrossed in writing, looked up. 'Huh?'

'How are we doing with that radio-link up with Havana?'

'General Taylor has it in hand –'

'Well tell General fucking Maxwell Taylor I want it in *my* hand before noon!'

The Kennedy family home,
Massachusetts
13th August, 1962

The young maid paused at the top of the stairs and tightened her grip on the breakfast tray she was carrying. Juice, coffee and scrambled eggs – the master of the house had been out of sorts recently and had taken to starting the day with breakfast in bed. The maid disliked going in to the old man's bedroom. Sure, he never actually touched her, but she could feel his half-lidded gaze devouring her uniformed curves. To her immense relief, a senior maid, ramrod-backed and grey-haired, took the tray from her half way along the carpeted landing and carried it to the door. The junior maid stepped lightly down the staircase – her feet suddenly rooted to the spot as she heard a sharp cry of alarm. Indecisive, she turned, twisting her face up towards the landing above. Another cry for help brought her running back up the stairs and along the corridor to the open door of the old man's room. Through it, she saw that the breakfast tray had been deposited hurriedly on the bedroom floor. Kneeling down beside it, her colleague was cradling the head of Joseph Kennedy Senior, his pale face – tongue protruding obscenely – lolling in her cupped hands.

Bobby broke the news to Joe Junior over the phone later that morning.

'He's bad, Joe. They say he might not pull through. Do you think we…?'

'I think we better run through that statement on Civil Rights that Sorensen cooked up for the press boys. We sure as hell need to hold the line!'

'We could cancel, Joe. Maybe we should…'

'No! We need to get this done first.'

The following day the three oldest brothers arrived separately (Teddy wired that he could not join them until that evening) and found themselves drinking rye on the rocks as a way of avoiding having to speak. Bobby was almost tearful, moving about the room and quite unable to sit down for more than a minute. He picked things up and put them down again without really looking at them.

'For fuck's sake keep still,' Jack barked, his face ashen with his own pain. 'Me, I have to walk about. This goddam back never gives me a minute's peace.'

'Sorry, Jack,' Bobby murmured.

Jack, ignoring his younger brother, turned to Joe.

'What's the latest? Goddamn doctors! They don't give away much.'

Joe shrugged. His voice was tired. Tired and distracted. 'No change.'

'That's it then. Let's do it.'

Joe emptied his glass, winced and nodded.

'Hey, guys, are you really sure about this? Jeez, if the old man recovers he'll go ballistic when he finds out –'

Joe and Jack did not even turn to reply to Bobby's nervous interruption. He followed them through the house and into their father's study.

'The day-to-day routine is all in hand. His post has been opened and sorted. Nothing urgent.'

'Thanks, Jack.'

'No sweat. You sure got your hands full right now.'

'So what now, guys?' Bobby asked uncertainly, uncomfortably conscious of being the younger brother – and being lower in the pecking order in the family hierarchy.

Joe unpocketed a small silver key. 'Time we had a look at the private stuff. There's a deed box we should investigate…'

'Christ, Joe, where's that been hiding all this time?' Bobby demanded.

Joe motioned to him to give him a hand hoisting the heavy deed box out of the safe and up onto the desk.

'Now think about this, the two of you. What's Pop gonna say when he finds out that we…'

'Came by to wipe up any shit he may be leaving for us to skid on? You know just how slippery the old devil was …is! Christ knows what we might find in here.'

'Joe's right, Bobby. Best *we* deal with things, keep them in the family. God knows what damage a loose-tongued lawyer would do with any of Pop's little secrets.'

Joe grunted softly as, turning the key with a soft, hollow click, he raised the lid of the deed box.

They began to extract every document, one by one, submitting each to a close and careful scrutiny.

'What kinda whore uses scent like that?' Jack growled, holding a bundle of private letters tied together with a pink ribbon.

Joe snatched the bundle and – without even checking the signature – tossed them aside angrily. 'Whore's the word.'

The deed-box was half empty, the desk top littered with the tell-tale debris of shady financial deals, rogue political pacts and the darker, intimate secrets of their father's devious affairs.

'What the hell...?' Joe wondered aloud. He was gazing down in puzzlement at an envelope which bore his own handwriting.

'What you got?' Jack grimaced. 'Someone had the nerve to put the squeeze on the old man?'

Bobby whistled.

Joe grew pale with anger as he realised that it was the letter he had written to Jane's parents back in 1945. He folded it carefully and slipped it into his pocket. He picked up another letter and examined its contents.

'Now what? Get all tangled with a dame as tough as him but smarter, eh?' Jack chuckled sardonically.

Bobby's voice was anxious. 'Anyone we know? Could they make trouble?'

'I don't understand... gimme a minute.' Joe waved Bobby away and, sitting in his father's chair at the desk, spread some financial records out before him and scanned them intently.

'Monthly payments. Not much, but regular.'

'Classic blackmail. Jeez, you think we'll need the FBI in on this, Joe?'

'How long?' Bobby asked.

Joe studied the paperwork carefully. 'Christ, almost seventeen years. Maybe a month or two more. But get this. These payments were made to O'Neill.'

Jack looked blank.

'What are you saying, Joe?' Bobby almost howled. 'Dexter? You mean Dexter and Mary? But...'

'Kinda keeps it in the family,' Jack observed drily. 'What kinda dope d'you think he has on the old man? Oh, shit. Do you think he... pop and Mary?'

'Wait,' Joe snapped, 'there's more. Look. From about the same time – seventeen years ago. Small but regular amounts going into an account in Cambridge.'

'Who the hell did Pop know up-state? Some campus girl; an intern?'

'Wait a minute. This account is in Cambridge goddam England,' Jack cried.

Joe's jaw-line tightened, his face was almost white, his mind groping towards a town three thousand miles away.

'Joe?' Bobby repeated his question but received no response.

'What the hell has the old man been up to?' Jack demanded.

Joe's hands tightened into angrily clenched fists.

'Cambridge, England,' he muttered gruffly.

Bobby, joining his two brothers at the desk, started to root about in the bottom of the deed box. Seconds later, he swore softly. 'Oh, shit. Look at this… and this… you guys. Pop got in over his head way back. Must have had a kid by some dame. Look. Adoption papers…'

'Holy shit,' was all Jack could manage.

Joe seemed to have retreated into a trance.

'Here it is,' Jack shouted, examining the documents he had snatched from Bobby's hand. 'It all ties in. The O'Neills. There was a kid. A boy. A boy called Patrick. And the date. Get a load of that. May 1945.'

Joe rose up abruptly. The chair tumbled over behind him. 'Give me that,' he snapped.

Jack handed the papers over into Joe's trembling hand.

'Get out. Both of you. Now.'

'Hey, you might be the fuckin' president but I've as much right to see…'

'Joe?' Bobby asked anxiously. 'What is it, Joe? What the hell's the matter with you?'

Joe wheeled away from the desk and strode out of the room, clutching the recently exhumed documents in a shaking fist.

Just over an hour later, Joe sat restlessly in a small room set aside for family visitors, adjacent to the intensive care nursing ward in the specialist stroke clinic. Two doctors had already entered the room, sat down next to the president, and in hushed, respectful tones, outlined his father's bleak prognosis as euphemistically as the harsh clinical reality allowed. On the other side of the door, an armed guard kept the Press men and excited, curious nurses at bay.

After a brief wait, he was ushered through the ward, past curtained-off bed-bays, some with bleeping machines, and into a private room. There, with a guard detailed outside, he was left alone with his father.

Joe Kennedy Senior, slumped in a bed with the cot-sides raised, was dozing gently.

'Wake up, you old son of a bitch,' Joe hissed, conscious of the guard on the other side of the door despite his boiling fury.

Joe Senior opened one lizard eye. It widened imperceptibly, closed and then partially re-opened. The other remained shut.

'Wake up, you goddam bastard.' Joe had to restrain himself from grabbing the cot-side and rattling it violently.

His father's body twisted slightly in response to the abusive outburst, but remained slightly lop-sided. A trickle of saliva oozed from the corner of his closed lips.

'You've got one goddam good eye, you bastard. Look at these!' Joe thrust the papers from the deed box under his father's nose. Was it his imagination or had the nostrils flared slightly in response?

'What you gotta say for yourself, eh? Nothing? Well I've sure got plenty.'

His father did not utter a single word – or even grunt – as Joe demanded to know, filling in the gaps himself, as outlined by the documentation. His mind swerved away from the very painful conclusions to be drawn from the payment orders, the adoption paperwork, the trail that led back directly to Jane. The questions he shouted were accusations – he was almost spitting his fury into the stricken old man's face.

'And what gives you the goddam right to go messing up people's lives, you evil old bastard. Huh? No, you can't answer that one, can you. Jesus Christ, if you weren't already in a fucking hospital bed I'd put you in one!'

As Joe started to cry – sobs of frustrated fury – the helpless body of his father seemed to squirm in the bed. The ooze of saliva from the corner of his mouth increased, leaving his chin wet with its shine.

Coughing and spluttering, Joe cleared his voice and approached his father once more, shaking the documents right under the old man's nose. Pushing his face up close, the young man's eyes were wide open and hot with his burning contempt. His father's one good eye darted away from his son's penetrating gaze. Joe Kennedy Senior grunted softly before exhaling laboriously in a low moan.

A nurse tapped on the door and entered. 'We heard raised voices. Is anything wrong?'

She advanced towards the bed. 'There now, we mustn't get ourselves all worked up, must we, hm?' she soothed, bending over the helpless old man. She turned her head around to Joe Junior. 'If you have any questions, Mr President, we'll be glad to answer them.'

'Does he know what I am saying to him?'

'Absolutely, Sir. It's just that he can't respond.'

'So every word I said went home?'

'I hope it gives you some consolation to know that we think he understood every word you said, Sir, yes.'

Joe grunted.

'How did you find him? Better than you expected?' she continued, wiping the old man's wet mouth with a tissue.

'Exactly as I expected.'

The president, feeling cheated and frustrated, walked out of the room. What had been that look in his father's open eye? Shame, or remorse? Joe Junior had the distressing notion that it had been somewhere nearer to contempt.

THE HAMMER AND THE ANVIL

15th August 1962

'Gee, Mom, is it Thanksgiving day already?'

Mary smiled and shook her head. 'You know it's not!'

'Then why all this for our usual tuna bake and cake?' Patrick continued, indicating the elegantly laid out dining table glinting with silverware.

Dexter joined them. He stood behind his dining chair, fingering the polished wood.

'Well tonight we are not having tuna bake,' Patrick's mother explained with a smile. 'I've got T-bone steak and home made apple pie with ice cream...'

'Gee, Mom!'

'Sit down, son. Your father and I want to have a little talk with you.'

Patrick flushed. 'You know, Uncle Will told me everything....I mean, he explained about girls and things last time we went out sailing... and we did human biology last semester...'

'I'm so glad Uncle Will talked to you about the facts of life, darling, though I think he might have said something to your father and me beforehand.'

Dexter coughed and took refuge in a sip of wine.

Patrick, unselfconsciously handsome and confident, suddenly looked concerned.

'Did Mrs Murray phone?'

'And why would Mrs Murray want to speak to me, hmm?'

Impetuously, Patrick launched his pre-emptive strike. 'We were only fooling around, honest Mom. We were just teasing the cheer leaders and one of them dropped her pom-pom so I picked it up and brought it to her... gee, I guess I shouldn't have gone into their locker room but it was full of steam so I didn't actually see anything so if Mrs Murray phones complaining about her daughter Becky it's OK Mom, honest...'

Dexter, about to punch Patrick's shoulder approvingly for penetrating the holy land of the cheer leaders' locker room, caught Mary's eye and, quelled, sipped another cautious mouthful of wine.

The steak was tender. Patrick ate wolfishly, but both Dexter and Mary merely picked at theirs.

They took turns, starting gently by breaking the news of Joe Kennedy Senior's massive stroke, then working round to telling Patrick that he was in fact adopted. Joe Kennedy's role in his adoption was carefully explained. Patrick cried softly before rising to kiss Mary and hug Dexter. They left the dining table, the meal unfinished, and gathered in the kitchen for mugs of coffee.

Patrick found himself reassuring Dexter and Mary as they struggled to console him. Nothing, he swore, would or could ever diminish the love he had and held for them both. They would always be his mother and father. Always.

'Especially when Mrs Murray comes on the warpath over Becky's pom-poms,' Mary O'Neill said archly.

Patrick blushed and grinned as Dexter ruffled the young boy's hair.

Then, inevitably, the curiosity won through. They had little to tell him – Joe Kennedy Senior had left them virtually nothing to share with their adopted son, now seventeen and eager to learn of his provenance.

'England?' he replied, disbelievingly. 'Gee! You mean I'm a sort of Limey!'

'Hell no!' Dexter grinned. 'Your... your father was an American pilot. Served with distinction and was decorated for valour, son.'

'Did he die or leave my... mom... Hey! Is she still alive?' Patrick flushed and averted his eyes shyly from Mary's loving gaze.

She gathered him into her embrace. 'It's OK. I understand. You can say 'mom'. I know you want to know and we will help you all we can but the truth is, darling, as we've told you, Joe Kennedy Senior fixed everything. Your mother was a very respectable young English woman from a good family and she... she was left with a baby. It happened quite a lot back then in the war. As Dexter says, your father was a brave man, a pilot. A man any son can think about with pride. You came to us as a tiny baby…'

Patrick hugged her. She kissed his bowed head.

'… and filled our world with love and happiness. We've thanked the good Lord for you ever since the day you arrived…'

'Except when you go chasing pom-poms and we get angry mothers on the phone,' Dexter grinned.

Man and boy exchanged friendly punches then hugged again.

'Uncle Will! Maybe he knows more. He was over there in the war. Flew missions. Gee, he might even have met my father, or known of him or knew someone who knew…'

Dexter stroked his chin thoughtfully. 'Maybe. Hm. Maybe so. It's a long shot, though. Still, no harm in it. He sure may have something to tell you.'

'Uncle Will has told you quite enough, young man,' Mary remarked with mock severity. 'Still,' her voice softened, 'it might be worth writing to him. Invite him down. The weather's going to hold. You could get a little sailing in.'

31st August, 1962.

Will sat in the darkness of his bedroom. The rain hadn't stopped all day. The air was dank and chilly. A bottle of rye, with the screw top undone, waited patiently for him. He had not yet poured out or tasted its contents. Next to the empty glass was a full ash tray.

Will stretched and sighed. Things were getting complicated. News of Joe Senior's severe stroke had come as a shock – but had led to unexpected difficulties. Over the last decade, Jane had written regularly – long tender letters. Will had read of her part-time lecturing post; the move to a simple cottage just outside the grounds of her college; the loss of her father and of the reunion with her mother. A Junior Fellowship at Homerton College and a flat of her very own overlooking the college quad and lawns.

Recently, there had been shy references to glimpses of Joe on the newsreels and television news. The letters had comforted Will but did little to lessen the burden Joe Kennedy Senior had placed on him. Joe Junior – for Christ's sake The President now – was a remote flickering image on the television screen: but always close to Will's heart. Will often consoled himself that he had been right to keep his secrets from Joe, such consolation coming from the fact that he had agreed with Jane that he would do so.

Later that evening, it was still raining steadily. The rye was almost finished. Will closed his eyes and sought escape in sleep, but rest would not come. Over the years he had trained himself to avoid the haunting memories and disturbing images distilled from the war years. Liz herself was just a sweet, melancholy remembrance. What kept Will awake was the knowledge that he had colluded in a huge and ugly deceit – the deceit perpetrated on Joe and Jane by Joe's evil old man. Now, he realized, he was at another cross-roads. With Joe Kennedy Senior out of play, was it time to get in touch with Jane once more? What about Joe? Christ! Will shuddered. Joe would have to be told everything now. And what the hell should he do about the kid, Patrick.

The phone by his bed jangled. Will ignored it. It did not stop. It'll stop after twenty chimes, Will thought, counting. Twenty six…twenty seven…it continued ringing.

Rye fuddled and close to exhaustion, Will stretched his hand out in the darkness and picked up the receiver.

A cool, female voice spoke, asking Will to identify himself. Will, bemused, obliged.

'Putting you through now, Mr President,' he heard the woman say.

X

1ˢᵗ September, 1962

After being waved through by the guard at the gates, Will pulled the Pontiac up in front of the Kennedy family home, the half-empty bottle of Jim Beam rolled in the seat beside him. It had been raining hard again, all morning. The wipers slapped across the windscreen noisily, their motion almost hypnotic. Will felt very tired. And not just tired – ever since the phone call the previous evening summoning him to a meeting with Joe Junior, he had felt uneasy. His breakfast of bourbon had not dulled the sense of foreboding weighing on his mind.

Will was shown to the library where he found Joe. The president of the United States of America was casually dressed and unshaven. There was no smile of greeting for Will. The rain was now driving against the long windows, sluicing the grey glass panes with a silvering blur. Joe was not drinking and did not offer one to Will who clearly had been. Joe frowned when Will asked for a large rye on the rocks. Joe's edginess was clear for Will to detect. It was in the rattle of the ice cubes thrown into the glass and again in the averted gaze as Joe disapprovingly presented Will with his drink.

Joe came straight to the point.

'You know about my father? Well, we had to go through his papers.'

'Papers?' Will echoed cautiously. Christ, he thought. Has the old man left a goddam paper trail.

'It was all there in fucking black and white. Adoption papers…'

Will paled and placed the glass of rye down on the table.

'Jane… Cambridge… Christ, Will. The dates… everything. I couldn't fucking believe it. Any of it. I mean… what the hell was going on back then?' Joe broke away and turned to the drinks tray. He poured himself a Scotch and tossed it down, neat. He spun round. 'That old bastard knew. He knew everything, Will. And fixed it up while we were stuck in Europe. Who knows?' Joe's voice rose angrily. 'Did he suggest an abortion? Would it have suited his book for Jane to get rid of my baby boy? Christ, Will. He lied. He got onto that goddam plane that brought us back and lied. Jane did not die. She had my child and my old man fixed it up so that no one would ever know and… say… is this getting through to you? Huh? Let me run it by you again. Jane did not die. She had a child… my child…'

Will snatched up his unfinished drink and drained off the glass in one greedy swallow.

He nodded, then wiped his lips with the back of his hand. 'I know…' he whispered.

Joe stood still then spread his arms out in appeal. 'You know?' he demanded, mystified. 'What do you know?' Joe was now sounding exasperated. 'How the hell can you know?'

Will froze, steeling himself for the imminent storm.

Joe's voice had tailed off. After a single curse that cracked out like a pistol shot he smashed his right fist down into the open palm of his left hand. 'Level with me, for God's sake. I've gotta get a handle on all this shit. What exactly do you know?'

Will stood up, uncertainly. He felt the drink flooding through his veins. He spoke slowly and softly. 'I know everything, Joe. Your old man lied to us. The both of us. Liz *was* killed, just like he told it to us. But not Jane. She did not die.'

'So how the hell do you know this, now?' Before Will could reply, Joe started shouting. 'OK, smart guy. Bet you didn't know Jane had my kid and was forced to give it up for adoption and…'

'Know all about that, Joe.'

'My old man tell you all of this?'

Will nodded uncomfortably.

'When? Why? I don't understand. Why the hell would he share a dirty little Kennedy family secret with you, William Ford? Huh? Tell me that! All of a sudden you were in his confidence, eh? Was it that way?'

'I guess.'

'Bullshit. He was a user, you know that. A fuckin' user.' Joe's eyes narrowed suddenly. 'Did he use you? Huh? How? What did he get you to do? No... you were with me when all that...' Joe threw his arms up in angry frustration '... happened. I need another fuckin' drink. You?'

Will nodded – immediately regretting his decision. This was getting pretty ugly. He could almost smell the rage in the library. He wished to God that he was miles away from these oppressive walls lined with leather-bound tomes. Miles away from Joe – now dangerously volatile and growing meaner by the minute. Joe's fury spoke through the clanking of the neck of the bottle against the thick crystal-cut glass.

They downed their drinks in unison.

Joe dragged his hand through his hair. 'Need you to do something for me, Will,' he said softly.

'I'll tell you all I know...'

'Sure... I know you will. But I want you to do something very special for me. I need you to go and see Jane. Go to England, Cambridge if need be, and try to find her. Talk to her, Will. Talk to her and bring her back to me. What d'you say, huh? You'd do that for me, Will?'

Will felt his mouth go dry. Jesus, he thought. It's coming. I'm gonna have to tell him everything.

'How about it? I can't go over there myself. You can see that. Not now. Impossible. Not with so much shit on my plate...'

Will took a deep breath. 'I've seen her, Joe. Talked to her.'

Joe frowned his confusion. 'What the hell? What do you mean?'

'Some time back. Your old man called in a favour. Got me to fly over and talk to Jane –'

'What the hell are you saying? You've been to England and seen her? When?'

'Just after you got married... and when things were starting to happen for you. Politically... you know. When all those strings your old man pulled started to add up to something...'

'I don't understand.' Joe's voice was now no more than a baffled whisper. 'What the hell are you telling me, Ford? Just what the fuck are you saying?'

'He was getting scared that she would see you in the press or news reels. He'd told her that you were dead... '

'Oh my Christ! How deep does all this dirt go? Will... talk to me... I really need to know...'

'Take it easy, Joe. Just listen to me. Your old man got Jane to give up the baby for adoption by telling her you'd been killed. He told her he knew a family who could give the baby a good life. She bought it – though it cut her up, Joe. Cut her up badly, but she saw that it kinda made sense...'

'Oh my God!' Joe slumped down in a leather chair as if pole-axed.

'I was dragged into it when one day out of the blue, he made the call. You see, Joe, I had a good job... thanks to your old man. He fixed it for me... I guess I felt I owed him... that he was calling in a favour. Told me to go over and see Jane and stop her from raising a storm once she knew you were alive and kicking...'

Joe stood up, his fists clenching and unclenching angrily. 'And you went and spoke to her? Just like that? He snapped his fingers and you went half way round the fuckin' world peddling more poison and lies? You bastard...'

Will stepped back as Joe lurched towards him. The first punch, a wild one, missed but the second smashed into his nose and upper lip. Blood flowed instantly. Will ducked and weaved, protecting his face with raised arms as he dodged Joe's furious fists. The library doors swung open and two neatly dressed young men filled the doorway. Will found himself staring down the muzzle of an automatic.

'Need any help, Mr President, Sir?'

'Everything's... fine!' Joe snarled. 'Leave... us. We're fine.'

'Very good, Sir. Thank you, Sir.'

The automatic was sheathed and both men withdrew.

'For Christ's sake, Joe, you know what the old bastard was like. Always shootin' lines and making it all sound OK. Said Jane would only suffer if she started to get in touch with you – mess up her life and yours – and there would be no getting her baby boy back...'

'Will! You never said... You knew and you never said...'

Will heard the dry sob in Joe's voice. Soon, tears of rage would be joined by tears of frustration and bewilderment. Already, the accusing voice held a rising note of resentment.

'Wise up, Joe. *I* didn't double-deal you! Your old man did. You know I'd never do that. Truth is, I was flattened by the whole thing. Flew over to England like I was in some kinda dream... and when I caught up with Jane...'

'How was she? Tell me...' Joe was pleading now, all his anger spent.

Dabbing at his bloody mouth, Will was eager to comfort his old friend. Later, as they sat side by side nursing their drinks, they consoled one another as they pieced together the painful puzzle bequeathed to them by Joe Kennedy Senior. Joe listened in silence as Will recounted every detail of his meeting with Joe Senior and his brief encounters with Jane in Cambridge. Before they parted, Will promised to do his best to bring together Joe, his war-time love and their child. The men's friendship was now over, they both knew that. A friendship destroyed by the one thing they still shared: being puppets manipulated by the machinations of Joe Kennedy Senior.

It was still raining heavily, hours later that day, when Dexter opened the door to Will.

'Say, honey! Guess who's here,' he called out, trying to conceal his concern at Will's split lip, at his dishevelled appearance and rye-shot eyes.

Mary joined them. She made no pretence of ignoring Will's condition.

'William Ford! You're drunk as a skunk! Oughta be ashamed of yourself. Really! And just look at the state of you.'

The men exchanged sheepish glances as Mary continued to cluck and chide. Patrick raced down from his room.

'Gee,' he gasped, staring at the dried blood around Will's mouth. 'Have you been fighting?' His tone was almost reverential.

'Uncle Will had an accident...' Mary broke in. 'He's just going to clean himself up while I get some coffee, aren't you?' Her tone was firm.

'Uh, I guess so,' Will shrugged.

'Go and freshen up. Coffee will be ready and then Patrick can show you the model plane he's been working on.'

Dexter shrugged his 'Don't ask me' look at his wife as Will went upstairs to the bathroom.

Mary frowned. She retreated to the kitchen with a gathering sense of foreboding. It was so unlike Will to turn up like this – bruised and clearly the worse for drink. It pained her for Patrick to see him in this state.

They sat in anxious silence around the kitchen table. Will refused the chocolate cake and winced as he sipped his hot black coffee through bruised lips. Patrick joined them, a model Liberator in his hand.

'What do you think of her? Isn't she a beauty?'

Will lowered his head down onto the table and swore softly. He crashed a clenched fist down, making the cups rattle in their saucers.

'Go easy there!' Dexter admonished lamely.

Mary was more decisive. 'Honey. Go up to your room. Uncle Will isn't... himself.'

'No,' Will grunted. His voice was thick and charged with emotion. 'Stay. Stay here, son. I've got something to tell you. All of you. Something very important.'

'Will!' Mary warned. 'I don't think...'

Dexter echoed his wife's concern. 'Just drink your coffee...'

'Best get it all out into the open,' Will sighed. He suddenly sounded exhausted. Turning to Patrick, he gently touched the model bomber, stroking the wing with his fingertip. 'Son,' he murmured, 'I got your letter. I'm here with some answers.'

'Letter?' Dexter demanded.

Mary raised a soothing hand. 'You remember, darling. Patrick wanted to know...certain things. So he wrote to Will...'

'Oh, that.' Dexter's voice was dull and slightly resentful.

'Gee,' Patrick cried. 'You really gonna give me some news about my...other mother and father?'

'Your... natural parents, darling,' Mary said softly.

Patrick gave her a quick reassuring kiss and then begged Will for information.

Will took a deep breath. 'I've just seen your... natural father,' he began cautiously.

Moments later, the stunned silence of the kitchen was broken by the crash of the coffee cup Dexter dropped as he discovered that the true father of his adopted son was in fact the President of the United States of America.

Cambridge, England.
29th September, 1962.

The library at Jane's College had a musty, slightly mousy smell. At the desk, Will was informed that she had in fact just moments ago withdrawn for afternoon tea. Yes, she would probably be partaking of some light refreshment in the Senior Common Room. No, telephonic communication was not possible between the library and the Senior Common room.

Lousy Brits! Didn't they just love to hear themselves talk. So many fuckin' words and all of them telling you nothing, Will thought to himself, retreating from the library readers' raised eyebrows and their loudly whispered calls for silence. A marble stairwell led his tired feet up to the closed doors of the Senior Common Room. Will hesitated, uncertain how to proceed. He heard laughter and, taking it as a good omen, opened the door and stepped inside.

'Will!' Jane's concerned voice cut through the chatter and tinkle of china.

Several faces turned to inspect Will and the voices in the room fell to a soft murmuring. Will ran his finger inside his collar then relaxed as Jane rose, gracefully crossed the floor towards him and, slipping her arm through his, led him towards a linen covered table stacked with cups and saucers. Despite her poise and self-control, Will felt her fingers gripping his arm tightly.

A college porter acknowledged Jane and inquired if she would like tea for her guest. Jane nodded. She was pale and tense. Her teacup rattled slightly in its saucer.

Will tried to ease the tension. 'Gee, you get tea served by that guy in the funeral parlour suit – how come?'

Jane smiled wanly. 'Tea has been served by a college porter for years. Will, really!'

Jane's exasperated tone had dipped into disapproval as Will had unscrewed a hip flask and tipped a good measure of rye into his tea cup. 'You look... tired, Will. Is anything the matter?'

Grimacing as he swallowed the rye-laced tea in one gulp, Will nodded. 'Yep. That's about right. I sure am... tired.'

'Was your flight delayed? These early autumn fogs are dreadful, I believe...'

'I ain't weary from the flight, honey, I guess I'm just... exhausted.'

Mentally correcting his grammar, Jane smiled. 'Have you just dropped in or have you come to see me for a special purpose?'

'Any more of that tea?' Will asked.

'Jane, my darling! There you are! I've been searching high and low for you – I say. Hello. Who's this?'

Will's tired eyes flickered up and narrowed at the sight of the handsome black-gowned academic who had joined them at their table.

'Oh,' Jane blushed becomingly. 'Sebastian, are your tutorials completed so soon?'

Sebastian grinned. 'Everything stops for tea!' he sang. 'Who he? Am I to be introduced to your... guest?'

'Do forgive me,' Jane apologised, recovering slightly before instantly losing again her elegant poise. 'Sebastian, meet Will. William Ford. A very dear friend... of a friend... a wartime friendship... Will flew bombers in the war... he is an American.' Her confusion was almost tangible. It intrigued Sebastian.

'Ah, the war. That would explain it,' he teased.

Jane's face flushed. She threw Will an imploring glance.

'Say, fellah, why don't you pull up a chair and join us,' Will said softly.

Sebastian held up both hands in mock-horror at the idea of doing such a thing. 'No, my good people. Can't stop. Simply must dash. I'm meeting a fellow in the quad and when I say a 'fellow' I really do mean a Fellow... ha ha ha! Supper later, Jane darling? She does a heavenly macaroni cheese,' Sebastian added in an aside to Will before striding off.

'So what's the deal with Sebastian and a macaroni supper?' Will asked laconically.

'It's just macaroni cheese... nothing special at all... actually, we are engaged.' Jane spoke almost defiantly.

'Oh, are you... actually?' Will had not lost the knack of mimicry.

Jane softened. Will had always been able to tease her and make her laugh.

'So there would be no use in my asking you to think about... a little trip over the pond with me, huh?

Jane's eyes widened. 'Are you seriously suggesting that I should... accompany you to America. Simply drop everything and fly back with you to the States?'

'Simply drop everything, including that macaroni cheese, and come back with me – and see Joe. He's longing to see you, honey.'

Jane shushed Will with a cautionary finger pressed up at her lips. 'Be careful, for goodness sake, Will. If anyone ever found out...'

'You mean anyone like… Sebastian?'

'You rotter, William Ford!' Jane flared.

Several heads turned towards their table at this, and somewhere in the hallowed depths of the Senior Common Room, a throat was distinctly cleared. Chastened by the note of reproach, Jane continued the conversation in a sustained and vehement whisper.

'Tell me about… everything. Joe. How is he? Still… unhappily married?'

'Not that anyone would notice,' Will murmured softly. 'But yes, I guess, he's still… unhappily married. Still married, still the president and still up to his neck in all kinds of problems… and now he wants to see you.'

'It's impossible. Surely you can see that, Will. And if he wanted to see me, talk to me, be with me…why the hell did he send you and not come himself?' Her voice rose sharply as she fired the question at him.

Will broke the fragile decorum of the Senior Common Room, raising his voice: 'How the hell can he come and drink afternoon goddam tea, when he's trying to run a country, huh?' to which several faces looked up in surprise. They moved away to a corner of the room and continued in an urgent whisper.

Jane spread her hands out in an impatient gesture of despair. 'This is impossible,' she hissed. 'Why the hell did you come here? All that… is past and gone… it's over, Will.' She reached out across the teacups and lightly touched his hand. 'Surely you can see that, can't you?'

Will's resolve hardened. He had come here to achieve a purpose. He owed Joe that much. Then it would be all finished with, all over. Like their friendship.

'I see a successful career as a lecturer and a macaroni cheese for a date tonight, but I can also see Joe at his desk, desperate to see you again…'

'Joe's not the desperate type!'

'What we're talking about here is his struggling with the weight of responsibility.'

'A burden,' Jane murmured.

'Guess you're right on the button there. And there ain't no bigger burden on this planet than the Oval Office.'

'But Will,' Jane reasoned softly, squeezing his hand. 'What possible help could I be to him. It would only stir up old memories, suppressed feelings...'

'You've forgotten your feelings for him?'

'That's not fair. Oh for God's sake! Just go, Will. Please. Just go... now!'

Will flushed. It was not a sudden rush of anger but the mantle of shame that suffused his weary face. He was about to play a card from the bottom of the pack. He knew he was about to play dirty – a trick which no doubt could have come straight out of Joe Kennedy Senior's deck of cards.

'You haven't asked me maybe why Joe needs to see you. Isn't that a bit... kinda weird? Could it be *you* want it all buried and forgotten?'

'How dare you say that, you... you bastard! You've no bloody idea of what I went through... losing Liz... the baby coming... my parents... Joe's hateful father...' Jane's husky voice broke. She gulped out the next few words. 'Having to let the baby go... my baby... our child... all I had left of Joe,' She broke down completely, her retching sobs drawing anxious glances of concern from the other academics.

Will stood up decisively. He spoke with authority in a low, firm voice. 'OK. That's it. Let's get out of here, Jane. Come on. We're leaving. Now.'

Jane was grateful to be led away out into the early autumn evening. On the crunching gravel of the quad they stepped, arms linked – throwing long shadows in the setting sun.

'What do you mean? How... when...?' Jane asked uncertainly.

Will was trying to explain how Joe had discovered the existence of Patrick after his father's stroke, adding, 'That's why he needs to see you. He wants you there when he... meets up with Patrick... but he wants to see you first.'

Jane stopped and turned abruptly. 'You mean he knows who... where Patrick is? I don't understand any of this, Will!'

'I've spoken to Patrick... just a couple of days ago. Told him all about you...'

'Will! I had no idea!'

'Patrick wants to see you. He's nuts about the idea of a meet – with you, of course, and Joe.'

'But it's impossible...'

Will breathed in deeply, imagining he heard the cynical cackle of Joe Kennedy Senior's laughter as he dug his hand deeper into his coat pocket.

'Patrick wrote you. Here. Here's the letter he wrote you.'

Jane sat down on an elm bench as Will walked through the echoing cloisters – giving her the time and privacy to read the letter from her son. When he rejoined her, her face was wet with tears. Will put his arm around her and asked, coaxingly, would she be able to take a seat on the flight over to the States in four days time. The seat – he omitted to inform her – that he had already booked.

Unable to speak, she merely nodded her assent.

Will turned away. It was done. There was no more to it. He had got Jane to agree to go over and meet Joe and their son. Will threw his head back and – longing for a couple of fingers of rye to pour down his parched throat – suddenly and silently wished to God that he had never, ever met a goddam Kennedy.

October 13 1962.
Washington D.C.

Down below, the tables in the hotel dining room were less than half filled. Upstairs, in her plush fifth-floor suite, Jane stood up once more and paced anxiously across the deep-pile carpet. Jane was not unaware of the special measures which had been put into operation for her visit. After being waved through immigration and customs at the airport, she had been whisked away in a limousine which itself had been shadowed by an unmarked car. At the hotel, the formalities were once again brushed aside and Will – thank heavens, a friendly face at last – had greeted her. The elevator had taken her straight up to the fifth floor. The bell-hop was polite but remained silent. She had thought suddenly that he was probably not a bell-hop at all. More likely to be CIA or something. There was a bulge under his jacket which was probably a gun. Jane did not know for certain but was reasonably sure from the eerie silence around her that hers was the only occupied suite on this floor. The two maids on duty were distinctly undomesticated and room service was supplied by a nervous waiter accompanied by a tough looking bodyguard whose eyes remained hidden behind his dark glasses.

Her suite of rooms was sterile. Spotlessly clean but bland in décor and utterly impersonal. There were pen and wash prints of American golfing legends on the dark cream walls. Will had escorted her to the door of her suite – promising to return. They had exchanged few words. Jane had been relieved to see him downstairs in the hotel lobby but had sensed a coldness, a reserve in his manner. She had also caught a whiff of bourbon on his breath.

There was a sharp rap at her door. Jane automatically touched her hair, patting it in a reflex gesture. Opening it, her eyes met Will's evasive glance.

'Will! At last! I thought you'd never come. I'm longing to talk…'

'No dice! Joe's on his way. Are you ready?'

'Yes... no... Oh Will, please stay! All of a sudden I don't feel... sure about any of this.'

Will's eyes softened. 'It'll be OK, honey. You look like a million dollars. Just relax. He'll be here in a minute.'

Will withdrew abruptly, leaving Jane standing at the open door. A smartly suited young man, his dark glasses glinting, emerged as if from nowhere and politely but firmly advised Jane to close the door and keep it closed. She stepped back into her suite but was too nervous to sit down. Jane suddenly felt constrained. To her relief, after a few more seconds, there was another sharp rap. Jane sighed and was approaching the door when it opened slightly to admit just the head and shoulders of the bodyguard. Peering round the room without entering further, he asked Jane if she was still alone. She nodded quickly.

'OK,' he called over his shoulder. 'All clear, Sir.'

Jane stepped back as the door opened further and the body guard entered the room. Behind him, the bulky frame of another dark-suited man loomed.

They both stood aside as if at a given signal, standing smartly to attention. Jane could not suppress a loud gasp as Joe, looking a little tired and strained, appeared in the doorway.

October 20 1962
Washington D.C.

Down in the bar Will sat nursing his second Martini. The reunion the previous week up on the fifth floor had not gone at all as he had expected. Will, joining the couple with champagne and roses after what he had deemed to be a suitable lapse of time, was perturbed to discover them, both with faces wet from tears, holding hands awkwardly in earnest debate. He had retreated hastily, feeling uncomfortable.

He drained the Martini and picked his teeth morosely with the cocktail stick. He had not met with either of them face-to-face since their reunion. He was here tonight to facilitate Patrick's introduction to his natural father and mother. Dexter O'Neill would be present. After that – Will neither knew nor particularly cared anymore. Everyone around him seemed to be talking about Cuba. The missile crisis. About shelters and pre-emptive strikes. The long reach of the Russian bear's red claws. Shit like that. Will snapped his fingers and ordered a third Martini. Cuba or no Cuba, he sensed his future lay somewhere on a bar stool.

Eight after eight. He swallowed his drink. In a couple of minutes Dexter would arrive with Patrick. Will saw it all clearly now – in sharp focus. The ride up in the elevator, flanked by bodyguards, their jackets bulging. Inside her suite, Jane, probably pacing anxiously. Then the pantomime with Secret Servicemen searching patently empty rooms and then, hey – let's hear it loud and clear for The Chief: enter Mr President, aka Joe Kennedy Junior. Will teetered gently on his bar stool. It surprised him that his third Martini had hit the spot so hard. It was only his third that evening...of a long day's drinking to come.

'Uncle Will.'

He turned and found himself looking into the shy, eager smile of Patrick. The boy's innocence in all this tempered Will's cynicism.

Will escorted Patrick and Dexter up to the suite adjoining Jane's.

Minutes later, having poured himself a bourbon, Will sat opposite Jane in her suite – so close that their knees almost touched, yet it felt as though there was nothing intimate between them.

'You're drinking too much, Will,' Jane remarked, coolly.

Will was about to reply, when Joe arrived with the usual flurry of security. Joe reached out and took Jane's hand, attempting to squeeze it and retain it. She shook herself free from his grasp.

Will left the room.

Joe spread his arms out wide as he apologised for not being able to see Jane since their last meeting. She did not acknowledge him when he told her that he had been wrestling with 'this Cuban business.'

They exchanged desultory politenesses for a couple of minutes. An air of unreality hung heavily between them. To their acute discomfort, they could not connect.

Their awkwardness was interrupted by Will who knocked, entered and asked them if they were ready.

Both Joe and Jane assented with curt nods in reply.

Will stepped into the adjoining suite and gestured to those inside. Dexter O'Neill emerged followed by Patrick.

Will coughed, as though either emotional or embarrassed. He coughed again – because in fact he was just a little drunk. Despite the unresolved tension so evident between them, Jane and Joe instinctively took a step closer and stood, not touching, but unmistakeably side-by-side.

'Mr O'Neill, I believe you have met...' Will began.

'Mr President, Sir, this a great honour...'

Dexter and Joe shook hands firmly.

Everyone turned towards Patrick, who stood overawed and rooted to the spot. His gaze went from Jane to Joe and back to Jane.

Jane, tears sparkling in her eyes, cried out, 'Patrick!'

Patrick brushed by Dexter and embraced Jane a little formally. Joe grinned – and with his eyes gleaming also he reached out to squeeze and shake Patrick's hand.

'Oh my darlings,' Jane sobbed, all her frustrations with Joe now completely gone. 'My very own darlings.' She hugged the pair of them so tightly she stifled their breath.

A little after 10.00 pm, back in the bar, Will was on his fifth Martini. The evening had proved even more difficult than their first meeting, he thought. After the tearful embraces and shy silences suddenly filled with questions, Jane had said something which had riled Joe – who had probably been pretty much on edge all day.

'Cuba seems to be managing without you tonight.'

Joe had taken it the wrong way. Will had tried to intervene – but had failed. The tension became palpable. At Joe's request, Will led Patrick back to the suite next-door, to where Dexter had retired, wrestling with his emotions. When Will returned, he heard angry shouting through the door before he knocked. Will was considering opening it, when the two bodyguards appeared, one each side of him, hands under their taut jackets. One of the guards knocked again, and must have mistaken something Joe had said as an OK to enter. He pushed the door open briskly, and they found themselves looking at Joe and Jane, standing face-to-face, engaged in a heated debate.

'That's right,' Jane had scorned, turning towards them. 'Just like your father, Joe. Can't do it without your henchmen, can you?'

Taking Will's empty glass with a smile, the barman asked, 'Ain't you got no home to go to, Sir?'

'Gonna stay put right here until it is all over,' Will slurred.

'Until what's all over? My vermouth?'

'The bombs. Might as well die with a Martini in my hand when the Cuban shit hits the fan...'

As Will fell asleep, slumped over the bar next to his untouched drink, Jane and Joe said goodnight to Patrick and Dexter. All their enmity evaporated, they sat down and talked... piecing together the events of late 44 and 45, remaining calm and rational. Jane cried gently, allowing Joe to hold and comfort her. She withdrew from his embrace and started to question him – about his return to the States, his choice of political career and his arranged marriage.

After a particularly lame response, Jane flared up again.

'You're weak, Joe. You should have stood up for yourself. Stood up against your father.'

'Like you did, I suppose, with your folks?'

'That's not fair. My God that is not fair!'

'And you're wrong, quite wrong, if you think that I never had the guts to stand up to him...'

'Easy to do when he's helpless in a hospital bed...Will told me about the stroke...'

Joe pulled her to him, forcing his face down on hers. There was a violence in his kiss. Jane responded with an open-mouthed passion.

They parted, Jane panting. 'Oh God, Joe! We belong... we should never have been... Why the hell didn't you try to find out what happened to me?' Her questioning broke down in sobs.

'I did... I swear I did... but it never reached them. My letter never reached your parents ...*and* now I know why!' he added grimly.

Joe reached out to embrace her once again but she shook her head and stepped back. He bowed his head and whispered a reply. The gentleness of his tone and the sorrow in it drew her towards him. Eyes closed, their faces inched closer, lips slightly parted for another reconciling kiss.

They drew apart abruptly as an urgent banging at the door was followed by the appearance of Joe's aide, Harrison.

'Sorry to interrupt...'

'Cut the crap, Harrison. What have you got for me?'

'McNamara on the line, Sir. Fresh developments...'

'Fresh? What the hell do you mean, fresh?' Joe demanded belligerently.

Harrison glanced briefly at Jane and then down at his feet.

'Well?'

'You're needed back at EX-COMM, Mr President,' Harrison said stolidly.

Joe turned to Jane. 'I gotta go...'

Jane burst into tears. Joe was about to try to console her when Harrison coughed.

'Sir!'

'Yeh? What?'

'There's vital new intelligence on Cuba, Sir.'

'New? Since when? Why was I not told?'

'It requires your immediate attention, Sir.'

THE HAMMER AND THE ANVIL

28th October, 1962
The White House.
15.07 hrs.

Most of EX-COMM were crammed into The president's Private Office, forcing Bobby to stand apart from his brother. Bundy sensed a rift developing between the two Kennedys and it bothered him. The last thing The White House needed just now was sibling strife. Others in the room secretly relished the tension surrounding the President, sensing that it was driving him into the ranks of the hawks.

Staffort appeared at the open door. His ashen face told them that his news was going to be bad. It was – the worst kind possible.

He blurted it out unceremoniously. 'We've hit one of their subs.' It was a bald statement. Staffort's voice held an angry, scared tone.

The announcement was greeted with a collective grunt of disbelief. Several in the room swore openly.

As Bobby groaned, his brother exploded angrily. 'I said no firing!'

Staffort almost bleated his response. 'We didn't open fire, Sir.'

'Then how the fuck...?' General LeMay snarled.

Staffort explained the incident. A destroyer had turned ninety degrees starboard in a manoeuvre intended to deflect off course a Soviet tanker which was clearly attempting to cross the quarantine line.

'They were probing, Mr President. Testing the limits of our resolve. It's a lethal cat-and-mouse out there. The destroyer cut a tight one across the tanker's bows... and rammed a Soviet sub skulking just below. Opened her up like a sardine can.'

'Holy shit! They're sure as hell gonna respond...'

Suddenly, a phone on Kennedy's desk jangled. Then a second – followed by a third. The President's Private Office reverberated with the clamour of urgent telephones. Within seconds, Joe, Bobby and George Bundy were each busy on a line. The rest of

EX-COMM strained in silence to catch what was being said. Then a phone outside the office, attached to the wall in the corridor, jangled demandingly. Staffort strode out and snatched it up. He stepped back into the room, the phone's flex at full stretch.

'Listen up, everybody,' he yelled.

EX-COMM listened. Those at the desk covered their phones with their hands.

'Reports coming in that they're firing at us.'

'Firing what?'

Other voices demanded – in cruder terms – just what the hell was Staffort telling them. He made his meaning clearer. 'The Soviet Field Commander has begun firing shells and missiles…'

'Missiles!' Joe Kennedy reacted. 'Conventional?'

'Affirmative, Sir. Conventional shells and missiles are being fired from inland positions out to sea at our blockade fleet.'

Staffort ducked out of the doorway as if he had been yanked into the corridor by the taut phone flex. He reappeared. 'Shall we respond? The Navy needs to know...'

Kennedy bellowed his orders.

'Return fire, with conventional weapons, at planned military targets' Stafford roared down the phone.

EX-COMM roared as one man. 'Fire!'

October 28 1962
The War Office (bunkered underneath The Pentagon)
18:49

With the exception of Adlai Stevenson, and with the addition of military advisors and other aides, all of EX-COMM sat around the huge oval table. A cloud of blue cigar and cigarette smoke hung low over their waxy, strained faces. Scattered across the table's green leather were coffee pots and bourbon bottles. They were mostly empty – it had been a long afternoon. Damage reports had come in revealing that two of the US Navy blockade ships had been sunk, the destroyers Leary and Charles P Cecil. And the aircraft carrier Independence had been badly damaged. Loss of life had been severe. Huge hanging maps, illuminated by tiny pin-points of different coloured lights, covered the walls around them. NATO allies were in greens, blues and yellows: foes were lit up in red. The eerie echo of ship-to-shore radio traffic whispering monotonously from the grey steel speakers was frequently interrupted by excited staccato chatter from airborne fighters.

General Maxwell Taylor was sitting hunched over a large, black telephone. It had a bank of red and green lights at its base. Taylor drummed out his pent-up frustration across the row of coloured bulbs with his fat fingertips.

In response to a question called out from the back of the War Office, Bobby Kennedy yelled back that they had at last established contact via a field radio link-up with the Soviet Commander on Cuba. This was met with applause, cheers and curses. Flushed with success, Bobby cracked a brief, strained grin over his shoulder at the EX-COMM team.

An angry buzzing, rather than a ringing bell, accompanied the red warning light flashing at the base of the telephone in front of Maxwell Taylor. The general blinked and froze. The excited voices of young jet pilots burst suddenly from the speakers on the walls. Their adrenalin surge was infectious. Taylor snatched up the telephone receiver and frowned – unable to cope with the Russian coming down the wire.

'Have we got a goddam interpreter in here?' he bellowed – the note of resentment in his voice unmistakeable.

One of the aides stepped up beside the General. 'That's me, Sir.'

Reluctantly, Maxwell Taylor surrendered the receiver, hating having to take a back seat to a young civilian at such a critical moment.

'Da!' the young interpreter responded, immediately holding the receiver up aloft and calling out aloud for Sorensen.

Sorensen listened intently above the crackle of static and then suddenly started to shout into the receiver. Taylor's head jerked up and his eyes narrowed suspiciously as Sorensen appeared to be frantically pleading in Russian with someone at the other end of the line.

The link was lost and Sorensen stared into the receiver in disbelief before putting it down.

'Commie bastards,' Maxwell Taylor snarled impotently.

A klaxon blared intermittently and two different bells jangled discordantly. Up on one of the huge electronic wall-maps, lines of red lights started to blink and arch out from the Rorschach blob of Cuba, crawling northwards, millimetre by millimetre. Bobby spun around and looked anxiously across to where his brother Joe sat poring over maps and papers with Sorenson and Bundy. The President raised his head. His impassive eyes met Bobby's expectant gaze. 'This is it,' the look between them said through the smoke-filled War Office. Everything they had struggled together to prevent – and more recently argued over – was about to break out and wash over them like Nemesis. 'Good luck, Joe,' Bobby mouthed across the space between them.

The fighter pilots' radio traffic crackled through the ether. The calmer voice of a strategic bomber pilot could be heard seeking an immediate update. Up on the wall, the tiny threads of red lights crossed the blue of the sea below in a slow but sure advance towards the American coastline.

All of the phones seemed to jangle instantaneously in a shrill cacophony. The field radio-phone in front of General Taylor remained inert. He snatched it up, his bulging eyes fixed on the encroaching track of tiny red lights. The vein in his neck thickened and the flesh over his starched shirt collar bulged as he began to shout abuse at the lines of red up on the wall. Then his gaze turned to where Joe remained seated. All eyes were now on the President who, sitting in rigid concentration, remained silent. His teeth were clenched. The muscle along his jaw-line tensed and spasmed.

THE HAMMER AND THE ANVIL

In front of Joe was a clear Perspex box. Beneath the casing were two desk-mounted buttons. A red one to launch a nuclear assault. A black one to abort any such strike.

'Holy shit, Joe!' Bobby shouted as he saw his brother's hand reach out and hover above the casing.

Others in the War Room gasped aloud as Joe Kennedy removed the Perspex shield.

'Oh my God' somebody whispered. Sweat broke out freely on those watching as the President appeared to touch each button in turn.

A siren rent the air with its sudden scream. A dull voice intoned the count-down to impact from the incoming strike.

'Fire! Fire, God damn it!' Taylor yelled.

'Jesus Christ Joe!' Bobby shrilled.

'We must... respond, Sir,' McNamara urged, his voice thick and scarcely audible.

The President's shoulders rose and fell raggedly as he breathed in deeply. He wished he was somewhere far away, a place remote from the fear, tension and anger of the War Room in the Pentagon.

The count-down continued. Heartbeats fluttered as it approached two minutes.

Joe jabbed his index finger down onto the red button, which began to flash angrily.

EX-COMM exhaled its pent-up breath with one gasp. Up on the wall, tiny white lights began leaving the mainland and heading towards Cuba, and the entire Soviet bloc. Tiny white lights stretching across the coastline signalling the outbreak of World War III.

The field phone in front of General Taylor buzzed angrily. He picked up the receiver and was momentarily stunned to hear stilted English being spoken down the line. He coughed, swallowed, and offered the phone begrudgingly to Joe. 'It's the Soviet Field Commander in Cuba', he growled in explanation.

Joe snatched the receiver to his ear. 'Yeah?' he rasped into the mouth-piece.

'Do you have good cards in your hand, Mr President?' a heavily accented Russian voice demanded. 'Do you hold a spade flush... eh, Joe?'

Joe swore softly. 'It that *you*, Anatoly? Jesus Christ!'

'Da. It is me. Your turn, Joe. You have to play your hand, it is so, eh?'

The count-down was reaching 90 seconds. Joe exhaled sharply and the hairs on the nape of his neck prickled as he pushed himself back from the edge of the table. He became aware that he was under Taylor's keen scrutiny. The general's shrewd gaze seemed to be burning into Joe's. 'You on fuckin' first-name terms with this guy!?' Taylor spat, his heavy jaw thrust out accusingly.

Joe closed his eyes. Images surged up in his mind. He thought of Patrick. He thought of Will. He ran his tongue over his teeth as if to wipe away a sudden sourness in his mouth. He tasted the rotten potatoes prised from the frozen fields in war-torn Germany. He relived his blazing wrath which had erupted before his bed-ridden father. He briefly savoured the cool delight of his first long kiss with Jane.

'Can we do a deal, Joe? My missiles for yours in Turkey, no?'

'No deal.'

'We have both fired our rockets, Joe. Maybe we should abort... I'm calling in that favour, Joe. You owe me.'

The President of the United States of America closed his eyes again and pictured the Soviet General's finger twitching over an abort button. But it was *not* the image of Melnyev's finger at the button that burned in his mind. It was the signet ring on that finger.

Joe squeezed the sweat from his eyes. He felt the sudden surge of hatred at the words of his one-time ally. *Favour.* His father had always dealt in *favours.* Always wheeling and dealing... calling in what he was owed.

And then he heard Jane's voice, her bitter words, the last time they had met, echoing in his mind. 'You're weak, Joe, you should have stood up for yourself...'

Over the abort button, The President's straightened index finger quivered…

FACT:

At 5.55 pm on the 12th of August, 1944, Navy Pilot Lieutenant Joseph Patrick Kennedy (eldest son of J.P. Kennedy Senior, US Ambassador to Great Britain 1938-1940) and Navy Radio Engineer Lieutenant Wilford Willy, took off from US 8th Airforce base at Fersfield, Norfolk, in the UK.

They were flying a US PBY-1 Liberator bomber-plane, packed with 21,170 pounds of British Torpex high-explosives – in effect, they were in a huge flying bomb. Their mission was to destroy the German 'V3 super-gun' site at Mimoyecques near the coast of Northern France. Once remote radio-control had been established by a 'mother' aircraft, the two men were to bale out, leaving the 'mother-ship' to guide their plane into a crash-dive onto the target.

It was believed that the V3 was only two weeks from becoming operational. It was thought that the super-gun was capable, once every twenty seconds, of firing a huge shell containing high explosive, or worse still, lethal gas (similar to Sarin), across the English Channel and into the heart of London. Its effect would have been devastating. What was not realised, until invading Allied troops reached the site, was that an earlier raid by RAF Lancasters dropping 'earth-quake' bombs had, in fact, been successful in damaging the super-gun, and that the Germans had already abandoned the installation.

At 18:20, as Joe and Wilford flew their Liberator over a field in Blythburgh, Suffolk (in the UK), they initiated a test of the mechanism for the switch-over to remote-control. Something went wrong. In two massive, consecutive explosions, the aircraft disintegrated, killing Joe and Wilford instantly.

No conclusions have ever been reached as to the exact cause of the tragedy.

Joseph Patrick Kennedy Jnr. was post-humously awarded the Navy Cross, the Distinguished Flying Cross (US) and the Air Medal. Lt. Wilford Willy was post-humously awarded the Navy Cross. Both of their names are listed on the *Tablet Of The Missing* at Madingley American Cemetery, Cambridge, England.

Had Joe survived the war, then it is almost certain that he, rather than JFK, would have fulfilled his father's ambitions to put a Kennedy in the White House.

Printed in the United Kingdom
by Lightning Source UK Ltd.
124527UK00001B/49-57/A